The Sea Brings Forth

# The Sea Brings Forth

*by* J A C K   R U D L O E

*Illustrations by Ingrid Niccoll*

**TRUMAN TALLEY BOOKS**
**E. P. DUTTON**
NEW YORK

TO

my family with thanks for their support,

understanding, and patience

# Contents

# List of Photographs

# ACKNOWLEDGMENTS

There are so many people to whom I owe acknowledgments and thanks that a just list would be far too long. My life as a collector has been an enriching experience, but it could take on real meaning and become complete only because there were scientists and interested persons in museums and universities who appreciated my efforts and urged me to continue.

However, there are people whom I must mention because they have been such an integral part of my life—particularly Dr. Elisabeth Deichmann of Harvard's Museum of Comparative Zoology, who spent so much time with me in her laboratory teaching me some of the fundamentals of taxonomy. Miss Charlene D. Long, Dr. John H. Welsh, and Dr. Ruth D. Turner of Harvard; Dr. William K. Emerson of the American Museum of Natural History; Dr. William A. Newman of the Scripps Institution of Oceanography; Dr. Thomas E. Bowman of the United States National Museum; Dr. Victor Zullo of the Marine Biological Laboratory in Woods Hole; and Mr. Charles E. Cutress of the Institute of Marine Science in Mayagüez, Puerto Rico, have all been my mentors.

Dr. Arthur G. Humes of Boston University made it possible for me to participate in the International Indian Ocean Expedition and thus enabled me to learn the importance of discipline.

I am especially grateful to Edward V. Komarek and Roy Kamorek of the Tall Timbers Research Station in Tallahassee, Florida. In my direst need they not only gave me sympathy and encouragement, but money as well, in the form of a continuous contract to supply their research station with a collection of marine organisms.

John Steinbeck, the renowned author and former co-owner of the Pacific Biological Laboratories, Inc., has encouraged me year after year to write this book, and to write other books, and by all means to continue my commercial collecting. And the anthropologist Colin M. Turnbull of the American Museum of Natural History has been a great support with his belief in my writing ability, even though he is revolted by what he calls "all those slimy little animals."

C. L. Stong of *Scientific American*, by publishing my articles and offering excellent advice, catapulted me into my writing career. There are others, too modest to wish to be mentioned, who assisted me with the preparation of this manuscript, reading, rereading, and even typing it.

But above all I must thank all the scientists, teachers, and other people who wanted to see the Gulf Specimen Company survive as an institution and have helped it do so, against great odds, by giving me their contracts and orders.

The Sea Brings Forth

# 1 The Biological Collector

It was almost dark when I arrived in Arcadia with my Airedale, Linda, and we had to push through the tall dead weeds in the front yard. The Airedale was happy that I was home again—that was all that counted with her. The door creaked as I opened it, and my laboratory smelled strongly of dust and mildew. Inside the air was still and penetratingly cold and clammy. The laboratory was rather chaotic, with moldy Petri dishes and dehydrated embalmed crabs still on the lab table. It was depressing. I hadn't expected it to be that bad. I had been away for four months with the International Indian Ocean Expedition in Madagascar.

When the Woods Hole Oceanographic Institution informed me that I had been accepted, that I was to participate as a biological collector at the Centre d'Océanographie et des Pêches in Nossi-Be, Madagascar, I dropped everything. I emptied my aquaria, left my Airedale with relatives, and was off. I wouldn't have missed that opportunity for the world, although I regretted having left at the height of the white-shrimp season. And now that I was back, I had to get my bearings, and it wasn't easy.

I felt a little more cheerful in the back rooms where I lived, with the lights on, my books around me, and the gas heater burning. I brewed a pot of coffee and glanced through the pile of mail that had accumulated. I put the bills aside for the time being and looked through the more promising mail. There were the usual purchase orders from the large biological supply houses and some from universities and medical colleges.

The shelves in my laboratory were about denuded of stock. Almost all the bottles and jars were empty. Only a few had some animals in them—one rattlesnake in formaldehyde, which still looked surprisingly good, one octopus, not so good, one jar filled with spider crabs, which nobody wanted, half a jar of sea cucumbers, and one jar with four sea horses, which everybody wanted.

The sea horses reminded me of my sea horse at the Museum of Comparative Zoology at Harvard. Oh how proud I had felt when I came across it in the collections of their Fish Department! It was in a black-capped museum jar with the legend "*Hippocampus hudsonius* De Kay, northern sea horse, taken on shrimp trawler *Elysium Queen* on the west shore of Tye Island, 6 meters, Anderson County, Florida."

And on the label was my name as the collector and my company's name. To me it looked impressive, although it was on the same shelf with fifty other jars of sea horses, from other parts of Florida as well as South America, Asia, and Africa, sent to the museum by famous explorers and naturalists, some more than a century ago.

I was proud of my sea horse, but as I looked at it I felt strangely remote from it. I had caught it in a shrimp trawl only the year before—I remembered how it felt when it wrapped its rough horny tail around my fingers—but now it was sitting in alcohol in a museum, and it looked as if it had been there forever.

As I continued checking my stock my thoughts went even

*The sea horses reminded me of my sea horse at
the Museum of Comparative Zoology at Harvard.*

farther back in the past. Four years before, when I had had to leave college, I thought that my world had come to an end. What was there for me to do? I had been majoring in biology, and I had always loved it. Even as a child I had been fascinated by natural history; I read prodigiously about snakes, birds, sharks, and sea turtles. I spent my vacation time exploring parks and the woodlands of New York.

When I left the university I was penniless and absolutely without any useful skills that would be helpful in getting a job. All my past preparation for life had been academic, and if I had completed my schooling I would have chosen a career in science. But as it was, my only working experience was as a third-class laboratory assistant, washing Petri dishes, counting sea-urchin eggs, test tube after test tube, and keeping frog tanks clean and weeding out the dead tadpoles.

But I was young and determined to survive; my world did not have to come to an end. There must be something I could do, something that I had a talent for. Then I remembered that on my last job, my professor-employer always bought frogs. He was studying the neuromuscular reactions of amphibians.

That was the beginning of my career as a collector. In waist-deep swamp water where cottonmouth water moccasins lurked, while swarms of mosquitoes feasted on me, I netted twenty-two large fat croaking bullfrogs. This professor desperately needed the frogs to continue his research, and he paid me nearly the same rate that he had paid the commercial biological supply companies. And so my first commercial enterprise netted me fifty dollars. In one night I earned more than a college technician did in one week. It felt great!

By hunting the North Florida woods and open fields I met my second order for the big "Georgia thumper" grasshoppers— they paid well, and so did the leeches and pond turtles for the physiology classes. Little by little my reputation as a reliable collector was growing in the local university. With my Airedale's help I was even able to produce a pregnant opossum within six hours' notice. Then one day a zoologist inadvertently took me out of the woods and put me into marine collecting—he ordered two dozen live pink shrimp.

I went to Elizabeth City, a fishing village, and found a soft-hearted shrimper, Preacher, and his captain, George Williams, who consented to take me out shrimping with them. After that one night out on the bay I fell in love with the sea and with shrimping, and I never went back to the woods again. To the fishermen the eels, sting rays, hydroids, and tunicates were just so much trash. To me this trash was something to learn about, something new and wonderful. Once you have felt the call of the sea, nothing else ever satisfies. I looked through the catalogues of the big supply houses and discovered that there was a demand for the fishermen's trash fish. I wrote to all the big biological supply houses, letting them know I could supply them.

So far I had dealt only with live animals. The supply houses wanted the animals preserved and well extended—in other words, looking more or less as they looked when they were alive. And so my education had not ended; even if it was not the formal, conventional type, it was still education. I had to learn about the animals—their phylogeny, their scientific names, and the techniques of extending them without their contracting into formless blobs, twisted or contorted. Step one in my education was to learn how ignorant I was. It was a gradual slow process of self-education; back to the library for books and more books on invertebrate zoology and marine fishes.

And there were times, too many times, when I was hard-pressed for money while learning. I slept on the shrimp boats during the day, collecting specimens at night. It was a hand-to-mouth existence, making a dollar here and a dollar there. But I was too stubborn to quit. And Preacher helped me out by teaching me how to shrimp—how to cull out the catch, operate

a winch, hang out the net, adjust the chains on the boards—
and as a deck hand I was expected to cook and to stand watch
and hold the boat on course while the crew took their rest.

For a time I lived an adventurous, carefree life as an apprentice deck hand and an amateur biological collector. There's no
denying the thrill of heading out to sea aboard a shrimp boat,
feeling the stiff south winds blowing in your face, watching
the great expanses of blue waters, and cruising the islands off
the northwestern Florida coast, shrimping all night, anchoring
up and sleeping all day, shrimping again and working westward
into Mobile Bay.

On Saturday night we went into port, showered, shaved, and
dressed up, and went off arm in arm for a night on the town. A
night on the town in that small town consisted of carousing
from bar to bar—all four of them.

We were usually awakened brutally in somebody's house in
the unreasonable hours of the early morning by somebody's
virtuous and indignant wife or sister and viciously dragged off
to the little clapboard Holiness Church for the good of our
souls. And a sorry-looking crew we were with our blackened
eyes, bruised knuckles, and pounding headaches. How the
pounding in our heads was intensified by the devout pounding
of feet and clapping of hands of the enthusiastic, pious congregation to the rhythm of the loud, tuneless piano! By the time
Sunday night rolled around, we gladly departed for the peace-
ful sea, away from the disapproving women.

Gladly, I worked with the fishermen, pulling their nets with
them, bare-backed, shoulder to shoulder, drinking with them
and eating in their homes, and spending my money as fast as I
made it. Always my thoughts were on the sea, the wonder and
the waiting for the nets to come up, the crackle of the boat's
radio at night, the good talks between the shrimpers as they
dragged their nets over the bottom, hoping to hit the shrimp
and to hit them right.

Gladly, I endured the sudden storms, the waves madly rocking the boat, showering the sea over the deck, the discomforts and sleepless nights on the craft. Even when I was wretchedly seasick—as the shrimpers said, "pink around the gills"—it was still glorious! I was a free man.

When I was not shrimping, I went out seining for specimens. Every morning, at the crack of dawn, the purse-seiners chugged out with their big boats, circling the offshore islands, watching the still waters for a ripple, waiting for the mullet to jump.

When the right moment came and the fish were cornered where they wanted them, the captain shouted, "Let's get her!" And as the boat circled the fish, the crew leaped into the shallows and fed out yards and yards of black webbing and bobbing yellow corks, engulfing the frantic schools of mullet, redfish, speckled trout, and mackerel. The beating and charging of fish against the webbing as the net was dragged up on the shore churned the water into foam as thousands of pounds of frantic fish fought the slowly shrinking-in webbing and were hopelessly engulfed.

I would stand with hands raw and sore from pulling the lead line and webbing, helping the fishermen haul their catch into the boats, while they in turn helped me pick out the "trash"— the cowfish, batfish, sharks, electric rays, sea hares, and jellyfish that I needed for specimens.

Then it was back to my house trailer in Elizabeth City with my specimens. I had to identify the animals and develop skills in preserving them. I spent hours anesthetizing sea anemones in preserving trays only to watch them contract as they died —making them worthless as specimens—because I had tried to speed up the killing process or had used the wrong method.

Each problem was unique, and each had to be solved. How could I keep a brittle starfish from breaking off its limbs? What was the ideal way of preserving the delicate comb jellyfish or how could they be shipped to Chicago and get there alive? This education was seldom smooth sailing. If the shrimp boats were not running I went skin diving for specimens—or beach-combing, but if the tides were too high, I had to wait two weeks for the right low tide. Sometimes it rained for a month, and then I was as much out of work as any fisherman. Some of the animals, like the comb jellies, were unpredictable; I never knew when I would see them come twirling, shimmering, and spinning into the bay again.

After six months of this happy life, I began to feel a gnawing discontent. I knew I did not want to be a fisherman, nor did I want to be a mere peddler of specimens. I still had a craving for books and knowledge, and I dreamed of becoming an important aid to scientific researchers and educators. By combing the beaches and by observation I learned something about the natural history of the intertidal animals, and with the books that I had been reading, I felt that there was something I had to offer to science after all.

Eventually I gave up my carefree life as larger and more important orders came in for live specimens. When I had saved up enough money I made a small down payment on an old army barracks. It had many failings—the floor sagged, the roof leaked, the shower was broken, and you had to be careful going into the bathroom; one heavy step and you would go through to the ground. But it had the advantage of being within my means and on easy terms. Also it was on the Gulf and I could buy specimens from the local crabbers. And I was in love with the landscape, because instead of the usual motels that bordered Florida's beaches this was practically virginal land. This town, which I shall call Arcadia, had never been cleared for civilization. The bay was bordered by tall, tall pine trees, massive branching water oaks heavy with drooping strands of Spanish moss, and ancient cypress swamps with big old alligators.

I had been supplying specimens under my own name, but with the purchase of real estate—never mind how shabby it looked; I had dreams of making it look important and significant—I called myself a company. But the company was only earning enough to keep itself going. And as businessmen know, all my earnings went back into the building, equipment, and supplies. Little by little I made my barracks livable and converted it into a rather primitive laboratory. As more orders came in, I repaired the roof and had shelves, sinks, and laboratory tables installed. But I had no surplus capital before I went on the expedition.

After I returned I visited large universities and research laboratories and obtained a number of good-paying contracts. There were cell physiologists who wanted live, fertile sea urchins. A biochemist ordered a pound of frozen amphioxi and some frozen tunicate larvae. A fisheries biologist at Woods Hole wanted a growth series of spadefish. A physiologist ordered live mantis shrimp and live sea anemones. Scientists in urgent need of horseshoe crabs for their research wanted to know how soon I could send them the first shipment.

But now I found Florida bitter cold, and I regretted my promise of immediate delivery. I opened a can of dog food for Linda, who ate it without any enthusiasm. She preferred people's food and liked to share my dinner with me, but I was in no mood to start cooking. I drank the hot coffee slowly, listening to the radio's weather report. The weatherman's smooth, cheerful voice said: "This has been the worst winter in Florida's history. The forecast is for continued freeze for the next four days, and then we can expect a warming trend and rain." Oh, great! The only specimens I could deliver would be frozen ones, if I could find them.

I had been very pleased when I was in Cambridge to find that my regular research customers were willing to order their teaching materials from me rather than from the major biological supply houses. They told me that they wanted to see me succeed in my venture because I had always taken a personal interest in their research, and they liked the way I went to the trouble of making sure not only that their specimens were the right ones, but that they arrived at the exact time for their convenience. I was dependable and consequently a valuable asset to their research programs.

But one and all they urged me to put out a conventional catalogue, instead of my usual economical mimeographed list, and they also advised me to sell the traditional marine animals of the North Atlantic which were used in dissection manuals and in teaching programs. Furthermore, some even promised to visit my laboratory in Florida or to send their students to me to work on their research in my lab.

From the expedition I had earned one thousand dollars. How far could one thousand dollars stretch? I thought dismally that it would take at least half that amount to put out a fairly decent catalogue, perhaps more. And the rest might go into the laboratory or a good seawater system, or perhaps the usual repairs.

Linda began to whimper. I let her out and sat down to try to figure out how I was going to make my laboratory a place where scientists would be glad to come to conduct their research. I needed capital, ingenuity, and luck.

It was late when I heard Linda at the door whimpering to come in. She was frozen. Tomorrow, I told myself, I would go out to Shiawassee and find out how the shrimpers were getting along. Much depended on them, the rest on what I could find on the beaches.

# 2 Oyster Season in Shiawassee

Vast expanses of blue waters and skies stretching on and on forever, weird tall pine trees like inverted mops, ragged palms and scrub bushes—that is the landscape of the Florida Gulf. It never fails to surprise me, so much sky and water merging into a cosmic blue. No matter where I travel or what I see, nothing can compare with it.

Usually spring begins in the latter part of February, but Florida was even colder than Boston. Biological collecting is a business dependent upon the seasons. Winter in the South brings low tides, lush growths of littoral marine life, and fattened oysters. Spring is the time of migrations, runs of pink shrimp, jellyfish riding the currents and washing up helplessly on the beaches. In July and August the desolate flats are seemingly void of life, save for a hermit crab or two leaving trails in the sand under the blazing hot summer sun. The shallow Gulf waters become a gigantic warm bathtub filled with lethargic rays and scavenging sharks. Finally fall arrives, bringing great schools of leaping mullet, redfish, and trout. Bryozoans and hydroids and tunicates and sponges blossom on the wharfs, pilings, and rocks. Conchs begin to appear on the beaches, plowing furrows in the sand. In the middle of October the white shrimp show up. Then all up and down Waterfront Street of Shiawassee and Elizabeth City trawlers tie up at the docks, their hatches loaded with baskets of shrimp. As winter progresses, more and more boats come into the docks and boat basins of the little north Florida fishing towns to reap the harvest of the sea—to mine the white gold.

When I returned, I saw no shrimp boats out in the bay or even working in the open Gulf, which was unusual for the early spring. The shrimp were staying way out in warmer seas. The oyster season, however, was in full swing, because oysters get big, fat, and tasty in cold weather, and Waterfront Street was throbbing with activity. I drove over the long bridge of the Shiawassee River with my Airedale beside me, over the drawbridge—which during the shrimping season would stop traffic every five minutes to let a shrimp trawler in or out, but now the watchman slept peacefully in the heated tower. I drove down the winding highway into town. Refrigerated trucks were parked all over Waterfront Street, loading sacks of live oysters for restaurants and metal drums of shelled oysters for canneries.

Waterfront Street is a long, wide street bordered on one side by the Shiawassee River, which runs out to the sea. Along the riverbank are fish and oyster houses—old, barnlike buildings of rusty corrugated iron, with docks where boats unload their catches. On the other side of the street are stores that sell hardware and appliances that fishermen buy. If you want you can buy a halyard, two hundred feet of shrimping cable, buoys and shrimp nets, purse seines, oyster tongs and oyster gloves and oyster-shucking knives, corks, ropes, and anchors, and beer-can openers. Almost anything you need or think you need to run a boat is for sale—mostly sold on credit; the appliance stores do a thriving business on paper during the off seasons. But when the shrimp come into the bay or the mullet start running as they should the dust-covered stacks of bills finally get paid off.

There are also places of refreshment for the weary fisherman—almost as many bars as there are marine-appliance stores. In the cold weather no sane person would seek refuge in any place but a warm bar where there is good company, a hot stove, and lots of draft beer. That was where the die-hard shrimp fishermen were to be found now, running up staggering credit bills. To these men there was only one kind of fishing, and that was shrimping; they wouldn't consider anything else.

But other fishermen were across the street at the oyster houses, unloading their catches and earning pots of money. The oyster season is short at its best, but if you work very hard, there is good money to be made. Around October, just before the first frost, families come from all over and live in crowded rooming houses and apartments to reap the harvests of the sea. They come to Shiawassee in broken-down Fords and rusted-out Chevrolets (the only makes they know how to repair), in pick-up trucks jammed with all their possessions, and whole families work the oysters, just as the migrant farmer families work the orange crop in the southern part of the state.

Fishermen come from Alabama and Mississippi, and from other parts of Florida, and some even drive over from Texas and down from Virginia. They are a fishing people and will not do anything but fish for a living. When they come to Shiawassee and Oyster Hill, they buy and trade boats, and anything that will float, no matter how decrepit or riddled with shipworms, is of enormous value. Exorbitant prices are paid for rickety outboard motors that should long ago have been retired to the scrap pile.

Rough, weather-beaten women with puffy red faces, wearing baggy trousers, hip boots, and heavy frayed sweaters, work beside their men. Usually two men work on every oyster boat; one tongs and the other culls. Both tasks are tedious and back-breaking, especially in the freezing weather. To reap the harvest of the sea, the oysters must be raked up with a heavy pair of tongs that resemble rakes with a scissors movement. It takes powerful back muscles and biceps to wield the tongs and lift the oysters into the boat. The man who culls breaks off the undersized oysters from the legal-size ones and throws them back to grow larger.

When I reached Shiawassee the day was almost over. The oyster skiffs had pulled into dock and were unloading their catch. The fishermen were shoveling loads of oysters into bushels. They received a dollar for each bushel, and some of the energetic teams could earn up to forty or fifty dollars a day. After the bushels were measured out, strong-backed young Negroes loaded wheelbarrows and brought them into the shucking houses.

Long wet cement tables lined the windows, and as each bushel was dumped on the table, the women, wearing thick oyster gloves, skillfully pried the oysters open, swiftly scooped the meat out into five-gallon metal cans, and dropped the shells out of special windows in the building. Mountains of oyster shells piled up higher and higher and still higher until they reached a peak and avalanched down to the ground in a flat, solid pile. Even the shells are sold for road construction; they give substance to soft sand and help fill in swamps and marshes.

The State Board of Conservation officers, dressed in light-gray uniforms and looking official and ominous with their conspicuous revolvers, walk in and out of the oyster houses to measure the catches and meet the skiffs as they dock. If they find a certain percentage under three inches, somebody is in trouble. During the oyster season, the conservation officers are the least popular officials in town.

I watched a big refrigerator truck back up to the oyster house where the Negroes were loading the oyster drums. And then Wally turned the corner of the fish house, singing loudly and cheerfully about a gal named Lou. He was wearing an old tan army jacket and a blue woolen cap pushed down over his ears. He had grown a big red bushy beard since I had last seen him. He was walking briskly, his arms swinging.

I wondered about the sudden growth of his beard. I rolled down the car window and called to him, and he stomped over and bellowed out, "Goddam, what are *you* doing here? Danny said that you was off on one of them tropical islands somewhere living it up with all them good-looking native women, laying up drunk all the time and getting pots of government money to boot. But old Cheesehead Williams said that was a lie—he's been telling everybody you was in jail—sent up the river."

He paused and listened to me explain at great length where I had been and what I had been doing. He solemnly shook his head and said gravely, "Did you escape or get paroled?"

I gave up defending myself. "What are you doing with that big bush on your face?" I demanded. "Turn beatnik?"

He stroked it lovingly. "Oh, that's my windbreaker. It keeps the cold air from coming down my neck and keeps some of them women from pestering me and stealing my hard-earned money."

A Negro, pushing a wheelbarrow past us, grinned and saluted mockingly. "Hello there, Captain Castro."

"Captain Castro?" I asked. "Did you join the revolution?"

"Naw, hell!" A wild gleam shone in Wally's dark eyes and his beard split into a grin. "Me and the State Board of Conservation had a little run-in a few months back while you was in jail—"

"I wasn't—" I broke in, but Wally went on, "Them sons of bitches pulled a fast one on me. They been out to get me.

They was hiding off the west end of St. John's Island, and when I came by pulling the net, they took off after me. There wasn't time to do nothing!" he said with disgust. "I was caught with my pants down. So I just took out my knife, cut the tow line, and let her go down. Then I started running. I was in that little fourteen-foot fiber-glass skiff of mine and must have had six hundred pounds of big white shrimp. I turned the throttle out wide open and that forty-horse Johnson just naturally hauled ass, but two of them wardens was right behind me.

"I kept circling, but their boat was faster than mine—they got those twin outboard sixties—and like I said before, I had that hull full of shrimp. So I figured they'd catch me sooner or later, but I wasn't going to make it easy. I kept circling and circling and they kept gaining and trying to cut me off, hollering 'Stop, stop, stop!' and I kept right on going. I was trying to get ahead of them and bail out that shrimp so they wouldn't have no evidence. Anyway I was still keeping a lead on them, bailing out shrimp, when that damn motor gets air-locked and I come to a stop. Right quick-like they was on top of me."

Wally paused and waited until I stopped laughing.

"But wait, I ain't even told you the best part yet. They was big-city cops, bigwigs sent down here special to catch people stealing shrimp, and they didn't know me for nothing. My beard was even bigger," he said, stroking it, "and when they grabbed my anchor line, they asked me my name and I said, 'I no speak-a da English!' They asked where I was from and I pointed out into the Gulf, 'Um-a from Cuba—Um-a from Cuba.' "

He bellowed with laughter. "They put it on the radio and said something about standing by until the Border Patrol got down here. Good God Almighty! It would have been the biggest laugh Shiawassee ever had, if that no-good stinker Bob Trammel didn't spoil it. That sorry, no-good sow's ear came rushing out in his big speedboat, and when he saw me he said, 'Goddamnit, that's Wally Kenmore. He's been pulling your leg.' "

Then Wally added with outraged dignity, "You know, them sons of bitches jumped into my boat, handcuffed me, and hauled me off to jail! But Jesus Christ—I sure had fun before that sorry Trammel spoiled it."

Even though I was laughing over Wally's exploit and he enjoyed the attention, I could not help but regret the stealing of shrimp. In the long run the shrimp will disappear from overfishing.

Every year scores upon scores of giant shrimp trawlers are built, and every year more and more boats attack the shrimp with huge, sweeping nets. There have been nights when I stood on a trawler and gazed with dismay at so many boats in the bay, all striking at the shrimp. Small boats and large trawlers, all brilliantly lighted so that it looked like a city floating on the sea, each one pulling one or two or even three big nets, all scouring the bottom.

Japanese fisheries biologists are way ahead of us in matters of conservation and have instituted spawning grounds where they farm shrimp as we do oysters. If we do not follow their example and put back the shrimp we are taking out, our shrimp will have the same fate as the oysters in "The Walrus and the Carpenter" in *Alice:* "They'd eaten every one."

The State Board of Conservation tries to protect nature's nursery grounds—the shallow bays and estuaries where the young, white shrimp mass together in great numbers. But the theft of juvenile shrimp is probably not the only reason that the shrimp are diminishing. Legal fishing for the large gravid shrimp in the offshore waters is far more devastating. One gravid female shrimp spawns, on the average, half a million eggs, of which only a small percentage survive their natural predators.

I changed the subject. "How's oystering these days?"

"It's been real good. I've been making plenty of money." He paused, then asked, "You still collecting bugs?" When I told him I was, he said, "Well, you should have seen the jelly-fish out there yesterday. Why, there must have been a million of those big stinging nettles. Can you use them?"

"You bet I can. I've got an order for two hundred."

"Well, come around one weekend and we'll get up a mess. You know I get a kick out of picking up that junk with you."

"Where's the shrimpers?"

"I imagine they're down at Metcalf's Bar. Ain't nobody shrimping these days. It's too cold."

"How about coming down to Metcalf's and having a beer with me?"

"Not right now. I'll see you down there after a while, I ex-pect. I got to collect some back money from the fish house. I got better than a hundred and fifty dollars waiting for four days' work. I'll see you later. Then you can help me pitch a drunk, if you want to," he offered generously. He pounded Linda quickly and jumped off, but she was faster and he got bitten anyway.

I left Linda locked up in the station wagon and pushed open the swinging doors of Metcalf's Bar. There was loud talking and laughing in the smoke-filled room. The shrimpers were there—those who had not gone oystering. Among them were Danny Yates, Preacher, David Clark, and Cully. Cully looked up glassy-eyed for a moment, then went back to sleep. They had been consoling themselves with beer, oysters on the half shell, crackers, and hot sauce, playing poker and talk-ing about their conquests with women—the usual subject of men in bars no matter where the bars are.

Preacher looked up. He was as handsome as ever with his deceptively angelic blue eyes. The name "Preacher" became him. If one removed his faded blue jeans, worn plaid shirt, and peaked cap and put him in ministerial garments with the Good Book in his hand, nobody would be the wiser. He looked so sincere and kind that one would, without hesitation, pour out one's troubles to him and feel perfectly safe in entrusting one's life savings to him. His real name was Oscar, but his mother had high hopes that some day Oscar would become a preacher.

When he learned that preachers earned very little and worked very hard and did not gamble, chase women, get drunk, and have fights, his interest in the higher callings dimmed.

"Hey, Yankee," Preacher shouted. "What kind of a bird is it that wears stripes and can't fly?"

The answer should have been a jailbird, of course, but I was annoyed. My pride was hurt. Here I had been around the world carrying an official gold-sealed government letter requesting that all officials render the courtesy due me as a member of the International Indian Ocean Expedition. And here were these unshaven, unkempt, beer-soaked fishermen teasing me. "Aw, go to hell," I snapped.

Danny shuffled the cards rapidly and drawled, "I told you I got a letter from Jack when he was in Africa and a post card from France. He wasn't in jail."

"Aw, come on, deal, Danny. Don't tell me, he was in jail and if he wasn't in jail he should have been," said George Williams emphatically, stroking his thick mustache with his stubby fingers.

Tiny's broad face curved into a calculating smile. "You ought to have come back with a lot of money, huh, Jack? How 'bout dealing in a few hands and putting some on the table?"

And Preacher called out to the bartender, "Nick, bring old Jack here a beer and one for me too since he's paying for it."

They had not changed a bit. And I felt, as I played cards with them and looked at their friendly, familiar faces, completely absorbed in the game, that my carefree days among them were numbered. I could not explain it. All I knew was that I could not stand still after an expedition, conferences, meetings, and lectures at the Smithsonian Institution and Woods Hole, speaking with scientists, traveling through Europe, flying halfway across the world to Madagascar.

My life could not continue as it had been before I left. I had to do something, either develop my small enterprise into a profitable business or take one of the positions offered me by the museums and universities, with a chance to complete my education. Whichever way I went, there would be a lifetime of hard, intellectual work ahead for me. There was no crystal ball, and I would have to wait and see what the gods had in store for me, but whatever I chose, I knew that I could not be a carefree deck hand again.

After we played a few hands and gossiped, I asked, "Any idea of when you're going out shrimping? I need some specimens pretty bad."

"There ain't a thing in the world out there anyway," Chass said disgustedly. "Not even stuff you can use—no sharks, sting rays, skates, or any of that junk. We made a strike a few days back and there wasn't nothing but a bunch of lousy little pinfish."

Danny told the bartender to bring two beers and put mine on his tab. "What kind of orders do you have this year?"

"Enough to keep me hopping when I get to filling them. Shock fish, sea snakes"—that is, electric rays and moray eels—"and a few pregnant sharks. Did you get any sea lice on that tow, Chass?"

"Sea lice" was the local name for mantis shrimp, which is the common name for *Squilla empusa*. A collector must know the scientific names used in the scientific world, and the common names that books and imaginative scientists give the animals, and lastly, and perhaps most important in locating the specimens, the local names like "sea lice," "shock fish," and "sea snakes."

Perhaps the local names are the real names, for when I think of sea lice, I think of a monstrous-looking shrimp creature that twists and flexes its jagged tail and cuts deep into any unprotected hand, drawing blood. I remember their beautiful opalescent queer-green eyes set up on high stalks and how they look waving their gills and claws in the piles of fish brought on deck. I remember how I first picked one up and how it slashed my fingers and I bled profusely.

"Sea lice" is a good honest name for them, because they are pests in a shrimp net. But the scientific name, *Squilla empusa*, clouds the impression. Perhaps *Squilla empusa* is a much better name for sea lice after they have sat in alcohol for ten years on the shelves of the United States National Museum, when all their color has been bleached out, and the memories of what it was like has been washed away—perhaps then they look like *Squilla empusa*.

"Them sons-of-bitches sea lice is always out there," Chass said, "but I'll guarantee that you ain't gonna get nobody to go out for *them*. What in the hell do you want with sea lice, anyway?"

"Scientists—they experiment with them," I explained. "They study their nervous system. Say, what about horseshoe crabs, Chass? I need them real bad."

Chass shook his head. "I didn't see a one. They must bury up somewhere in this cold, or they go way offshore—one."

"Well, if I were you," Danny said thoughtfully, "I'd just tell them scientists that you can't get none of that stuff until the weather warms up. If they know so much about shark guts and sea lice, they ought to know that you can't get something when you can't get it, and there ain't nothing you can do about

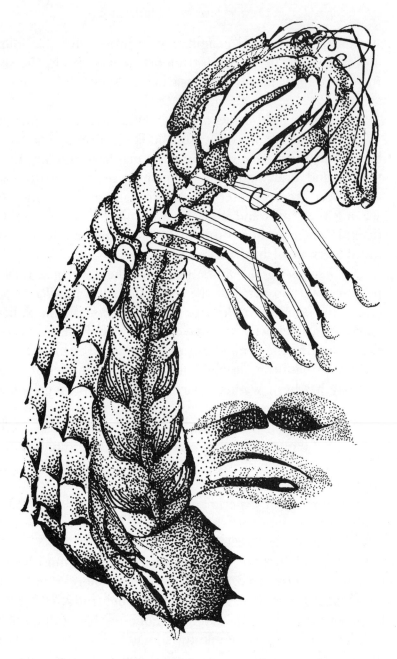

SQUILLA EMPUSA—The Mantis Shrimp
*"Sea lice" is a good honest name for them, because they are pests
in a shrimp net.*

it. It's colder than a well digger's ass in Alaska out in that Gulf."

"They say that's *my* problem—I'm the collector. I'll pay you a dollar for every crab you bring in, if you can get them in the next couple of weeks. I need forty right now."

Preacher exaggeratedly choked on his beer and looked up with surprise. "Well, I'll be damned. I never thought I'd see the day when you'd be paying us for that junk." He began to tease me, reminding everybody that he had known me when I was a snotty schoolboy and that he had had me scrubbing down his decks and washing his dishes, and had taught me how to head shrimp. Everybody laughed when he related the time I first went shrimping and he told me to pick up an electric ray and I did.

But he didn't tell the rest of the story—how I avenged myself by giving him a rattling good kick to his posterior, which he returned with interest, and how I retaliated by turning the deck hose on him and the fight was on. I waited until Preacher merrily subsided. Then I went on to explain to the shrimpers that I would no longer have as much time to be out on their shrimp boats, and in that case, I thought it was only fair that I pay for any specimens they brought in on my special request.

"Sure," said Danny. "That's reasonable enough. You do pull your share of the work, and I always say"—he turned to the other shrimpers—"if he can make something out of that trash we cull off, I'm glad for him."

Chass nodded. "I got no objections to making a few extra dollars. But it seems to me that's a hell of a drive for you to make from Arcadia to here. Seems like you ought to move away from that mangy bunch of crab pickers."

Then he launched into bitter and fluent cursing at the Arcadia crabbers, and he was helped out liberally by everybody, including drunken Cully, who hated the Arcadia crabbers passionately. The moment he heard them mentioned, he half lifted his head from the bar and started mumbling. "God-dam crabbers . . . they can stick everyone of them f'in crab pots . . . goddam chicken-assed sons of . . . chicken-assed sheriff . . . stinkin . . . crabbers . . ."

He continued on and on and on with the rhythmic regu-larity of a chugging train until it got on Chass Parker's nerves. The big shrimper thumped him and said, "Shut up, Cully. Drink your beer and go to sleep."

Ordinarily this might have invited a rousing good brawl. Nobody told Cully to shut up. But right now he was too far under to resent being told how to behave.

There had been a long-standing feud between the Shia-wassee shrimpers and the Arcadia crabbers. The two industries could never agree on where to set the boundaries so that they could keep out of each other's way.

"How about it, Jack?" prodded Preacher. "Why don't you move away from that little hole? I know an old oyster house that's up for sale for five hundred dollars down, and you could turn it into a good lab."

"Not until Shiawassee puts in a real airport," I replied.

It was almost dark when I left the bar, and the street lights had come on. Most of the oyster skiffs were empty and tied to the dock, but I could hear the sounds of oysters being cracked out in the brightly lit oyster houses. Some of the oyster fishermen had gone into the bars, and truck drivers, tired of freezing and waiting for the oysters to be shucked and loaded, had gone into the bar for a bit of cheer too.

A few hefty middle-aged prostitutes, bespangled with ear-rings and cheap fake-pearl necklaces, wearing little makeup and heavy coats, met the tired oystermen at the docks, and if the girls were lucky, they walked off arm in arm to the bars or to decrepit boardinghouses down the street. And through the darkness I could hear them giggling or chattering in their drawling voices, and the rumbling, low tones of the men.

But next to the bustling oyster houses were long blocks of silent, deserted shrimp and fish houses. Not even the cats kept vigil. The river waves lapped up gently against the docks and the hibernating shrimp boats. Their masts were naked, all the nets had been stored, the wire fish baskets and boxes were put away. They waited and slept until spring would finally come.

Until the weather warmed up and the shrimp boats were on the move again, all I could do was to comb the beaches, fill some of the backlog of orders, and stock up some of my supplies from the flats.

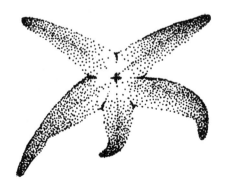

# 3 Collecting with an Airedale

I drank the scalding coffee hastily and dressed warmly while Linda padded anxiously beside me and looked up pleadingly as if to say, "You're taking me with you, aren't you? You won't leave me again, will you?" Her stubby tail wagged ingratiatingly.

It was still dark when I loaded my station wagon with buckets, shovels, plastic bags, rakes, and Linda, who insisted on coming with me wherever I went, especially since I had deserted her for so many months and left her with relatives. There was hoarfrost on my overgrown lawn and etched on the palmetto scrub. The water in the ditches was covered over with a thin layer of ice. I pulled the hood of my jacket up over my head against the bitter north winds and drove ten miles down to the best collecting beaches.

Early spring in North Florida is a wonderful time to go collecting. The strong north winds combined with the low tides push the water far back and expose great expanses of tidal flats. Combing the lonely sand and mud flats with my dog, I was in my own world, cold or not. I enjoyed collecting when there was much to collect. Had the flats been barren of life as they were in the hot summer, I would have been uncomfortably conscious of the freezing weather and after a short while I would have quit. But now the flats were rich with animal forms, and I was so absorbed and enthused that I was not aware of the biting cold and my smoking breath.

In the past I had often gone out collecting with friends, visiting professors and graduate students. I enjoyed helping them with their projects and showing them the wonders of the North Florida beaches. In this cold weather there were few visitors, but Linda was good company. Like me, she was an ardent collector. She ran ahead, stopped, sniffed the sand, and sudenly began to dig vigorously. With her paws she fairly excavated the beach until she found the conch. She trotted up to me, wagging her stubby tail, dropped the large conch at my feet, and waited a moment for my praise—"Good girl." Then she was off again. A sudden spurt of water attracted her attention. When she heard the bubbling of the terebellid worms, she cocked her ears, listened intently, and dug furiously and futilely; they were just too deep.

In the dawn, with the red sun rising over the bay and golden glints sparkling on the gently lapping waves, I walked along the edge of the sea and in the shallows, collecting the animals I needed. Sea cucumbers, starfish, conchs, clams, cockles, sponges with brittlestars and snapping shrimp, pea crabs—so many, many creatures were everywhere, just for the picking. It seemed no time at all before I picked up a quota of large hermit crabs, many of them carrying lush growths of *Hydractinia*. Some carried an extra bonus of reddish commensal sea anemones, *Calliactis*, and since they were worth fifty cents apiece, I felt well rewarded.

With Linda at my heels, I walked along the beds of eelgrass looking for the tiny knifelike slits that brachiopods make. Seeing a brachiopod, one might think it is some sort of bivalved mollusk because of its shell, but it is not. It is a separate phylum, anatomically different from all other animals. It is a most essential laboratory animal, since one genus, *Lingula*, is the oldest surviving genus of any present life form, having remained virtually unchanged for four hundred million years. I was finding *Glottidea pyramidata*, a Gulf Coast brachiopod which is very closely related to *Lingula*. The tips of its shell rising up to the surface of the mud between the eelgrass roots caused the characteristic little slits.

On the mud flats I recognized these little hints and clues that Nature left me; these were my stock in trade. It requires a specialized knowledge to dig up each specimen and isolate it from its substrate. Over the years I had become an ecologist and a naturalist in my own way. A sudden spurt of water from the sands told me of the presence of an angel-wing clam. Every little hump and trail and burrow in the sand left a message. Two tubes spaced a foot apart protruding above the eelgrass, which might look like mere brown twigs to the untrained eye, were a parchment worm; that small mound of sand was a burrowing sand dollar; and this furrow was made by a moon snail. I could see the trail of the hermit crab as it dragged its stolen snail shell over the mud. That little hole was the burrow of a mud eel.

*Cerianthus*, a curiously purple sea anemone, rode up to the top of its long fleshy tube and blossomed with long tentacles that waved gently with the ebbing tide. I stood and watched its beauty for a moment, taking in this exquisite creature while it was still alive, for in a short time it would be a lifeless and colorless entity in formaldehyde. Then I reached down to snatch it. A sudden spurt of water broke the silence of the morning and the small, purple anemone rocketed to the bottom of its long tube, but to no avail. I leaned on the shovel and with one mighty pry, sand tube, anemone, and all came up and entered my collecting bucket.

Cerianthids were widely scattered on the flats. I walked along slowly, searching for the beautiful waving maroon tentacles and digging the animals up as I came upon them. Now and then I dug up a large, ugly-looking scale worm called *Poly-dontes*—it lives in a very similar tube, and only slight differences in the degree of sliminess and sandiness distinguish the anemone's tube from the worm's.

Sea gulls flew over the water, picking up the fat round sea urchins from the flats. They carried them high up, splattered them on the earth, then feasted on their oozing, rich gonads. All they had left me were twelve sea urchins. A long sipunculid sausage worm sticking its little pink nozzle out of its sandy burrow had to be painstakingly pulled out. It was like a tug of war with the odds in the worm's favor—at least in the sense that it might tear apart, rendering it useless to me. The beautiful bright-red-and-green cirratulid polychaete annelid has a medusalike head with lively long thin tentacles—I needed all my cleverness and skill to excavate the worm from the mud without breaking it. And some worms, like the long pink nemerteans, either broke into pieces at the slightest irritation or would abruptly vomit their proboscis.

A collector's work is different from a fisherman's, although both search the sea. The fisherman feeds man's appetite for food, the collector feeds his appetite for knowledge, his curiosity. A classroom biology instructor wearing a laboratory gown and rubber gloves pries open the lid of a big drum and neatly lays out many odd and interesting creatures of the sea for his students to look at, to probe and dissect.

And perhaps for the first time the students look upon a rubbery white squid with bulging black eyes and long tentacles covered with sucker disks. They see the pale sea anemone *Cerianthus*, faded pink nemerteans hardened in formalin, speckled orange crabs, and a long, striped moray eel with its mouth fixed permanently agape. And as these animals are laid out on the black-topped laboratory tables, the students learn of other creatures besides themselves that live in their world. As they scrutinize and handle lumps of coral with tiny polyps expanded, or study the circulatory system of a preserved dogfish shark, they wonder about the environment they live in.

Perhaps they never wonder how the specimens got into the laboratory. Perhaps they never know that a biological collector, wading among the rocky tidepools of the Pacific, gathered these fragile, feathery hydroids and spent hours relaxing their delicate polyps to make them look lifelike and natural.

They probably never know the man on the rocky New England coast who patiently and carefully pried the red starfish they are examining off the rocks and wharf pilings. But that doesn't matter at all. No one is apt to think, while eating delicious shrimp at the dinner table, of the fisherman who caught them in his trawls. And that is the way it should be.

One afternoon, as I was sleeping comfortably on the shrimp boat *Elysium Queen*, Danny Yates woke me and said: "Come on, Sugar. We've got to catch some shrimp tonight—there's a whole lot of people to be fed." And so it is in collecting—there are a whole lot of minds to be fed.

I was also collecting sea cucumbers for a specialist who was trying to settle a controversy concerning the identification of sea cucumbers by analyzing the chemical structure of the blood instead of comparing anatomical structures, which are the traditional keys used in taxonomy. A biochemist, visiting the local marine laboratory, collected a series of the most abundant sea cucumber, *Thyonella gemmata*. Some of the holothurians were fatter and had thicker-branched tentacles and longer tubed feet, and he called them "stouts." The others were thinner and had fewer-branched tentacles and shorter tubed feet, and he called them "thins."

He examined the blood of both the "thins" and the "stouts" and found some important differences. He declared that the "thins" and the "stouts" were sibling species; if they were, he had reason to conclude that he had discovered an entirely new species of sea cucumber.

Since sea cucumbers are traditionally identified by the shape and size of their spicules, the biochemist sent a good series of preserved "stouts" and "thins" to a sea-cucumber specialist who promptly identified both of them as belonging to a single species of *Thyonella gemmata*, based on the arrangement of the spicules.

The specialist, interested in the biochemist's results, suggested that he not be hasty in his conclusions but raise the sea cucumbers over a period of five years, testing their chemistry and noting their morphology to see if there were any blood changes due to age differences, feeding, or sexual maturity. Furthermore, if they were truly sibling species, as he claimed, he should conduct further experiments and try breeding them. True sibling species cannot be interbred.

Disregarding the specialist's advice, the enthusiastic young biochemist published his paper, with photographs showing the "stouts" and the "thins" and illustrations of the differences in their blood. He suggested that one of the sibling species should be named in honor of the sea-cucumber specialist.

The eminent specialist, to prove conclusively that the "thins" and the "stouts" were the same species, requested that I get up a large series of *Thyonella gemmata* starting from postlarval stages and ranging up to the largest specimens that could be found.

On my hands and knees I searched for the characteristic tiny double holes among the sand in the eelgrass beds, and after scraping the sand and mud grains away from the roots of the eelgrass, I exposed a tiny sea cucumber not more than an eighth of an inch long. I picked it up with a delicate needle-point forceps and put it in a vial of alcohol. I found more like this, and still more. Then I found some a quarter of an inch long, and still more up to half an inch long. Finding the infants was the hardest part. I could not blame the biochemist for not finding any that small.

But the big *Thyonella gemmata* ranging from five to nine inches long were all over the mud flats, covered by just a few inches of water. The sausage-shaped sea cucumbers poked their floriated heads out of the mud, waving their tentacles as they snatched up bits of plankton. They were so dense that the littoral looked as if it were peppered with little clumps of ferns. If you watch a sea cucumber closely, you will see a most fascinating feeding process. They sweep the water with their eight long, sticky, finely branched tentacles and capture bits of planktonic life, then they wipe the food off with two smaller tentacles, much as a child licks sticky candy from his fingers.

To assist in the identification, I made sure to extend every one of their floriated crowns. I couldn't do this with the infants, but I had developed my own special technique for catching the big ones and keeping the tentacles distended. Sneakily I brought my hand down through the icy waters and swiftly clamped my fingers behind the tentacles, strangling the sensitive animal so it could not draw its floriated crown back into the body. Then I tied a rubber band tightly behind the tentacles and dropped them into alcohol.

If I made one wrong slip and didn't snatch a sea cucumber just right, it drew in its tentacles and contracted quickly down into the mud. My Airedale walked along with me looking uncertain of herself—this was not her sort of work. She stepped among the sea cucumbers, stirring up the mud and causing them to contract. "Linda, go away!" I ordered. "Go back to the car."

She looked hurt and wandered off to dry land. I had to work fast now, because sea cucumbers are light-sensitive, and with the sun rising higher they were contracting farther down into their burrows. The tide was beginning to creep in, and when I was satisfied with my series of cucumbers, I carried my jars to the dry beach.

Linda was happy again now that I had abandoned the sea cucumbers. She raced ahead, her ears flapping in the wind, pounced on a spider crab, raced back, and dropped it at my

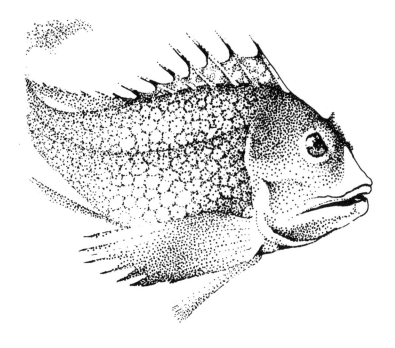

*I hadn't expected to find a poisonous scorpion
fish stranded in a tide pool.*

feet. I thanked her, then released it while she was digging frantically, making the sand fly, for no particular reason. I continued collecting other animals, filling my buckets with *Molgula*, the lumpish brown sea squirts, and *Echinaster*, the orange starfish. Periodically I made a trip to the station wagon to load the collections, then returned to the flats again for more.

I had expected to find all the animals I was looking for, since I had years of experience looking over these same beaches and tidal flats. I hadn't expected to find a poisonous scorpion fish stranded in a tide pool. But there it was, splotched orange and brown, with its bristling spines in the shallow water, so well camouflaged in the sea weeds that I might have stepped on it if if hadn't suddenly flapped its tail and splashed. I was very happy to see this nasty little creature, because I knew a paleontologist who wanted to compare recent scorpion fish with fossilized bones of ancient ones chipped out of sedimentary rocks.

If I had gone collecting fully equipped to handle a scorpion fish, with dip net, tongs, and a special container, undoubtedly I would not have found one. Now the problem was how to catch it. I could not just pick it up—the needlelike spines can cause excruciating agony if they penetrate the skin. I had not forgotten that just a few months before I had been stuck by the spines of a rabbit fish in the Indian Ocean, and my hand had felt as if it had been soaked in gasoline and lit. The burning pain had lasted all day, and at one point I almost fainted. I had no desire to repeat that experience.

But how could I capture a poisonous scorpion fish without dip net or tongs? I had to use my ingenuity. The shovel was ineffective; as soon as I scooped the fish up, it flipped off and fell on the damp seaweed, where it leaped and wriggled furiously, doing a wild little dance. Linda saw it and got excited, as Airedales do, and rushed in to bite it. The fish would have given her a mouthful of venomous spines which might have killed her, but I was quicker and snatched her by the scruff of the neck and threw her off, roaring, "No, Linda, no!" She landed on all fours, the whites of her eyes gleaming insanely and her ears flattened back, and charged again.

Linda and I had to have it out. I was determined to settle it once and for all. Airedales, no matter how intelligent and sensible, can be very stubborn and knot-headed, especially when they are determined to bite something. Finally I had to resort to the shovel. Linda felt no pain. The shovel was even less effective on her than it was on the scorpion fish. I abandoned the shovel and hurled her to the ground and sat on her and cursed her until she was subdued.

An observer who knew that I was collecting specimens for a livelihood and who witnessed the roaring battle between me and Linda might wonder why I tolerated so stubborn a bitch. But her bad behavior was only temporary; at other times she was a sweet dog and extremely useful, and in one case, if it had not been for her, I would have been unable to fill an urgent order for a cancer-research foundation. The researchers had found that pen shells, *Atrina rigida*, have an amazing resistance to cancer, and they wanted a large quantity. If the order had come during the winter or early spring, I would have had no trouble finding them; the tips of their valves are easily seen in the bare eelgrass beds. But the order came in the middle of the summer, and the eelgrass was knee-deep and every occupant was thoroughly covered over. After searching endlessly through the eelgrass, I accidentally stepped on a pen shell; its sharp valves jabbed into my bare foot. I dug it up and showed it to my dog. Linda sniffed it, padded on, stopped, and began digging. Sure enough, it was another pen shell. I praised her highly, and with her usual enthusiasm, she dug up the quota of fifteen *Atrina*. She was also good at rounding up ghost crabs but horseshoe crabs were her specialty.

Now that I had finally settled things with Linda, and she was restored to her usual sanity, I turned to the scorpion fish, which angrily bristled its spines. I placed the empty pail on its side and with the shovel nudged it toward the opening; it twisted and writhed, with its ominous dorsal spines erected. I kept my distance and urged it on again, and after three tries I succeeded, while Linda stood by and looked on wistfully.

I had to be cautious in carrying the scorpion fish back to the station wagon—it was a very active fish, thrashing and leaping in the bucket. By this time the tide had come in, covering the eelgrass, and the morning was gone. I was happy but exhausted. In collecting it is easy to work way beyond your endurance because the work is so interesting and there is so much to do. However, all these animals would have to be preserved in my laboratory and put into specimen bottles and drums—the scorpion fish would be frozen to make a skeleton—and my work would not be finished until late at night.

Back in my early naïve days, as a rebellious ex-student, I thought that by leaving the university and becoming a collector I had ended my days of hard work, study, and routine. In the university I followed a routine that had been established for me. Since I was required to do little on my own initiative, I had no headaches. My guidance professor worked out my curriculum with me, I attended classes on schedule. I awoke in the morning to an alarm clock, which gave me time for morning ablutions, a quick breakfast, and an eight-o'clock class.

My eight-hour day was parceled out into hours, half hours, and even quarter hours, giving me time to change classes, trotting rapidly from end to end of the big sprawling campus. There was time for everything if I kept my eye on my watch, time for the library, time for lunch, time for another class, time for chemistry lab, and so on, and even time to stop and talk with a friend.

As long as I was in the university I disliked having my life so scheduled and so mechanized. I was enduring all this to earn something I never quite understood, called credits. As many times as credits were explained to me, emotionally I could not accept them as symbols for what I knew. For the life of me, I could not see how racking up credits made me one bit smarter or added to my knowledge. My advisers advised me that credits were a means to an end and that if I wanted to make biology my lifetime career, I would have to acquire a diploma, or what was called in the inner educational circles a "union card."

I finally realized the value of scheduling one's time and developing a routine only after I left the university. I vividly remember the first night I left my comfortable city apartment with my portable typewriter and other possessions and moved into a little rented trailer in the dull, quiet fishing town of Elizabeth City.

Across the street from my trailer was the Holiness Church. I could hear the preacher droning on, the inflection of his voice rising and falling, the shouts of the congregation with hallelujahs galore, and "Praise the Lord" with barrelfuls of amens, with the joyful singing and stomping of the congregation. And at last it was over—silence. Suddenly I felt empty and lost. There was no reason to go to bed early, nor was there any reason to wake up. There were no classes to attend. My time was all my own and I did not know what to do with it.

This is a universal problem that must be faced in one's lifetime sooner or later. A college graduate who has received his diploma and all honors is suddenly thrust out into the world to fend for himself. They call it an adjustment period when servicemen have finished their term and are told to adjust to the civilian way of life, to forget the routine of the military. Some go to pieces and cannot adjust. Some seek careers within the confines of the routine; they become officers. In the university they become graduate students, then professors. It matters not whether one leaves a routine situation honorably or dishonorably: the aftereffect, the so-called freedom, is the most difficult period of all.

As I paced around in my tiny trailer, I began to doubt the wisdom of collecting specimens for a living. Could such a life have a practical future? That night I slept fitfully, made restless by bad dreams of a hallful of disapproving deans, all looking alike, sitting behind big impressive desks and pointing accusing fingers at me, all chanting in unison: "You are not college material." And in my sleep I could still hear the well-rehearsed speech that followed in their deep authoritative voices: "There are some who will be able to make it through the university and some who do not have the ability. This is regrettable! But those who do not have this ability must get out and make room for those who do. Have you ever thought of going to a trade school?"

The next morning I felt as lost as a fetus thrust out too soon from the warm, protecting, nourishing womb. I had to draw my own breath, get my own bearings, and adjust to the real world.

For four weeks I lived a depressing and aimless existence, sleeping at odd hours and too much, lumping around the trailer, sometimes reading, and generally feeling sorry for myself. But hard work soon broke that up. I had begun supplying specimens from the shrimp trawls.

When I finished with the specimens that I had collected on the flats in the morning, I looked through the lists again. Many of the orders could not be filled until the shrimp boats started running, many were seasonal on the flats, and others, such as *Aplysia* or the ctenephores, were unpredictable, but I was not unduly worried because the large biological supply houses were quite flexible with their purchase orders—they could and did wait until I could fill them. But now that I was determined to put out a conventional catalogue and expand my business, selling to the big commercial biological supply houses was one positive and quick way of raising the money to pay the printer.

# 4 Searching for Horseshoe Crabs

Even after I met most of my back orders, I went out every day with my buckets—I was building up stocks of preserved specimens. But the one animal I sought the most was not here, not in the northern Gulf or even in warmer Miami. All the orders for horseshoe crabs I had solicited while I was in Cambridge I could not fill. Daily I was receiving urgent letters, purchase orders, and telegrams, even long-distance pleading phone calls, telling me how much depended upon the immediate delivery of *Limulus*. But I was helpless.

In the cold weather *Limulus polyphemus*, the horseshoe crab, moves out into deeper, warmer water, and it comes inshore during the spring. Usually shrimp trawlers scooped up all the horseshoe crabs I needed. But there were no shrimp boats going out in Shiawassee or Elizabeth City because of the continued freeze. The only boats working offshore and in the bays were the crabbers. I would have to appeal to them.

At the boat landing of Arcadia Harbor their trucks backed down into the water because the boxes of bait were so heavy.

It took all the strength of the big muscular fishermen to heave the weighty boxes over to helpers who stacked them neatly in the boats. In the cold weather we were all dressed alike—hooded jackets, identical sweaters—but the crabbers wore rubber aprons and thick leather gloves.

The uniformity in dress was the result of buying from Miss Hopkins's Grocery and Fishermen's Supply. She sold only to local fishermen and their families—her store was hidden away in the back woods next to the bay, far from strangers and tourists who might make unusual requests for strange goods she never carried. I was flattered when she let me have a charge account with her; it meant I had been accepted.

At the landing old Andy, warmly muffled, held the boat steady while William, his helper, and Beaufort Caine loaded the long wooden skiff.

"How are you doing, Mr. Andy?" I greeted him.

And as usual he nodded slowly and replied sadly, "I ain't doing no good, not a bit of good." His voice was pitiful, whining. He shook his gray head and sighed. "This cold weather ain't doing my rheumatism a bit of good. It's about to kill me."

I shook my head in polite commiseration. I never knew what to say about his condition. Should I say, I'm sorry to hear that, or You're looking fine anyway, or I hope you feel better, or what?

Old C. D. Pearson came to my rescue and tossed off, "Ah, don't you believe him. He's as healthy as a hog fattened on corn and swill. You couldn't kill him with a meat ax!"

Grateful to C.D., I grinned and said, "How's crabbing these days?"

Redheaded Ramsy Johnson replied indignantly, "Crabbin'? We ain't crabbin', we're starvin'." He jerked a box of alewives off his truck and dropped it in the stern of his big, wide skiff. "There ain't no crabs out here no-way. You crab all day, pull two hundred traps, and don't get but one or two boxes.

They're paying seven cents a pound now, which is good, but dern them crab houses, they charge us so much for bait, we cain't hardly make a livin'." He snorted with disgust and leaped up on his truck.

The two crab companies in Arcadia buy bait fish during the summer for a piddling sum when fish are abundant and the market is glutted; a single strike in hot weather brings alewives, a herringlike fish, in by the ton. These are stored in the companies' huge freezer lockers and resold for two or three times the original amount, often to the same crab fishermen who caught them.

C. D. Pearson and his partner, Tony, and a number of other crabbers were all echoing Ramsy's complaints.

"Well, I know how you can make some extra money," I said cheerfully. "You can get me some horseshoe crabs and I'll pay you a dollar apiece, and I'll take fifty crabs."

There were no takers, not even a gleam of interest among them.

I thought I could tempt them by raising the price. "A dollar fifty," I said to C. D. Pearson—he had a small hand shrimp net he sometimes pulled from his crabbing skiff, and once he had sold me some brittle stars. "I'll go as high as that if you'll hurry and go pull your little trawl or something."

Paul Slobe, Jr., jumped off the truck, came up quietly behind me, and said scornfully, with arrogance in his voice, "A dollar fifty! Shoot! The kind of money you make off them you ought to be paying five or ten dollars apiece."

I looked around at the men's faces. Nobody added to his remark, but I could see that most of them were agreeing with him.

When the construction men had been working on my barracks, putting up a new roof, replacing the rotten floorboards, building a bathroom, and installing sinks and lab tables, the townsfolk had walked past hourly, gaping and meandering in, telling me who had lived there before—how terrible the roof had leaked—and then trying to appear casual while they probed politely to find out what I did for a living. Finally I had been forced to put up a sign stating that this building was a biological-specimen company that sold marine life for research only.

The sign worked a miracle. I was not a game warden to interfere with their poaching alligators, deer, and range hogs, and I was not a federal agent, so everybody felt comfortable. At least I was in some kind of business, even if they were not sure just what kind of business it was. But with all the money I was spending, it must be a very good business and I must be immensely rich.

Of all the people in town, Ramsy Johnson, Paul Slobe's first cousin, never worried about my financial state. He said, "Ah, don't pay any attention to Paul. He's always shootin' off at the mouth, and you know he ain't got a bit of sense." He added thoughtfully, "I been thinking. I just finished rigging up my boat for shrimping and I was going to catch my own bait fish— I can't go on paying their price."

He looked hard at Paul Slobe, Jr., who had a dull, uncomprehending look in his eyes; his thick lips were slightly open as if he were overwhelmed by the process of having to think. He knew if he came back with an answering insult, even if he was able to think of one, Ramsy would instantly come back with something far more humiliating, and he would have to counter that one too. It would take time to think up a good one. And he was never very good at thinking, even though he had a high school diploma. He had only used his head as a weapon in football; he bowled over the opposing team, butting them in the stomachs with the zeal of a billygoat, and became football champion. The school won the pennant that year. He deserved his diploma.

Paul's face was brick-red, and he was puffing with anger. He would have liked to hit Ramsy for his insolence, but from past experience he knew Ramsy would sidestep every one of his swings and come in with mean, smashing, cutting fists. However, Paul was not defeated—he saved face by jumping up on his truck, stacking two one-hundred-pound bait boxes on top of each other, and lifting them both to his chest (something nobody else could do). He climbed off the truck with the load and staggered over to his boat.

Ramsy laughed and said, "I just happen to know of a deep channel where I know I can get those horseshoe crabs, as cold as it is, and seventy-five dollars won't hurt none."

Ramsy had the distinction of being the first fisherman to try shrimping in the conservative village of Arcadia. All winter long he had worked on converting a worn-out party boat into a shrimp trawler. He had overhauled the engine, installed a winch, wired it up with a radio, and bought a shrimp net. In hidebound Arcadia, Ramsy was considered a rebel. Unlike the conservative crab fishermen, who had their pride, no job was beneath Ramsy's dignity if he got paid well for it. He considered money far more important than pride.

Two evenings later, Ramsy and his brother Bubba pushed into my laboratory carrying a fish box covered with canvas. "Where should I set them?" Ramsy asked. He was followed by his wife, her sister, her sister's husband Beaufort, who was also carrying a large pail sloshing over with water, two small children, and two half-grown barefooted boys. I never knew what relationship they bore to Ramsy, but there were always so many children and dogs running around in Arcadia that I had long ago given up on who belonged to whom.

I led the way back to the small shipping room and looked happily at the catch. There were sixteen healthy horseshoe crabs, covered with some much-needed flatworms. In the water-filled bucket were two big lumps of *Astrangia* coral, five dead sea horses, one live sea horse, two dozen stinging *Dactylometra* jellyfish (probably the reason for the premature demise of the sea horses), and three yellow boring sponges. Ramsy had brought all these to me because he thought they were pretty and I might need them. He was right.

Ramsy and his family followed me from room to room as I sorted out the animals. I put the live sea horse and the coral into the bubbling aquarium, and the dead sea horses, the live sponges, and the jellyfish into their respective jars of embalming fluid. "I'll write you a check for thirty-seven dollars," I said.

Ramsy nodded and said, "What's in that jar?" He pointed to my display shelves, which reached from the floor to the ceiling, and to a bottle that was labeled *Moira atrops*.

"Those are heart urchins," I told him. I liked answering Ramsy's questions. He always showed a healthy curiosity, and what's more, he remembered everything I told him.

"I've been fishing in these waters all my life and I ain't never seen half the stuff you got here. And near about everything I do see that's worthless to me, you can turn it all into cash money." There was wonder and admiration in his voice.

If there had been more men like Ramsy in town my business would have grown like a garden weed. However, among the other crabbers, Ramsy was also considered a bit of a nut. "Oh, him!" they would say. "He's always out in the bay ex-peermintin' with something or other."

The crabbers were remembering the time when the crab house owners had decided to discipline Ramsy for independently selling his crabs at the boat landing to tourists and making a good profit. The traditional punishment for this offense was to refuse to buy crabs from the offender and to discharge the wives and daughters in his family from the factory. It was customary after an appropriate lapse of time for a committee of the crabber's relatives to appeal to the owner, who would allow the crabber, chastised and submissive, to return to work.

Not so with the rebellious Ramsy. His wife obtained a good-paying job with the State Department as a shipping clerk, and he went out dredging for scallops—a thoroughly radical departure from the conventional fishing in that area. Unfortunately the scallops were not abundant enough. But Ramsy, stubborn and determined, still continued his private enterprise. He dug fiddler crabs and seined for minnows and grass shrimp, and sold them to sports fishermen for bait, also at a substantial profit. Ramsy's rebellion ended when Mr. Paul Cowell stopped him one morning at the post office and asked in a genial, fatherly tone, "How you been, Ramsy? How's your old lady and the young'uns?"

Ramsy mumbled a noncommittal, cold reply, but Mr. Cowell, undeterred, continued, "Where have you been keeping yourself, Ramsy? We've been a-missin' you. Why ain't you coming around selling us your crabs?" Mr. Cowell rambled on, before Ramsy could reply, because he was afraid the redheaded young man might tell the truth instead of muttering the usual "Oh, I've been feeling poorly," or "My old lady's been sick." The crab house owner said, "We've been busy something terrible, and we sure could use Mary-Sue to pick crabs."

Ramsy did not believe in holding a grudge; he was too practical. Having pride and holding grudges was too expensive. This way he could go on working for Cowell, his wife could pick crabs on weekends and holidays, and he could continue with the bait business.

When I handed Ramsy the check he looked satisfied. "Much obliged. If it don't blow too hard out there, I'll be back tomorrow. Maybe I'll get all of them. Is there anything else you need?"

"Yes," I replied. "I need three thousand fiddler crabs—a

thousand male crabs; the other two thousand can be mixed sexes. I'll pay you fifty dollars if you can get them before next week." That was a high price for fiddler crabs, but with the ground frozen and the crabs staying far down in their burrows, it would be rough digging for them.

"Why, sure." Ramsy's voice was buoyant. "I'll get them for you Sunday. Let's see, that will make it about eighty-five dollars. I'll put this whole brood"—meaning his family—"to work digging them out."

Before the week was over, go-getter Ramsy did it again. I had all my horseshoe crabs and fiddler crabs, not to mention a number of other useful specimens. Ramsy was richer by one hundred and forty dollars. I canceled all further orders for horseshoe crabs with the fishermen and removed the little want ad I had placed on the bulletin board outside the post office. With the demands for horseshoe crabs met, I could relax and wait at my leisure for warmer weather and the shrimping to begin. For the time being, I believed, I could forget all about horseshoe crabs.

But there were five fishermen who did not forget about the horseshoe crabs and did not read the bulletin.

When the waters had warmed up and winter was finally over, with small schools of fish in the bay, C. D. Pearson, Bennie, Herbie, and Tony went in fat Roscoe's big crabbing skiff to seine for alewives and mullet. They were hoping to get at least ten boxes of alewives—five boxes would be enough bait for all of them, but they hoped to sell the other five boxes to the crab houses at three cents a pound, which would pay for the gas and oil for running the boat and the trucks, and this way, Roscoe had reasoned, their bait wouldn't cost them anything.

It was a sunny day. The air was pleasantly warm and there

was enough breeze to make the fishermen comfortable. Old Roscoe sat on the bow squinting and peering over the still, greenish waters watching for a ripple, some sign of fish. He motioned to Tony to cut the motor. Tony yawned, nodded his head sleepily, and slowed the motor to a crawl. Old C.D. stood up in the center of the boat, shaded his eyes from the sun's glare with both hands, and gazed at the wide expanse of bay waters for a sign of fish.

The sea broke over a sand bar. Roscoe spoke softly. "It appears to me like there is a right smart school off the south end of that reef."

Impatiently Bennie said, "Come on, let's get 'em." He was a thin, impulsive young man with a quick temper.

"You just hold your horses, boy. If you strike now, you'll lose better'n half of 'em." C.D. spoke slowly and quietly. "The tide is rising, and in a few minutes they'll be down at this end of the reef."

Herbie laughed, lit up a cigarette, and said, "It's deep as hell at that end of the reef, Bennie. You'll get us all drowned."

All Tony said was, "Give us a cigarette, Herb, I'm fresh out." Once he had the cigarette between his lips, he had nothing more to say, and when Roscoe told him to stop the motor, he took a deep drag from his cigarette and obeyed.

The boat drifted. The men had long since run out of any conversation. It had been a long, long morning, and there had not been a sign of alewives or other fish anywhere. And having impatient, irritable Bennie with them made it more difficult until Bennie fell silent, worn out with fatigue. All the men smoked cigarette after cigarette, now and then breaking the monotony by passing the water jug. On the water when there are no fish, but only the anxiety of waiting and watching, time passes so slowly that a day's work seems like a week.

It was lunchtime. Roscoe eased the anchor over the side and sat down. He picked up a paper bag, pulled out a sandwich made of cottony-soft white bread with a thin slice of hog-head cheese and a generous slab of mayonnaise. His hands, like all the fishermen's, were thickly callused from years of pulling in heavy seines and crab baskets. He looked at his sandwich with disgust. "I declare, my old woman makes them sandwiches worse and worse every day." He bit into his sandwich and munched on it.

C.D. fared better. He was a widower, and his daughters had packed his lunch with hard-boiled eggs, a generous sandwich, and a fluffy piece of cake with pink icing which they had proudly baked themselves. Bennie was eating a store-bought sandwich wrapped in cellophane—for he and his wife, Lucy Mae, had had a fearful row, and he had been sleeping on the living-room couch for the past three nights. Herbie, being a bachelor, was also eating a store-bought sandwich and a bar of candy.

All four men watched Tony enviously while he ate his lunch. Being a newlywed, he was eating last night's left-over thick crusted fried chicken—he ate it with relish, smacking his lips and sucking the bones. Then he ate the cold biscuits thickly spread with margarine and jam. He topped it off with a huge chunk of chocolate cake.

Unconsciously, the fishermen were following his every mouthful and running their tongues over their lips. A little sigh escaped fat old Roscoe every time Tony reached into the greasy bag and pulled something out. When he finished, he threw the bag into the sea, belched, wiped his lips on his sleeve, and said with satisfaction, "That Polly-Ann sure do know how to cook, mmm-mmm!"

Herbie smirked insinuatingly. "That ain't all she knows how to do, is it?" He giggled.

The others laughed with him, and old C.D. shook his head sadly and said, "Lord alive, that *is* the truth. That boy is so weak in the morning, he can't hardly pull up them crab baskets. I'm near about thinking of getting rid of him."

Tony blushed deeply. "Aw, get out. Shoot! Y'all are jealous."

Roscoe interrupted their laughter and teasing. "I just saw some mullet jump. Look sharp . . . that school of alewife is moving. Here come the fish." He spoke sharply, and hand over hand he snatched up the anchor rope. "Tony, crank her up. Let's get 'em."

Tony sprang to his feet and jerked the starter cord, and the motor came alive. The monotony, teasing—everything was forgotten in the rush of activity and the anticipation of a strike. C.D. and Bennie jumped into the shallows with the net, dragging it toward the sand bar. It took all their strength to pull the huge, cumbersome net through the cold, resisting water that was as high as their chests. The boat moved slowly away from them as Herbie and Roscoe helped the net spill out over the stern, keeping it from tangling. The boat and net were forming a wide semicircle, which would be completed when it reached the other end of the sand bar.

With the semicircle completed and the fish walled in by the two-hundred-and-fifty-yard seine, Tony beached the skiff, jumped into the water, and helped Herbie and Roscoe to close the semicircle by dragging their end of the net up on the sand bar. Now that the fish were walled in, they lunged against the webbing, but they were trapped. The lead line hugged the bottom—there was no escape there—and the bobbing corks kept the webbed wall above the surface.

On each end of the seine were two men slowly pulling up their ends of the net by gripping it by the lead line and webbing, dragging it up onto the sand bar, their feet slipping and digging into the sand, their backs and shoulders straining. The rhythm and coordination of fishermen pulling in a seine is a beautiful thing to watch. When one man has pulled his share of the slack net up on the beach, he drops it, walks back into the water, passes the man ahead of him, grabs another portion of the net, and strains again toward the beach. The man behind him now piles up his share of the webbing, drops it, and goes out into the water again to get more. Simultaneously, on the other end of the net, the same action of beaching the net is being accomplished.

The fish were being compressed and crowded toward the center of the net; mullet leaped high and splashed back into the trap. Some leaped high enough and cleared the corkline to freedom. The semicircle became smaller and smaller and more and more slack webbing was piled up on the beach while the fish were forced into an elongated bag that the fishermen call a "pocket." Roscoe waded around the center outside of the net, watching for snags, pressing the lead line down with his foot. The men on each end of the net were complaining—the seine was exceptionally heavy. It felt like they were pulling in a whale.

Bennie was groaning, "Damnalmighty, we *sure* must have struck fish!"

Roscoe, who had been inspecting the net, shouted out, "Fish my butt! We struck all the dern, nasty old horseshoe crabs. We must have hit everyone of them in the bay."

The men at both ends of the net felt sick when they saw ten, fifteen, then twenty horseshoe crabs all balled up and tangled in the incoming webbing, flexing their abdomens and dagger-like telsons, their little pincer claws clutching each mesh, getting more and more entangled. And this was just the beginning of these crabs. The fishermen were helpless. It was a five-hundred-dollar net, and once struck, it had to be pulled in no matter what was in it, even if it was a frantic eight-foot hammerhead shark, lunging and snapping viciously at the fishermen's feet.

The more the net was pulled in, the more crabs appeared.

And when the agonizing, hopeless strike was over, on the beach was a small hill of horseshoe crabs, and only two or three hundred pounds of alewives and some mullet, barely enough to bait their crab traps.

The five fishermen felt like crying. They had to untangle each and every horseshoe crab. At first they killed the crabs with hatred and anger, bending them backward, smashing their carapaces. Old C.D. was too weary to stay angry. "Don't bother killing them things, it will take too long," he said in a complaining, whining voice. "We'll be here all night."

Roscoe nodded grimly and said, "He's right, boys. Just let's throw them out."

Bennie said thoughtfully as he was disengaging a horseshoe crab, "I'm thinking. That scientist fellah might want these crabs. A month or two ago he asked me to get him some, said he was going to pay all kinds of money for them—I don't recollect just how much."

Fat Roscoe scratched his bald head and frowned. Then his face beamed, showing a gap in his yellow front teeth. "Why sure, I most forgot. My son-in-law Ramsy got three dollars apiece for them. The way I heard it, he made three hundred dollars in one night."

Tony almost swallowed his cigarette. He and Herbie had been picking out what fish there were and pitching them into the boat. "Three hundred dollars!" he repeated with excitement. "Why that's enough to make a down payment on a house trailer."

Herbie was doing mental calculations—he was good at that. "If Jack is paying three dollars apiece, why we must have fifteen hundred dollars right here."

C.D. was realistic. "Oh, bull! I heard him. I was there too. I heard him say that he would pay a dollar and a half. I didn't hear nothing about no three dollars. He only upped the price if

I would pull my little shrimp net for him, and that was still cold weather."

Some of the hopeful light went out of their eyes and the joy out of their hearts, because seven hundred and fifty dollars was not fifteen hundred, and divided five ways it would only be a hundred and fifty each, Herbie figured.

C.D., however, was philosophical. "Well, hell, that ain't bad for one strike, considering we weren't going to make anything."

Everybody's face brightened except Bennie's. He had been giving the matter further serious thought. He lived next door to the scientist. He had tried to get the better of him a few times and had found the Yankee a little too shrewd. "I sold some frogs to him once," Bennie said thoughtfully. "He said he'd pay seventy-five cents apiece for live bull frogs. But when I brought him a passel of them, he said they was grass frogs, or leopard frogs I think he called them, and said he couldn't give more than twenty-five cents for the live ones and told me I could keep the dead ones."

"Was they grass frogs?" asked Tony curiously.

Bennie laughed. "Yeah, that's what they was. I didn't think that smart-assed Yankee knowed the difference. That's what I'm thinking about what we're gonna charge him for these horseshoe crabs. He goes down to the bay all the time—he must have seen them by now."

"That's right. I've seen him diving in the water when it was freezing out. He was getting those little old pieces of rock coral right off the landing docks. He must be crazy," said Herbie with a sneer.

"Crazy, hell!" said C. D. Pearson. "You ought to be that crazy. He gets plenty of money for that junk. One day I saw him down there at the landing netting jellyfish and he told me he gets a quarter apiece and there must have been ten million out there."

Poor old C.D. had not thought to ask how many of the ctenophores could be sold. Had he found out that only six hundred could be marketed, he would not have been so impressed.

Old Roscoe suddenly became angry. "Well, the hell with that son of a bitch. I ain't gonna go no lower than fifty cents a crab. It don't pay for us to fool with them. But we'll see what we can get out of him. I might just talk him into going seventy-five."

That evening when they returned to the landing, the pitiful amount of fish was packed into boxes and Bennie drove off with the bait in his truck to store them in the cold room of the crab plant. C.D., Roscoe, Herbie, and Tony had tossed the crabs into the truck. Tony took his place at the wheel, C.D. sat in the middle, and Roscoe was just about to climb in when old Andy and William's skiff glided up to the landing loaded with boxes of blue crabs. After William beached the skiff, old Andy clambered painfully out and looked at Roscoe's truck filled with clonking, clattering horseshoe crabs. "What in the *hell* are you going to do with all those horseshoe crabs!" he asked, his eyes wide with astonishment.

"We're going to sell them to that scientist fellah," said Roscoe, with an air of importance that comes with wealth.

"Did he give you a order for 'em?" Andy eyed them with disbelief.

"Well, no, but we figured he's about done used up all the crabs he bought from Ramsy."

"Roscoe," said Andy dryly, "you old fool! He ain't eatin' them. I doubt he'll give you a dime for that load, not if he didn't order them."

"Don't you go callin' me an old fool," Roscoe retorted indignantly. "Just because you go out fishin' with that beatnik professor don't make you no professor." Roscoe, offended, hoisted himself into the truck next to C.D., and Herbie swung up on the running board, and Tony drove off. Their spirits rose high as they approached the specimen company's barracks.

I was in the yard filling the final orders from the large biological supply house for horseshoe crabs. First I graded them as to size. The largest and the most handsome sold for seventy-five cents each, which I considered a substantial price for two hundred horseshoe crabs. The medium-sized ones sold for fifty cents, and only one hundred were wanted. I hurried, because the truck line was due to pick up the drums. After sealing the two drums I was ready to stick on the labels when I heard a complaining, belching muffler, and a car door slammed twice.

I looked up and gulped. "Oh, no," I thought miserably, "they wouldn't dare!" I shuddered when I saw the pick-up truck filled with horseshoe crabs and the four happy-looking fishermen.

I had collected my crabs on one particularly stormy day. The usually calm waters on Tye Island near Arcadia were whipped up angrily and whitecaps danced on the gray sea. When the tide had reached its highest point and flooded into the ditches along the roadside, the horseshoe crabs had swarmed up to the water's edge in hoards, in copulating pairs. Huge females with males hooked to their abdomens had pushed up on the beach, crawling on top of each other. The shoreline had been thickly bordered with horseshoe crabs for a mile, as far as I could see. I had gotten the crabs while the getting was good, dumping them into the back of my station wagon and going back for more, and more and more. Every available drum was packed with them; I had enough to last for two years.

I felt sick when old C. D. Pearson called out joyfully, "Hey, Jack. We got them horseshoe crabs you been wanting." Smiling with toothless gums, he went on, "We got all you need. Where do you want us to set 'em?"

"I don't want them," I said, recoiling. "I don't even want to look at them. I've been working on horseshoe crabs all week."

"You can't go giving orders, then canceling them thataway," said old Roscoe heatedly. "We ain't going to charge you but fifty cents a crab."

I shook my head. "I can't pay that. I can't sell them. Those crabs have been so plentiful this spring that the market for horseshoe crabs dropped out."

I tried to explain to them that there was just so much I could sell no matter how plentiful the animals were. Then, desperate for words, because they stared at me impassive and unbelieving, I compared my business to the seafood business—a glutted market for mullet was no different than a glutted market for horseshoe crabs.

They did not budge. They stood there with their mouths tight and disapproving. And I resented them for it, because they were making me feel like a wretch.

"All right," Roscoe said coldly. "We'll take fifty dollars for this load."

I tried to control my temper, but I could feel myself getting edgy. "I just told you I don't want any horseshoe crabs. But I'll pay you fifty dollars if you pick these little flatworms off the crabs' undersides, and help me flatten and preserve them."

I picked up a crab and showed them the little white worms oozing and sliding over the flapping gill books and the scrabbling ambulatory legs.

All four men protested loudly. "I wouldn't fool with that mess." "Ugh! Them nasty little worms—hell no." I think it was Tony, or perhaps it was Herbie, who yelled at the top of his voice, "I'll tell you what you can do with them worms and them crabs . . ."

"All right, all right," I said, trying to soothe their outraged feelings. "I'll give you ten dollars for that load. You can dump them in the frog pond."

"Hell no," said Roscoe. "I'd rather throw them in the junk

yard. I know damn well that you'll make five hundred dollars pure profit on them." And without another word the four drove off toward the dump.

Shortly afterward the freight truck rolled up and two big men got out. "Hi," one greeted me. "What are you shipping out today?"

"Just some horseshoe crabs. Get them out of here—I've seen enough of them to last me a lifetime."

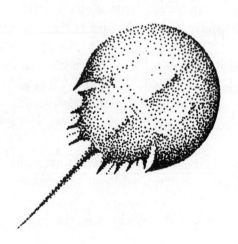

# 5 The Awakening

I sat cross-legged on the docks in front of the Yates Brothers' Shrimp and Fish Company holding Chass Parker's net taut while he brought the mending needle over and under the webbing. All of the Shiawassee shrimpers and their deck hands were either on the docks or on their boats getting their shrimp riggings ready. Mending of nets is like a masculine sewing circle—you have a chance to sit and gossip, drink beer, smoke, and cuss. There is a special wedge-shaped tool—the fishermen call it a needle—used to weave the nets, and a special skill is required in mending: the meshes are tied carefully and tediously with intricate knots. They must be square and woven to just the right size. It takes two men to repair a net, a man to wield the needle and a man to hold the webbing taut.

When the mending is finished, the nets are dipped in a creosote tarlike mixture to keep them from rotting in the salt water. Wood is heaped under big iron pots of creosote and set ablaze; its tangy smell hangs over everything. With the black mixture hot and soupy, the nets are dipped in sections to make sure that every inch of webbing is preserved. Then the great black nets are hung up to dry over the fish houses.

"There's mostly big shrimp out there now," Chass was saying, "but mighty few. George Williams tried to drag a couple of days ago and the most he got was fifteen pounds after two strikes."

"What kind of trash was there?" I asked. "Did he get any sharks or skates or anything I can use?"

Chass took a swallow from a can of beer. "No," he said. "George said they was mostly pinfish and a million goddam crabs. I expect there's a few skates out there, though. They come in early and leave when the weather gets warm." He pointed to a projecting corner. "Here, hold that part. I got this finished."

While we were talking, I could hear the sounds of boats being made ready for the spring run. There was the noise of straining machinery pulling a monster shrimp boat up on the ways, the rhythmic clanking of hammers and chisels scraping the barnacles from a boat's bottom. I could smell the fresh copper paint used to protect bottoms from the voracious shipworms.

Tired, sleepy engines were coughing and spluttering. Diesel fumes dominated the pungent salty air of the Shiawassee River. Captains, down in their engine rooms, tinkered and tightened, putting in new oil filters, installing new batteries or reviving the dead ones. Steering cables had to be checked, and the little repairs tnat were not made last fall at the close of shrimping season were now being attended to. There were a few major repairs that were beyond the captains' mechanical abilities, so expert marine mechanics tore down engines and replaced stripped gears and burned-out bearings.

Throughout the years I had grown to know all the local shrimp boats by collecting specimens on them at one time or another. I learned that shrimp fishermen live in a world of their own, a world of shrimp nets, ticker chains, and block and tackle. They are as close-knit a community as you will find anywhere, completely familiar with each other's boats, their faults, their virtues, and with them I knew whose boat was well designed with a strong solid bottom and whose boat was top-heavy and rocked badly in rough weather.

These are important and very real things to the shrimper. We knew who was a good captain and took care of his boat, kept the decks painted and the engine in top mechanical condition, and we knew who were the slobs. All too well I knew the shabby Greek rigs that ran on indefinitely with a little chewing gum, pieces of string, and if anything serious was wrong, adhesive tape, some bailing wire, and maybe a prayer. These tired old barges never quit, although the captain often had to stop pulling the nets far out in the Gulf of Mexico, climb down into the greasy engine room, and repair some malfunction.

The well-off Yates Brothers' Shrimp and Fish Company owned the brand-new double-rigger *Supreme Lady*, but she had deep-rooted, serious troubles. She was cursed! The big double-rigger was always ailing—a burned-out engine requiring a seventeen-hundred-dollar overhaul, or a stripped clutch that cost six hundred dollars to repair, or some other drastically expensive trouble.

The *Supreme Lady* was one of the most beautiful boats in Shiawassee. It was always freshly painted and had the most modern operating equipment, an automatic pilot, new sinks and stove, and a high-powered radio. She was built to take the open sea and stay out for months. But her stays were brief and often disastrous. Twenty shrimp boats could be dragging the same area, but only the *Supreme Lady* would tear her nets to shreds and bend the heavy steel boom as if it were a paper clip. Once she had sunk down to her masts in the river and they had had to rewire the whole electrical system.

Her owners were proud of her looks, but I believe they

would have liked to see her sunk for good with all her insurance paid up. However, with all the money they had invested in her, they had no choice but to go on investing more, hoping this time they would get all her kinks straightened out and perhaps the curse lifted.

Helping Chass mend his net was relaxing, and Chass made the chore easier with a plentiful supply of beer. Chass had a tremendous capacity—his beer bills were higher than anybody's in Shiawassee, but few people had ever seen him drunk. Since he was entangled with all his webbing, he sent me to fetch two beers from his ice chest, and soon two more cans floated out into the river. Chass was saying, "It's been a hard winter, and that water is still plenty cold. But if we have a few more warm days like this, I believe the shrimp will start to show up. If you want, you can come out with me next week. I'm fixing to make a trial run."

I was glad to hear this. Even with one strike I knew that I could get many of the specimens I needed. Letters and inquiries were inundating me. "Why haven't we received the shark tapeworms?" "When can we expect our order for batfish filled?" "Have not received mantis shrimp—were they lost in shipment?" And so on.

I told Chass about my troubles. He nodded cheerfully and said, "I expect I'm gonna come over to Elizabeth City. Be down at the boat by Tuesday week and we'll go out for sure. But there ain't no shrimp on this side of the bay no-how. I declare, this damn fog every evening is keeping a lot of people from trying anything. A man can lose his boat, rigging, and religion and everything else out there when he can't see the hand in front of his face."

Not that the loss of religion meant anything to Chass—he lost it on the slightest provocation—but his boat was a serious affair. The weather had been misty every morning and every evening since the warm weather had begun. Even as we sat on the docks mending the nets, I could feel the air start to get heavy, and a light fog was already beginning to form around the Shiawassee Bridge.

While we were talking, I looked at the out-of-town shrimp boats tied to the docks. The big boats from the Carolinas, Texas, the southeast coast of Florida, Mississippi, and Alabama were permitted to use the docking space because they agreed to sell their shrimp to Shiawassee fish houses. They were rigged up to shrimp the year round. They too were waiting. There was good camaraderie among the Alabama, Mississippi, and Shiawassee shrimp trawlers. They were even related through marriage. Many a romance ended in marriage while waiting in port.

However, the captains and crews of the big rigs from the Carolinas, Texas, and the east coast of Florida were considered strangers, and treated as such. Later, when their faces became familiar and both the out-of-towner and the Shiawassee shyness wore off, things would be friendlier.

I felt sorry for the young deck hands on the strange trawlers. They looked so forlorn and lost with nothing to do in the quiet sleepy town. There were pool halls and bars, but most of the deck hands were under age and even beer was denied them. There were plenty of girls in Shiawassee, but they were not friendly to strangers. And while waiting for the shrimp to run there was no money to buy love. The young deck hands generally had little or no education and just drifted from port to port.

There were the professional deck hands, those who understood shrimping and would do nothing else for a livelihood. Then there were others, romantic adventurers who tried shrimping for a season or two, hoboes who thought they would give it a whirl for the winter, and there were a few fugitives who signed on a shrimp boat as a good hiding place from the law.

But no one, adventurers, professionals, fugitives, or teen-age deck hands, could stand the waiting part. The hardest work, culling the biggest catch in the roughest sea, is nothing compared to the hardship of being isolated in a strange port with absolutely nothing to do except wait, wait, and wait. After a while even conversation dries up, the damp, soggy playing cards are impossible to shuffle, and the ancient worn-out magazines have been read and reread.

In my travels on the east coast in Florida for specimens I worked out my own method of breaking down the cold barrier between myself and the shrimpers. If there are any jellyfish in the bay, I will lug my pails, long-handled dip net, and preservatives down to the dock and give the staring shrimpers a noncommittal nod. They will return my nod in the same manner. Not paying any attention to them, I will begin dipping for moon jellyfish. By this time they are staring curiously and openly. It's not fish that I'm catching, just saucer-shaped jellyfish. Their necks are beginning to feel the strain from their peering and trying to see more. They see me quite plainly put the moon jellies into basins of harsh-smelling embalming fluid. I can see the curious captains and their deck hands out of the corner of my eye, as I pack the jellies into a drum as if they were made of precious jewels, and then seal the lids tightly. I hear footsteps approaching, then a curious voice: "Would you mind telling me what in the hell you're doing?"

And that night I feel the delightful winds of the Atlantic as the shrimp boat pulls its heavy nets over the sandy bottom of the east coast.

The fog was increasing over the Shiawassee River and the air took on a chill. I helped Chass carry his net over to the *Portia* and left it piled up on the deck. His boat was alongside the *Elysium Queen*, whose captain, Danny Yates, was hammering away at the winch pulley and cursing bitterly.

"What ails her, Danny?" Chass asked sympathetically.

"The belt keeps slipping and I can't for the life of me figure it out. Everything's gone wrong today," he said disgustedly.

"Everything?" I asked.

And Danny told me his day's sad story. His father, who owned the big fish company, was also a minister in the Methodist Church, and naturally he disapproved of all swearing and especially drinking. Danny had been happily working on the winch with his deck hand, Jimmy. They had just bought a sixpack of Falstaff and had settled down for a lively day's work. They hadn't even torn open the cardboard to get at the first beer when Jimmy looked up and saw Danny's father walking briskly along the dock with his usual stern expression. Danny, in a panic, tossed the sixpack over the side just an instant before his father stepped aboard.

The old man heard the splash and said suspiciously, "Did you drop your hammer, son?"

"Yessir," said Danny respectfully, pushing his hammer under him and sitting on it. "I sure did. Sure was careless of me."

His father looked around suspiciously and sniffed the air for a trace of the devil's brew, smiled benignly and approvingly, and walked off.

Chass laughed. "You're lucky he didn't catch you, though—you'd have to put up with a sermon for the next four hours, huh?"

Danny looked wretched and grunted disgustedly. "Goddammit, Chass, I still need a beer—you got one?"

"Sure am sorry, Danny. I'd sure give you one, but Jack here drank every bit of it," said the old liar.

Danny laughed and then looked at me. "How about loaning me a couple of bucks? If I go home I'll have to ask my wife for the money and she'll know it's for beer, then there'll be all kinds of hell to pay before I get the money."

"That's a mean woman he's married to," Chass put in.

I yielded, and Danny said gratefully, "I'll sure have it back

to you next time you go out with me, sure will." Turning to
his deck hand, Jimmy, he said cheerfully, his voice vibrant,
"Come on, Sugar, let's get us a beer and get on back to work."

All of Shiawassee was back to work. And I too had to get
back to work, because if I didn't print up and mail my catalogue I never would find the time, energy, and creative frame
of mind necessary to get the job done. When the shrimp came
in the waters would be littered with them.

Sometimes you can see the shrimp when they pelt against
the boat's hull as they jump and splash out of the water. At
night the waters are streaked by fiery flashes of luminescence as
they bolt and dance through a sea of phosphorescent plankton
—a most wonderful sight. Even oyster skiffs pull shrimp nets
behind roaring outboard motors, and old waterlogged row-
boats are called into service to trawl through the rich waters
with hand nets. There is money to be made, good money, for
the markets are still high.

Tired captains and deck hands throw ropes down to dock
workers when the boats come in. The nights are hard but satisfying after dragging up nothing but shrimp, hundreds of
pounds, baskets and boxes full of shrimp. Mysteriously word
gets out: "They're catching shrimp off Shiawassee." And
boats come from all over into the eastern Gulf to reap the
harvest of seafood gold.

At the shrimp and fish companies, squeaking, rolling con-
veyor belts pull up baskets of shrimp on a ramp and strong
men with bulging muscles lift the baskets and dump them on
long tables inside the cool, corrugated-iron fish houses.

Then, after the blast of a siren, Negro women, old men, and
children file in and circulate from fish house to fish house,
standing around the long cement tables with their fingers flying
as they snap the heads off shrimp. The women sometimes sing
melodiously as they work, often breaking off with intermittent
chatting and gossiping, while the shrimp heads part from their

bodies with a steady rhythm of snap-snap-snap. More shrimp are dumped on the tables, and the shrimp pickers continue pinching off heads.

Drums of shrimp heads are dragged outside to the docks and dumped into the river, and the dark waters become cloudy with shrimp juice as the heads sink down into the deep. Thousands of excited minnows charge around frantically, snatching up the tidbits.

Perspiring men load boxes of iced-down shrimp tails, which are taken to the markets. Captains and deck hands wait in line for the fish house owners to pay them for their catches. As soon as they are paid they return to the boats, change out of their shrimp-soaked pants, curl up on the bunks, and sleep to await the trip out that night. There is no time to spend their money. They too, like me, have to get while the getting is good.

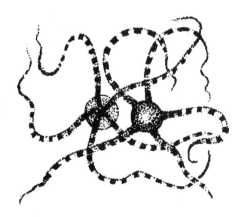

# 6 Potluck

In the evenings I worked on my forthcoming catalogue. Since I was determined to expand the business the catalogue was of prime importance. It had to be attractive—well written and designed. It was due to go to press in six weeks, because I had to allow enough time for the universities and schools to plan their summer and fall research and teaching programs.

I was listing only the largest and most prevalent species of nudibranchs, the more conspicuous barnacles and crabs, the most abundant and easily obtained marine fish. I listed only the animals I was reasonably sure I could collect when they were ordered. And it was not easy, not by a long shot. How could I make *Pennaria* hydroids come alive and mean something? In a world of jumbled scientific terminology and new terms being evolved faster than chicks in a hatching factory, I found everyday English more satisfactory. I wanted an inland instructor who had never been near the seashore to have an idea of what *Pennaria* really looks like.

Under a dissecting scope the polyps of *Pennaria tiarella*

look like clusters of innocent snapdragon flowers. Their movements are snakelike, swaying and nodding. Then when some unsuspecting little planktonic creature seeks shelter or food among the lovely white petals, it gets stung to death and digested. In summer *Pennaria* becomes even more beautiful and strange. It sprouts pink, oval-shaped medusae buds alongside the polyps, and when full with ripeness, they break away and float gently out to sea with the ebbing tide.

Of course all this could not be put into a catalogue. It had to be condensed, like a telegram. So I pretended to myself that each extra word cost a dollar. I had to reduce *Pennaria* to these inadequate words: "A bright pink hydroid. Medusae buds develop alongside the hydranths. Available April through October." And then their price.

In the catalogue I also featured special package deals, economical shipments which were based on realistic collecting. It simply meant that when I went collecting on a tidal flat, or went skin diving, I filled my buckets with a variety of animals that were abundant that particular morning. The beach and shoreline is always changing—each season has its callers and visitors. One spring morning the Portuguese man-of-war may be blown ashore and piled up on the beaches. Pelagic sea slugs which inhabit floating sargassum weeds may be available one day and gone the next. And one day during the winter the tide flats may be full of the great orange polychaete worm *Lysarte brasiliensis*, oozing and sliding through sand that was barren just a week before. Just as suddenly *Thyone mexicana*, the thin-skinned sandy sea cucumber, is found everywhere.

There are the old reliable residents that stay around through the seasons whether it is hot or freezing. On the low tide while I was filling my buckets with such basics as moon snails, crown conchs, starfish, sea cucumbers, and sea squirts I could always pick up the sporadic visitors for my package-deal collecting order. If an unusual nudibranch slug, common in the Caribbean,

floated up to the northern Gulf, the students whom I supplied
might have an opportunity to watch the graceful animal waving its plumed fronds, folding and opening its blue-and-orange-
spotted skirts like a ballerina, as it glided across the floor of the
aquarium.

And on this same day while I was picking up clusters of red-
beard sponges, or digging up acorn worms, I might come upon
the leathery tube of the scale worm. I wanted the instructor
and his students to share the experience I had with this animal when I first found it.

I shall never forget slitting open the tough, leathery tube and
watching in amazement as the largest scale worm I had ever
seen slithered slowly out. I felt as astonished and transfixed as
Aladdin did when the genie rose slowly and enormously out of
the lamp. The long, long worm slowly came out with a snakelike movement, covered with mucus and slime, and slid into the
pan of seawater. I had mixed feelings toward this worm. It was
almost dragonlike, and there was something repulsive about it.
Like the mythical dragon it had scales. There were two rows
of armored, blue-tipped, brown-spotted scales that seemed to
have a waving movement of their own on twelve inches of
sinuous, writhing worm, and the head was crowned with snakelike tentacles that moved in rhythm with the rest of the worm.
It was horrible-looking, yet looking at it in another way I saw
a deep beauty in its colors and rhythm.

If the students, following my instruction sheet, observe the
scales closely, they may see something even more surprising
and fascinating. Under the scales, adhering to the worm's
body, may be a number of small reddish snails no bigger
than the tip of a matchstick. Their shells resemble a flat,
coiled-up spring. These are *Cochliolepis parasitica;* they are in
the same class of gastropod mollusks as the heavy-shelled
whelks, the gaudy, lively tulip shells, and the crown conchs

found foraging on the beaches, oyster reefs, and tide pools, devouring clams and each other.

The moon snail, slowly traveling under the damp sands with its enormous, slimy, membranous-looking foot, searching for a clam, bumps into another burrowing, hungry snail, the ear shell, and the fight is on. The death struggle ensues until one kills the other by rasping away on the flesh and shell with its sharp radula, a long ribbon of teeth unsheathed from the thrusting, extending proboscis, or each tries to smother its adversary with its overwhelming, expanding foot.

I know who won when I see an empty moon-snail shell washing up on the beaches, and then I think of the tiny parasitic snail who comfortably solved its struggle for existence by latching onto the well-concealed scale worm. These little vitrinnelid snails have evolved into the highest form of existence—parasitism. Contrary to popular opinion, parasites are not animals that have degenerated. True, they may have lost the use of certain limbs, but they have developed a more useful organ, like a big sucking mouth or appendages that can dig in and cling; they have evolved above the free-living forms.

I look at the fish copepods with their shrunken legs, grotesque sucking mouths, and long strings of reproductive egg sacks. They have evolved into their highest possible form. Once upon a time they were just ordinary shrimplike creatures who fended and found food for themselves.

I often wonder how we, the human species, will ultimately evolve if we continue making machines and computers our hosts. Will our legs become shrunken from mechanized transportation, and will our heads become grotesquely large and our stomachs swollen?

Now getting back to the fascinating scale worm and its parasites, I had to consider whether I should feature it in my catalogue. More often than not, months would go by before I happened upon more scale worms. I could institute a search for them, but only on special order, which took it way out of the economy class.

The idea of a packaged assortment had come to me when I

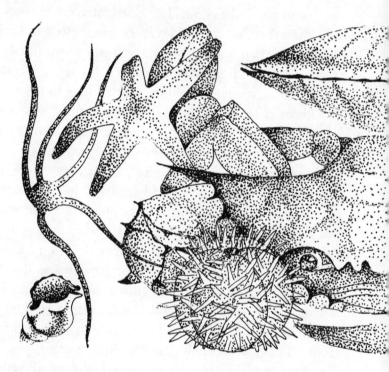

*The idea of a packaged assortment had come to me
when I was visiting Woods Hole. The instructor
gave me a carte-blanche order for an assortment of*

was visiting Woods Hole. An instructor of invertebrate zoology who had been teaching his course using embalmed marine animals, colorless and reeking of formaldehyde, found his students dull-eyed and bored. He gave me a carte-blanche order for an assortment of living marine invertebrates that could be found on the beach at low tide in a single morning's collecting. He felt it was the closest thing to actually taking his students to the seashore to see a live creeping starfish or a moon snail.

A second professor wanted to abandon preserved materials

*living marine invertebrates that could be found on the beach at low tide on a single morning's collecting.*

entirely, so he asked me to have live animals in phylogenetic order flown up in time to meet laboratory schedules. The first week it was sponges; the second, coelenterates (hydroids, jellyfish, corals, sea anemones, etc.); the third week, flatworms; and so on. Both men implored me to throw in any exotic or unusual creature like the giant scale worm because they would enjoy looking at it themselves.

The spring mornings in North Florida were thick with fog. The tides were good and low, and one morning I took advantage of it to get up a good collection for the assortment orders. I wanted to get in as much intertidal collecting as I could before the shrimping season really started. The fog drifted slowly over the beach; at times it seemed like I walked into the middle of a cloud. The water was glassy-smooth, and the fog hung like thick coils of smoke over its surface. The rising sun was trying to burn through the thick moisture, which clung to me and to the shrouded trees and palmetto scrub. My vision was necessarily limited, and I could not see very far down the beach. As I walked through the mists I could not help seeing the huge, dying jellyfish *Rhopilema verrilli*, some of them as big around as washtubs, stranded by the outgoing tide.

They are Southern jellyfish that float about in the ocean currents and occasionally drift up to New England. Not much is known about them—where they come from and where they go—but their migrations along the western Florida coasts are consistent. I had seen them year after year during the winter months, but I did not intend to list them in my catalogue. These heavy, massive jellies would be impractical to preserve and costly to ship, and they were too large for any normal aquarium. Small specimens of *Dactylometra quinquecirrha* were more popular and more suited for classroom study. They had been in last week, and I was hoping to find a few stragglers for the assortment order.

However, as a collector, I filed away in my mind the seasonal occurrences of *Rhopilema*, because a few were infected with a small, interesting parasitic pink sea anemone. Also, someday a biochemist might need a large volume of medusa tissue to make a protein or mineral-salts analysis. And should there be a demand for a great mass of frozen coelenterate eggs, I would go in search of *Rhopilema verrilli* immediately.

I picked up four of the smaller live chunks of sea pork that had washed ashore, and then went on looking for live whelks and cockles. This was mollusk week, so Linda was encouraged when she dug up six large Venus clams, *Mercenaria campechiensis*, which make good dissecting specimens. I don't know how she did it—whether she nosed them out or whether she saw their keyholelike slits in the hard-packed sand—but she was good at finding them and blood clams, *Arca umbonata*, which I was always pleased to get because I knew students would be interested in them. When you crack open this clam, you will be shocked to see its bright-red blood trickle down your fingers. I also knew the instructor would be pleased, because he could demonstrate *Arca* as one of the most primitive forms of bivalves.

Linda padded up to me, dropped a whelk at my feet, and waited for my lavish praise. I was too busy to pay any attention to her, because I was laboriously digging up a long pink nemertean ribbon worm, *Cerebratulus lacteus*. To keep it from breaking in two, which would make it useless as a demonstration specimen, I carefully splashed seawater on the shovel and then slowly washed out another six inches of worm from the sand, and then more gentle splashing of seawater, until finally I had all the sand washed away.

I thought wistfully of the Cape Cod region and even Boston Harbor where these worms were so common that fishermen dug pailfuls for bait. Later on when the full summer season was upon us, and collecting slacked off, I was hoping I could go to the Maine coast and get a stock supply of traditional Northern specimens for my customers. These nemerteans were scarce and smaller on the Gulf beaches, but they were always in demand and would serve the zoologist's teaching course.

I decided that there were enough locally to offer them as live specimens in my catalogue.

Linda watched the tedious operation of removing the ribbon worm impatiently. She pitied my slowness and stupidity. If I only left the digging up to her superior ability she would have that silly worm out in no time. So she lunged in helpfully with scrabbling paws and tossed sand and four pieces of the worm into the air. I sat on the sand bitterly contemplating murder and wondering if the shovel would be sufficient. Linda was a sensitive dog; she walked stiffly away, insulted and sulking. I knew when she was sulking because she wouldn't even glance at me.

She pretended she saw something that was far more worthy of her attention. A flock of saucy sandpipers were picking up worms on the high beach. This was irresistible; these brazen birds had to be taught a lesson. And she was off in a flash, her ears flapping back in the wind with the joyful, hilarious look that only Airedales have. The sandpipers seemed to enjoy the chase as much as she did. They flew off screeching down the beach, waited until she bounded up to them, and then flew farther down and back again, with Linda panting and racing until they led her back to me. After an hour of this invigorating exercise, she forgave me and came back to watch me dig for sea anemones.

I happened upon a sand bar where there was an aggregation of the large gray burrowing sea anemones *Bunodactis stelloides*. I proceeded to dig some up for a stockpile and orders. Linda was good at this digging; between us we managed to fill a bucket of slimy, contracted blobs that would flower out later in the seawater aquaria.

*Bunodactis stelloides* was not a traditional sea anemone like *Metridium*, which is found on wharfs and jetties of the New England and North Pacific coasts. Instructors purchase *Metridium* by the hundreds for routine dissection in zoology classes. But I had had an uphill job trying to create a market for *Bunodactis*, which was seasonally abundant on the Gulf. After a specialist in the Smithsonian Institution identified my specimens as *Bunodactis stelloides*, I sold a number of them to museums, because once they were officially classified they were a valuable addition to the worldwide collections of anemones.

The first year the sales of these anemones dragged. They didn't pay for the time involved in collecting them until I convinced a physiologist at Harvard to try the live anemone for classroom demonstrations. He became an enthusiastic customer and advertiser for *Bunodactis stelloides* once he learned what an amazing anemone it was.

Unlike the popular North Atlantic *Metridium senile*, which is delicate and has to be kept in chilled aerated water, tough little *Bunodactis* adjusts to any temperature, blooms magnificently in stale seawater at room temperature, and lasts for years. What is more, it makes a superb specimen for demonstrating muscular contractions. When the sensitive *Metridium* is given an electrical stimulus it promptly draws in its tentacles and often remains contracted. It takes hours or even days to expand again, whereas *Bunodactis* just as promptly, draws in its short, stubby gray tentacles but opens up two or three minutes later. Repeated electric shocks do not affect its ability to respond, and it can be used for demonstration over and over again.

*Bunodactis stelloides* was gaining a reputation, and I was already giving it a special description in my catalogue and planning to have it photographed.

When I was almost finished getting up the live-animal collection from this beach, I turned my attention to the massive, firm jellies lying scattered at the edge of the sea or draped on the rotting pine stumps and began looking for specimens infected with the parasitic anemone. I examined ten jellyfish and found them negative, but on the eleventh I found a number of half-inch-long pink anemones lodged in the canals. They were definitely alive, because they slowly contracted and stretched in the midst of the firm tissues of the hanging lobes and umbrella.

These anemones were not destined for the beach-potluck order—they were much too valuable. A year before I had sent a sample to a zoologist at the Smithsonian Institution, who identified it as *Calamactis*, a genus of actinian, or sea anemone, known only from the Gulf of California. Was it possible that the specimens from the Gulf of Mexico were a new species? The specialist reported that they were parasitic only in their juvenile stages. But no one knew what they were like in their adult form and where the adults could be found.

I knew almost all the anemones from my collecting locality, and never once had I encountered the adult *Calamactis*. Before the species could be determined, the juveniles would have to be raised successfully in aquaria to adult form. Therefore the actinian specialist had ordered two dozen living juvenile *Calamactis* last year.

But unfortunately, by the time I received his letter the jellyfish were gone. Another year had rolled around, and now the jellyfish were back with the infant parasitic anemones. I dug my fingers into the slimy, firm jellies and flipped the heavy bodies over, looking for more infected specimens. I carefully squeezed out some little anemones into a glass jar filled with seawater and held them up to the light admiringly. They were orange or pink cone-shaped creatures crowned with a ring of blunt tentacles.

All I needed now were two clusters of *Molgula occidentalis*—sea squirts—and my collecting would be finished. I drove to a little sheltered inlet near Elizabeth City where *Molgula* abounded. If all went well the specimens would be on the plane that evening.

# 7 The Alewife Fisherman

The inlet flats were luxuriant with the lumpy, potatolike *Molgula*. They were brown and covered with a thick sandy test, or skin. Every now and then one shot out a stream of water like a toy water pistol, particularly when I handled it. They grew in large clusters with as many as twenty-five in a group or as few as five.

The heat of the sun had not quite burned up all the fog in this low-lying area, but I could see the ghostly figures of two gill-netters shaking fish out of the net webbing, like shaking sand out of a blanket. They might be getting spadefish, which I had been urged to collect, so I slipped into my waders and went out to their boat. "Get much of a strike?" I asked conversationally.

"We didn't do too bad," said a young man with a red weather-beaten face and bushy yellow hair, dressed in blue jeans and a faded red sweater.

He looked familiar to me, but I could not place him. Perhaps I had seen him somewhere before, but he looked so much like every other young man in the fishing villages that I was not sure. He had to be kin to somebody in Arcadia or some other nearby fishing village, I reasoned, because everybody in the area was closely related.

Before my trip to Madagascar I had thought nothing of the resemblances, but now I could not help wondering about them. All the people looked the same, young or old. They had

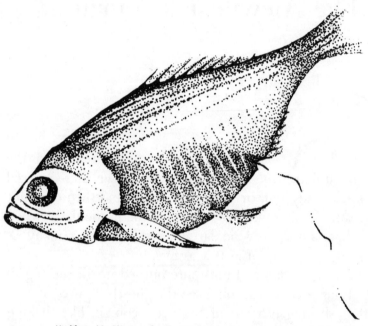

*"Alewife?" I asked. "I guess you're bait fishing."*

the same close-set blue eyes and the same features in their narrow faces—the old men had a few wrinkles and sparse gray hair, their hands had more and thicker calluses, and their faces were more weathered and drier, but their features were definitely the same. Almost all the young fishermen had bushy, strawlike yellow hair except for the few who had bushy, strawlike deep-black hair. The black hair had been introduced by a tribe of Gypsies who had settled in Arcadia many, many years ago. They had intermarried and were totally absorbed.

The young man in the boat picked up a handful of fish and threw them into a box.

"Alewife?" I asked. "I guess you're bait fishing."

"Well, I should think so," said the young man, staring hard at me. "You can't eat them, they stink too bad. Although some people catches them to feed their hogs."

"Yeah, we use them to bait the crab baskets," said the other fisherman, who was fat and middle-aged. He peered at me from under his old straw hat. "You that scientist fellah, ain't you? You lives next door to my daughter's husband Bennie Topper, in Arcadia." He nodded, looking satisfied.

I knew I had seen this fat fisherman before. Of course, he was Bennie's father-in-law, and I had seen him often in Arcadia, but I had never had occasion to speak to him. In the course of my work I often met people who were familiar to me as I traveled all over the coast of northern Florida, stopping at all the fish houses, examining fish caught in nets. And I had become a familiar figure to the fishermen, for often they were striking their seines along the same beach where I was digging in the eelgrass with my shovel and buckets or capturing jellyfish with a dip net in the shallows.

I said heartily to the fisherman, "Oh, yeah. Bennie's a fine boy and a darn good neighbor."

The alewife fisherman had an expressive face, and now he wrinkled his nose with anger. "A fine boy! A good neighbor!" He spat into the calm sea. "Who are you trying to kid? He's the sorriest son of—" And he broke off into a long string of curses, never using the same curse twice. "And my poor Lucy Mae had to take her young'uns home to her mama. She's staying with us in Elizabeth City, right this very minute." He was glaring at me.

I knew I had started off on the wrong foot with this fellow.

Now how could I get out of it? In this case, I decided, honesty was the best policy.

I shrugged my shoulders and said, "Well, I don't think I'm much of a diplomat these days. I'll never run for mayor if Arcadia ever decides to have one."

The fat man laughed. "I don't see why not. You couldn't be no worse than some of them crooked politicians."

Now that the fisherman seemed in a better humor, I said, "I'm hunting for spadefish today. You didn't happen to notice if there were any in the net?"

"What's spadefish, Uncle Will?" the young man asked, his pale-blue eyes looking puzzled.

"I believe it's them little flat-looking things with black and white stripes, Eugene. Angel fish some calls them—that right?"

I nodded. "Yeah. They average about six inches inshore, but I'll take all sizes."

"I'm satisfied that I saw a couple when we were hauling the net in," Uncle Will replied, jerking the fish through the webbing and tossing them in the box. "Why don't you take a look?" he invited. "They're somewhere in that mess." Engrossed in untangling the net and piling it into the boat, he pointed to the catch without looking up from his work, adding, "Now watch out for them dern hard-headed catfish and those stingarees. They can sure mess you up."

Not once have I waded out to a fisherman's boat and not been cautioned to watch out for sting rays and catfish. And usually the fisherman would roll up his blue jeans above his calves and show me the deep white scars and pitted marks where a sting ray had lashed its barb when he stepped on it while hauling in the net.

I promised I would be careful and climbed into the boat. I began looking through the greenish-yellow fish that were piled high, pounding their bodies against the boat, struggling helplessly to get back into the sea. I kept a wary eye out for the sea catfish, *Galeichthys felis*. Sea catfish have poisonous dorsal and pectoral fins, and if you get jabbed by one, the pain is agonizing—as Linda later learned. I saw several large catfish and carefully put them in my plastic bucket, because they were males carrying the female's large marble-shaped eggs in their mouths. After a few months the eggs hatch, but the two-inch-long young remain in the father's mouth until they fully absorb their egg yolks. I was hoping to get up a good series of these peculiar paternal catfish and preserve them in a natural position with the young still in their mouths.

Linda had wandered out to me, stepping daintily and looking about curiously. "That your dog?" Uncle Will asked, suddenly interested. "Why, that's an Airedale. They make fine bear dogs. Ever hunt her?"

"I'm afraid I don't get much time to go hunting these days," I said with just the proper tinge of sadness and regret in my voice. To confess that I did not like hunting and killing animals for sport would border on blasphemy, for hunting is a part of these people's basic culture.

When the first day of hunting starts, every store in town puts up a CLOSED sign and every man and boy takes to the woods. In the schoolhouse of Chadd County, where all the Arcadian children went, there are many empty seats—only the girls in their colorful starched dresses are present. The hunting virus is highly contagious; it spreads to the men teachers and even to the truant officer, who are all absent—because of sudden illness, naturally.

The woods are filled with mangy, screeching, yelping hounds, with hunters running, leaping over palmetto scrub, wading through icy streams, yelling to their dogs. Old men limber up and hop to it, blasting away with shotguns. The little Florida deer flee in terror. Squirrels take to the treetops, even to the tops of the tallest pine trees, and coons will not show their faces. The hogs, squealing and grunting, run into the palmetto scrub, away from the packs of insane hounds who are out for the first time after being penned up all summer—skinny hounds with their rib barrels showing distinctly, mangy yellow hounds, beagles, feists, and anything else on four legs that can pretend to be a dog and can bark. And woe unto any animal, domestic or wild, that wanders into their path. And poor Linda stays locked behind the screen doors, moaning and whimpering enviously when she catches the sound of the hounds baying.

As the fishermen talked of dogs and hunting, I sorted out alewife after alewife and tossed them into the fish box. I found spiny boxfish, a cowfish, and many catfish, but no spadefish.

Eugene lifted a sting ray, properly holding it with his fingers clamped into the pits behind the eyes so it couldn't whip its venomous barbed tail into his hand. "You need any stingarees?"

"Oh, thanks," I said, pointing to my bucket. "Just drop it in. I'll tell you what else I'm looking for. Did you ever see any fish with a large bulge—a kind of swelling on it?"

Eugene shrugged his shoulders. "I don't know, I never noticed. Did you, Uncle Will?"

Uncle Will scratched his unshaven cheeks thoughtfully. "Now and then, when I'm cleaning a mullet, I find one with a lump on it. Not too often. Why?" His blue eyes were narrow and suspicious-looking.

"They study them at the medical schools. Doctors want to know how fish get cancer."

Uncle Will nodded with approval. "If we get one I'll drop it off at your place. My wife's sister, the one who lives in Perry, just died of cancer, just two weeks back. Poor woman! She wasn't but forty-two and she left ten young'uns." Uncle Will sighed heavily and we both shook our heads sorrowfully. Suddenly he seemed more interested in what I was looking for. He reached into the pile, parted a few golden alewives, and produced a small spadefish. "This what you're looking for?"

"That's it," I said gratefully. Now I could start filling my spadefish order. Spadefish, *Chaetodipterus faber*, have a most unusual bone structure with modified swelling around the pelvic fins that makes the bone look like a swollen drumstick. A fisheries biologist at the Woods Hole Oceanographic Institution wanted a growth-range series to determine when and how this peculiar bone formation began—are the fish born with it, or does it develop suddenly when the spadefish matures? At the end of the year the biologist learned that the tilly bone, as it is called, develops only after the fish has grown eighteen inches or more. After that the bone formation swells enormously.

As I continued culling for more spadefish, I heard both fishermen laughing. Linda had snatched a small pigfish and was gulping it down greedily. "That dog sure likes to eat fish." Uncle Will laughed. "I never in all my life seen a dog eat raw fish like that."

"Only when she can steal it." I never could curb Linda's thievery when it came to fish. I stared hard at Linda, who instantly dropped the fish and tried to look innocent, wagging her stubby tail cheerfully. "If I give her fish for dinner," I explained, "she won't touch it, but just give her half a chance to steal it, she'll eat until she bursts." I knew that as soon as we turned our backs to continue with our work, Linda would gulp the fish down.

We worked in silence. Eugene kept staring at me in a strange manner. I could feel his eyes on me even though he was busy with the fish and the net. I tried to disregard his puzzled look of inquiry, but it bothered me. He would scratch his stiff, strawlike hair with his fishy fingers and then abruptly return to his work.

Although I did not find many spadefish, in the pile there

were other desirable specimens, such as sting rays and the cat-fish with the young in their mouths. Suddenly Eugene asked, "What's this ugly-looking thing?"

He handed me an alewife. Clinging to the inside of its mouth and crawling halfway out was a large isopod, looking like a big white grub with black eyes. "Oh," I said gratefully, "I've been looking for these things. It's a kind of a parasite, akin to the sea roaches that run all over the docks—only this kind lives in a fish."

A look of revulsion passed over both fishermen's faces. "We call them leeches," Uncle Will said. He continued to jerk fish after fish out of the net and toss them quickly into his bait box.

I removed the isopod, which immediately transferred its hold from the fish to my finger. I wrenched it free from the bleeding finger, but instantly it attached itself to my other hand and began to dig in. With a violent shake I threw it into my bucket. I felt sorry for the poor fish for having such an ugly creature in its mouth.

I had been surprised, and pained, by this insectlike creature's vicious ability to dig in and hold on. I didn't think that this information was ever listed in the taxonomic descriptions, al-though I was sure that there were elaborate and detailed pic-tures of the isopod, *Olencira praegustator*, showing its jointed legs with its ugly hooks.

The isopod had already been identified for me at the Smith-sonian Institution. There were times when it was so prolific that I could fill a deck bucket with specimens, and so I could list it in my catalogue both as preserved and live. But first I had wanted to read all about it. I was expecting a recent paper on it, the modern dull taxonomic description that would illus-trate mouth parts and body and tail segments and describe in dry detail its hooked legs.

But what I had received was Benjamin Henry Latrobe's paper of 1797 at the Trans-American Philosophical Society in

Philadelphia. His intimate first-hand account and description of the isopod makes enjoyable reading. While "confined by illness for several days at the house of a friend" near the York River in Virginia, he studied the "insect," which he named *Oniscus praegustator:* "As soon as he was free from my grasp, he immediately scrambled nimbly back into the mouth of the fish and resumed his position. In every instance he was disgustingly corpulent and unpleasant to handle; and it seemed, that whether he have obtained his post, by force, or favor, whether he be a mere traveler, or a constant resident or what else may be his business where he is found; he certainly has a fat place of it, and fares sumptiously every day."

Latrobe was an accurate and careful observer. Often I have found the isopod clinging to the roof of an alewife's mouth, and I have preserved many in that position. But I read Latrobe wistfully, for naturalists no longer write so entertainingly. I often wonder if modern taxonomic descriptions must be so painful and dull.

"What do them bi-ologists do with those leeches?" Uncle Will demanded.

I explained simply how scientists examined each parasite, identified it, and kept a record of its geographic distribution. Eugene paused, his pale-blue eyes fastened on me while I explained the importance of learning about these specimens. I doubt if he understood all I was saying, but he appeared awed by it. I knew the Chadd County school had an excellent science teacher, and Eugene looked as if he had been taught at least enough about science to kindle an interest in it.

Not so with Uncle Will, who looked at me sharply and said, "What's them scientists doing to keep the leeches from getting into the fish's mouth?"

"Nothing," I admitted, "not yet. They are just learning about them."

Uncle Will snorted contemptuously and said he thought

learning about a leech or a parasite was not enough. "It sounds like a bunch of crap to me," he said fiercely. "What a way to spend the taxpayer's money! All them big scientists sitting in the government-supported universities, drawing fat salaries and doing nothing to earn it."

I had heard similar arguments before, but none quite so harsh. From time to time I came across cynical fishermen who were skeptical of the benefits of modern science. These people had lived in their little fishing villages all their lives, just like their fathers and their grandfathers before them, and nothing would change them; all they knew was fish, nets, boats, and trucks, and that was all that a man needed to know to live. Anything outside of their own world they viewed with suspicion and distrust. Their women married young, had babies early, and worked picking crab meat, cleaning fish, or shucking oysters, and that's all they knew.

But Eugene's high school science had not been entirely lost on him. He began to tell his uncle how science was responsible for everything—the motor that ran their boat, the engine in the car. And they had been shooting rockets and men into space, he had seen it on television, and science was curing people's ailments.

But Uncle Will stubbornly said he didn't see how people were any better off now than they were when they didn't have all those things, and anyway, if Eugene wanted a good education he could put his mind to learning how to build a good boat and set traps and other useful things. Eugene's face registered doubt and confusion, and we let the subject drop.

Once again we culled the fish in silence, and after a while I found another spadefish and Uncle Will tossed me one too. He looked at me searchingly and said, "You sell them things, don't you?"

I nodded and his fat, unshaven face beamed with approval. He said he was glad I was earning money at my work, not drawing fat government salaries at the taxpayer's expense. His tone was friendlier. "We've been getting twenty or thirty of those kind of fish most every day. If you just want them, you ought to go out crabbing with someone."

"That's a good idea," I said. "I think I'll go out with old Andy."

"You're the scientist who has that specimen company over in Arcadia," Eugene said brightly. He had finally placed me, and his face came alive again. "Yeah, I remember. You were the one who was getting those bats out of the roof of the schoolhouse a few years back with Herbie and Tony, weren't you?" So that was why he had been staring at me so hard.

"Yes. I used to sell bats, but not any more—they're too much trouble to fool with."

We talked about bats. I told him that bats are known carriers of hydrophobia and that I would have to get rabies injections if I were going to continue handling them. Then the subject switched to rabid foxes and coons in the summertime, and how Uncle Will had had to shoot one of his hounds because it was foaming at the mouth.

There was nothing left in the catch to interest me, so I thanked Uncle Will and young Eugene, called Linda, and returned to my station wagon. I thoroughly injected the spadefish with formalin so their viscera would not macerate.

Spadefish are vegetarians and have characteristically long guts, making them far more difficult to preserve than carnivores. When preserved improperly, the spadefish may appear thoroughly hardened in embalming fluid, but actually it is rotting and stinking internally and soon becomes bloated. It would have been better to remove the viscera, but the order from the Woods Hole Oceanographic Institution stated that they had to be internally injected and the viscera well preserved.

If I wanted to get the order filled, I would have to go crabbing. That night I went to the airport to deliver for flight the
live shipment of specimens for the invertebrate-zoology
courses. And before I went to bed, I made arrangements with
old Andy to go crabbing with him in the morning.

# 8 Crabbing for Specimens

Old Andy always wore a great droopy straw sun hat, even in winter or in the fog, and his skinny shanks were swamped inside his long hip boots. Young William, a raw blond youth, steered the crabbing skiff while I sat in the middle looking at the choppy waters of Arcadia's harbor. We had rounded the mouth of the river and run along the sandy white beaches of Tye Island, where strings of crab buoy corks bobbed above the surface.

William cut the motor and we drifted up to the pots. Old Andy said to me, "You'd better get back in the stern, so you can pick your specimens out as soon as we pull them up."

I clambered back to the stern and watched William snatch up the cork buoy and pull up the rope with his gloved hands. Old Andy rose with difficulty. His movements were slow and painful as he put on his rubber apron. He was afflicted with arthritis. "Oh, Lord," he groaned, flexing his aching fingers and rubbing his back, "let me get my old age in order before we catch some crabs." He helped his old age along by meticulously unwinding a towel that was wrapped around his medicine. His medicine was in a whiskey bottle, and it was his own special concoction—one part medicine (some sort of Grandma's herbs) and nine parts cheap bourbon. He took a large gulping swallow, cleared his throat loudly, smacked his lips, then meticulously rewrapped his medicine and safely stowed it into his lunch box.

In the meantime William had brought the rope up, coiling it carefully in the boat, and at last a wire crab trap rose to the surface. Fifteen large blue crabs scrambled madly about, clattering against the wire.

"Why, it sure looks like we're hitting them, Mr. Andy," William said. "Sure does!"

Andy nodded. "If we keep catching them this-a-way, we'll be making some money." He released the rubber strap that held the trap closed and shook the crabs out into a fish box. Then he opened the bait hold, which was filled with fish bones from yesterday's bait, and stuffed it with fresh alewives.

William was already pulling another trap up by the time Andy had finished baiting the first one. Then he tossed the crab basket over the side and attended to the new catch. There was a long black shark remora in it. Andy dumped the fish and crabs out into a wooden fish box and gestured at the remora. "You'll have to pull it out somehow," he told me. "I didn't bring any tongs out with me. Had two in my truck, though—I should have thought of it." He handed me a long wooden stick. "Here—use this to push them crabs around so they won't latch onto you."

"That's all right, Andy," I replied, reaching into the box of crabs and pushing them away from the fish. "I'll get them out somehow." But this was easier said than done, for all the crabs were angry at being cheated of their lives—they were lured into the traps by the delectable smell of fresh dead alewives, and then pulled from the water and dumped into wooden crates, where they pinched each other into a great tangle, tore off claws and legs; and all were fated to be dropped into huge vats of boiling water at the crab house. And when I reached in for my shark remora, an army of claws raised aggressively and snatched at my fingers. But at last I managed to get hold of the fish's tail and yank it out, shaking off the claws that had latched onto it. Perhaps of all the crabs in the sea, the common

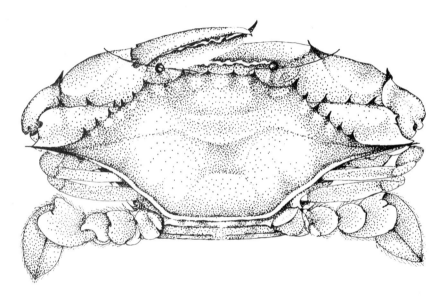

*Perhaps of all the crabs in the sea, the common blue crab,* Callinectes sapidus, *is the most aggressive and vicious.*

blue crab, *Callinectes sapidus,* is the most aggressive and vicious.

When the fish was free, I scrutinized it and found a small white parasitic copepod clinging to its tail. I took a vial from my collecting bucket, filled it with alcohol, and borrowed William's long sharp knife to remove both copepod and tail.

"What are you getting off him?" William asked from the

bow, stopping his chore of pulling in baskets long enough to watch me.

"They're parasites—fish lice," I told him. "A kind of shrimp-like animal that sucks the fish's blood."

"Damn!" William said. "I been fishing all my life and I ain't never seen them. Why, I don't know the very first thing about them."

"You ain't supposed to," Andy said firmly. "That's why you's crabbing for a living and he's selling specimens. The good Lord made all kinds of people that knows a whole lot of different things. If you knew about those bugs he's a-picking off that fish, why you wouldn't be out here crabbing."

"Don't you know about 'em, Mr. Andy?" asked William respectfully.

"No, I don't," Andy came back. "And I don't need to know about them. If'n the good Lord meant for me to know, by God I would have knowed natural-like. So you just go back to your crabbing."

William pulled up the next pot. It had four crabs in it and three striped spadefish.

Andy looked disgusted. "I thought for sure we were gonna catch the fool out of them old crabs, seeing how those first pots came up." He dumped the crabs and fish down on the deck so I could pick them up and save all the spadefish.

The spadefish were crawling with *Argulus*, and I happily picked them off with forceps and dropped each tiny animal into a vial.

Andy asked, "About how much do you get for those, Jack?"

"About five cents apiece," I replied, catching the last of the fish lice as it scurried over the writhing fish's body.

William was amazed. "Damn! You sell those too?"

I nodded, and he continued, "I sure wouldn't have the patience to pick them off, but you must be making good money."

Andy said, "That boy earns his money, William. It's kind of like a doctor—you got to go to school and study that mess, read a lot of books, before you know what to sell. If he gets high prices for that mess, he deserves it." Of course Andy's attitude toward my work pleased me, but later, when he ran out of bait, he changed his mind about its value.

He turned back to his own troubles, and after a while he said as he grabbed onto a bobbing cork and began pulling it, "Come on, O crab. Old Andy made these baskets. Come on, fill them up."

William added sarcastically, "Crabs don't give a damn who made the baskets. If they're going to come, they'll come. If they ain't, they ain't."

"No sir," said Andy. "No sir. They know Andy here made these baskets, and now they're gonna come fill them up." He administered to his arthritis with his medicine and spluttered and choked. The fumes of his medicine were strong.

The next basket was packed with crabs and a few conchs, and they filled up the fish box. I pulled out a new box, and they began dumping the loads into it. Andy and William had two hundred pounds of alewives, and they had roughly four hundred crab baskets out, half of which they were going to check.

The day grew on and the sun rose higher, burning away the morning fog, and it soon became unbearably hot with our warm clothing on. We exchanged the water bottle often, and bit by bit, with crab basket after crab basket, the big wooden fish boxes were getting filled with crabs and the boxes of bait were dwindling.

We had already pulled up over fifty pots and switched to another string of traps near the hill when Andy and William suddenly became angry. "Some son of a cow has been raiding our pots again," Andy said bitterly. And there was the evidence—the alewives in the bait cage were completely eaten, only their rotting skeletons remained behind, and there was not a crab in the basket. The entrance to the trap was left open, the thief not having bothered to close it after he raided the crabs. Andy baited the empty trap and lowered it.

They pulled up the next pot and found that it too had been raided. "Do you have any idea who's doing it?" I asked.

"Hell, we know who's doing it," William said, "but we can't prove nothing. Looky at that boat yonder. That lousy George Slobe steals from everybody's trap." He stuffed three alewives into the bait cage.

I looked at the man checking crab pots far out in the bay, too far to tell if it was his own line he was checking or somebody else's. "But that's against the law, isn't it?"

"Hell yeah, it's against the law—but you gotta prove it first," Andy said. "If the State Board of Conservation was worth a damn, they'd be out looking to protect other people's property instead of just hitting a man with fines for every little thing."

"Shoot," William said with disgust. "There ain't no law here. You gotta take the law into your own hands. I'd like to have me a .30-.30 out here and put a bullet into his ass. Then I'd cut him up into little pieces and bait the pots with him."

"And you'd get caught too," said Old Andy sagely. "Yessiree."

"Why?" I asked.

"Cause," Andy said, "some other sonofabitch would go stealing your pots and he'd find the wrong kind of bones in it, report it to the sheriff, and that would be your ass right there. You can't trust nobody out here." He spat into the calm sea. "The hell with this crab line—it's all stripped out and a waste of time to check. G'wan over to the next crab line, William— maybe he ain't got to that yet."

We moved off and worked around the mouth of the Paradise River, down along Indian Point and out past the shoals, where the salinity was higher. Andy predicted that we would be getting more conchs and different-looking animals in the baskets, and he was right.

As soon as the dripping crab pot came aboard, I immediately saw two large flame-streaked box crabs, *Calappa flamma*, moving about feebly. They are one of the most exotic-looking crabs in the Gulf. They look as if they might dwell on the very bottom of the ocean depth—or, because of their brilliant orange and white colors, like some garish coral-reef creature. The fishermen called them rooster crabs.

The frenzied blue crabs in the basket scuttled and ran in all directions when Andy emptied them, but the box crabs hardly moved. I had seen them before in the shrimp nets, and they were always sluggish. I had no particular use for the crabs at the moment, but they were so odd-looking that I thought it would be well to preserve them. Sooner or later someone might order them.

"Crabs got them bugs in them too?" William asked.

"Some do," I said. "They've got a barnacle that lives in the gills."

"Do they, sure enough?" Andy asked incredulously. "A barnacle?"

"Let's see it," said William.

"I'll have to break open the shell of one of these blue crabs to show it to you."

Andy looked a little unhappy at the prospect. "It don't do no good to go messing up the crabs. Fish house don't like it when they're broke up. But I want to see too," he decided.

I picked out a blue crab from the fish box, holding it by its rear paddles so it couldn't pinch my fingers, and then I smashed its carapace with my knife. When I was sure it was dead, I removed the crushed shell and exposed the gills and pointed out the little orange barnacles that were growing on them.

"I'll be damned," said Andy. "I fooled with crabs all my life, and I ain't never noticed those things before."

Commensal barnacles on the gills of crabs are well known to the marine biologist. The particular species that we were examining was *Octolasmis mulleri*, which lives on the gills and in the gill chamber of almost every portunid crab in the Gulf of Mexico. Sometimes their infection is so thick in the gill chamber that it's hard to see how the crab respires at all. One investigator counted over five hundred barnacles in a single crab. While the barnacles occupy a large portion of the surface area of the crab's gills, and their stalks even bore holes into the crab, they are not considered true parasites, because the barnacle takes its food from the water in the crab's gill chamber, not actually from the crab itself.

But I found another barnacle on the box crabs that proved to be one of the most interesting finds of my career as a biological collector. The box crab has two long flat chaele—claws—that it presses up against its carapace, reminding one of a miser hoarding his gold, counting it over and over. On this box crab there was a bunch of small gooseneck-type *Octolasmis* barnacles growing between the chaele and carapace. When I sent them to the barnacle specialist at Harvard, they were identified as *Octolasmis tridens*, only recently discovered in the Indian Ocean, and there was disagreement as to whether my specimens were a new species or a related form.

The outer line was proving better for the fishermen, and soon the stacks of empty fish boxes were being packed with crabs and the fish in the bait boxes were lessening. The afternoon moved quickly and time went faster. Sometime in the course of it, Andy explained his theory of relativity. "Lorda-mercy!" he was saying as he baited a trap and dropped it back into the sea. "There's days when there ain't nary two or three crabs to a pot, and you got to run them lines anyway or the crabs will die. And you keep pulling up those pots with just a few little old crabs in them—why, there ain't nothing heavier. Every one of them baskets weighs a ton empty. Don't it, William?"

William agreed that it did. "But," Andy went on, "when those crab baskets are full, and you're getting thirty or forty crabs to every pot. But shoot, you don't think nothing about snatching one basket up right after the other. Then they don't weigh nothin a-tall."

And that's the sort of afternoon it was for the crabbers. The boxes filled up—they had nearly a thousand pounds of crabs—but the bait was running out. Their day would end when the bait was completely gone.

A large gray shark appeared and followed the skiff while the twin outboard motors pushed us over from cork buoy to cork buoy. As William pulled in the baskets, the shark swam up alongside the boat. It seemed nearly as big as our skiff.

I was going to throw him a catfish, but Andy said, "No, you better not waste no bait. We're gonna need every bit of it to bait these pots, since the crabs are running so good. In fact, you might start dressing them catfish out for us—if you want to. Just cut the head off and split their belly open so they won't bloat up in the trap. Catfish make good crab bait when you cut them up right. Be sure they don't fin you."

Moments later William pulled up a crab trap that had, in addition to twenty two crabs, two large flounders. "Welcome aboard," William said gleefully. "I sure am glad to see you fellows."

"They'll make good eating," I commented.

"They sure will," said William, holding them up lovingly. "There's nothing better. Why you just take some flounder and fry 'em good and crisp in some hot grease, eat 'em with hush puppies and grits—that's the best meal in the world. There ain't nothing I'd rather have than flounder."

Andy said nothing but baited the trap with the last of the

alewives. The next trap he baited with catfish, and the following two traps. Then he said, "Hand me them two flounders, William."

William gloomily gave Andy his two flounders, and Andy, with grim determination, cut holes in them so they wouldn't bloat and lowered the pot back into the water. I knew Andy didn't like taking the boy's flounders, but bait comes first.

William sadly cut the motor down and we drifted up to the next cork buoy. Andy pulled it up, emptied the crabs, and gave me a long calculating look. "Do you need *all* them fish?" I had a pile of shark remoras and a few pigfish that were host specimens for the parasitic copepods.

I looked over my pile and not very graciously yielded two remoras, which he put in his trap. Remoras, *Echeneis naucrates*, are elongated, torpedo-shaped fish with a peculiar dorsal fin that has been modified into a sucker disk, which enables it to hang onto sharks and other large fish, getting free transportation and greedily snatching up the big fish's leftovers. Frequently they attach themselves to scuba divers and become quite a pest.

Because of the fish's adaptations, it is of considerable interest to classes studying the evolution of biological forms, and although I had no immediate order for shark remoras, I found it a good practice to keep up a stock of preserved specimens so that when an order did come I could fill it immediately.

Andy looked at my remaining four remoras. "Them pilot fish sure make good crab bait," he said. I gave him another remora and two pigfish, rather reluctantly.

"I have to keep some pilot fish, Andy," I said defiantly. I would have adamantly refused to part with any if I had known that two weeks later I would receive a good-paying order for twenty-five remoras.

Andy was eyeing my ice chest, packed with twenty-eight

spadefish. "You wouldn't mind parting with some of those angelfish, would you? They sure do make good bait."

"No," I said emphatically. "That would be mighty expensive crab bait!"

"How much do you get for them things?" asked William.

"Enough to make a mortgage payment," I replied.

"That is mighty expensive crab bait," Andy agreed coldly. "You'd better keep them. But you got more of them pigfish," he challenged. Gone was his reverent attitude toward science.

It was his boat, so I coldly handed him all my pigfish and all but one remora. But not one spadefish would I yield. He baited the last crab basket and we started for home.

I resented having to yield up my catch after having spent the whole day in the broiling sun, culling specimens out of boxes of angry pinching crabs. Except for the spadefish I salvaged, it made the day seem futile.

William sat between the two outboard motors, holding the boat on course. The tide was falling, and the waves were now breaking over the oyster reefs and sandy shoals. Andy, overcome by fatigue and probably too much medicine, pulled his big straw hat over his eyes and leaned over the boxes of crabs, which were covered with wet burlap sacks, and drowsed off.

The silence continued. It was a long, long trip back to Arcadia, and from time to time William and I looked at Andy, who was snoring peacefully, and then we looked at each other and grinned. I thought of how different shrimping was from crabbing. In shrimping we had a mutual understanding. The captains were grateful when I helped cull catches—in exchange they even helped me save my specimens. But crabbing was a two-man team, and everything they caught in the pots was used—either put in the traps for bait or thrown into the crab boxes to increase the weight and cheat the crab houses a little.

The warm sun and the long, monotonous trip back, the rhythmic roar of the outboards, and the sameness of the landscape, the scrub pines, sand dunes, and the brilliant sun on the blue water soon made me follow Andy's example.

I awoke with a sudden jolt that knocked me forward on top of the crab boxes. Fortunately there was a thick layer of wet burlap between us.

"Wa-what's happened?" asked Andy in alarm, scrambling upright and blinking his eyes.

"I reckon I fell asleep, Mr. Andy," William said apologetically. "It appears we run aground." The boat was halfway up on a sand bar.

"I declare, I was asleep too," Andy remarked. "It looks like old Jack here was the only one awake." He turned to me. "You should have hollered when you saw us coming up on this reef."

"I was asleep too," I confessed, and we burst into laughter.

"We'd better get this boat off the reef quick or the tide'll leave us high and dry," Andy said after he recovered.

William and I jumped into the cold water and pushed the boat off, and we returned to Arcadia in high spirits, Andy and William with a thousand pounds of crabs (netting them forty dollars for a day's work) and I with an excellent series of spadefish. And a Woods Hole order was completed.

# 9 Trial Run

The waiting for shrimp continued. For a week the fogs came and lifted, and came again. Chass and the other shrimpers brought their boats over to Elizabeth City. Chass had not yet acquired a permanent deck hand, so I was filling in. The fishermen sat on their boats in the basin and passed the time playing cards, drinking beer, or reading magazines, hoping the interminable blanket of cold damp white mists would clear by the time the sun set. But each night they climbed into their pick-up trucks and old cars and drove off, disappointed, through the thick fogs, back to Shiawassee, hoping that the morrow would bring good weather.

Every day I drove down to the boat basin with specimen containers and bottles of Bouin's fixative solution, formalin, and alcohol and waited with the other shrimpers for the weather to clear, waiting to meet my commitments.

One afternoon the radio of the *Portia* spluttered and crackled loudly through the damp air. Chass had tuned in to the channel of the out-of-state trawlers that were shrimping late that afternoon twenty miles east of Elizabeth City. We were all anxious to know what the weather was like. But they were not talking about weather. We heard snatches of talk about a submerged airplane wreck that was someplace out in the bay; they were hoping their nets wouldn't tangle with it.

A sudden burst of laughter floated up to us from the *Elixir*, moored one boat away from the *Portia*. Nobody turned his head or seemed the least bit interested. Chass turned the radio dial to get better reception and said impatiently, "I wish to hell they would say something about the weather out there."

"I imagine they're off Shell Cove if they're talking about that airplane wreck," Wally said dispiritedly. He seemed unusually depressed as he glumly drank his beer. Another wild burst of laughter and joyful shouts came from the *Elixir*. And yet we all felt strangely subdued. I couldn't help wondering about it.

"Those Alabama boats don't know where the hell they are." Danny laughed sardonically. "They could be anywhere from Gull Point to Tarpon Springs." He crushed the empty beer can with one hand and tossed it into the water and then popped open another.

I had started making up a stock solution of formaldehyde when more shouts of laughter and gaiety stirred my curiosity. I had to ask about it, even though I noticed that all the captains and their deck hands were studiously ignoring it.

"What's the excitement over there?" I asked Danny Yates, jerking my thumb in the *Elixir*'s direction. "Is Preacher having a party?" Preacher had become the captain of the *Elixir*, which was a Yates Brothers boat.

Danny laughed mirthlessly. "You're damn right! Preacher is having a party. The sheep grew back a new coat of wool and they're fleecing him."

I was puzzled for a moment. I didn't know what Danny meant, and I was about to ask when my glance fell upon the big shiny creamy-white Cadillac parked among the pick-up trucks, old coupes, and old station wagons. Then it dawned on me. "Aha," I said. "So Sam is back. Some people never learn."

Chass waved his hand as if he were brushing off something unpleasant. "That stupid Yankee can't learn. He hasn't got any sense. Personally, he hasn't got enough money and he can't get up enough money to play poker with me. I'm picky about who I—"

I didn't hear what else Chass had to say because another shout of hilarity drowned Chass's soft speaking voice. Then a loud voice said, "Come on, Preacher, shut up and deal. It's getting late." And then I heard Preacher's loud drawling voice return with, "Aw, shut up, you fat Greek." Sounds travel easily and distinctly over the water. "How many do you want, Sam?"

Sam was like a fish out of water, trying to get along on land and not quite making it. He had one of the biggest and finest homes on the beach, a big car, two big boats, and big everything, but he failed to impress his neighbors. He tried to make friends among the fishermen, but they detested him—he was just too vulgar, too ostentatious, too loud, and too self-centered, and he had the unpleasant habit of belittling and disparaging everybody and everybody's possessions.

I didn't like Sam Wells either, but I was curious about him. I could not understand why he continued trying to make friends among the shrimpers, because he had never been a fisherman, and they snubbed him in the most humiliating manner. Except for the unholy three who were fleecing him now, nobody even said hello to him. Once I heard Sam hail Cully, who turned around and said in his high-pitched voice, "I don't know you, mister!" and turned and ran up the plank to his boat.

I left my formaldehyde solution for a moment and edged to the portside, craning my neck to see into the *Elixir*. Then I boldly climbed up on the rail for a better view. And there was a sight to behold! Preacher was looking more angelic and benevolent than ever under his peaked cap. Tiny, resting on his big haunches, looked wolfish with glittering eyes, and George Williams, leaning his chin in his hands, looked greedily porcine. The three card sharks were sitting on the bare deck while Sam Wells was enthroned on Preacher's best new life preserver. I could hear Sam's voice distinctly. It was rasping, rumbling, and boastful against the soft, honeyed Southern drawls.

I knew they were cheating Chicago Sam—he had retired and moved to Florida from Chicago—because when Tiny rubbed his left ear with his big hand, nobody took chances and Sam won a slim pot. When Preacher cast his innocent blue eyes heavenward, the betting rose fiercely and so it would too if George Williams rubbed his walruslike mustache.

Chicago Sam had the floor, no doubt about it. The three fishermen listened to him with rapt smiles, and at the end of Sam's anecdotes, they would guffaw with laughter, practically rolling all over the deck while Sam happily joined in the merriment. Preacher, overcome, slapping his thighs, managed to take a fast peek at the distracted humorist's cards. And still howling with laughter, he said, "Oh, lordy, that's a good one. I'll match your ten dollars and raise you fifteen."

I always spoil things for myself. I couldn't help giggling. Sam looked directly at me, and a shadow of annoyance and dislike passed over his face. And I caught a split-second warning look from both Tiny and George—it distinctly said, "If you don't clear out of here, we'll skin you alive and boil you in oil."

Still laughing, I returned to my solution of formaldehyde. "How's it going?" asked Danny. "As if I don't know."

"It's funny as hell," I laughed, "but it's kind of creepy too."

Jimmy looked annoyed. "I wouldn't play nothin' with that old Preacher. I swear he has a periscope at the end of his nose.

Someday, somebody's going to flatten it for him; they're going to make him look like a bull dog."

There were no other comments about the card game. And a gloomy pall settled down upon the waiting captains and their crews. The thick overhanging gray clouds and the cold mists matched their mood. I felt there was a distinct feeling of shame about the three rascals. Almost everybody there was related to them by either blood ties or through marriage. And I couldn't help sharing the shrimpers' feelings, because I liked Preacher, George, and Tiny—they had been practically family to me. I think we all blamed the stranger in our midst, Chicago Sam, as if he were responsible for their downfall.

Chass, still working on the dials of the radio, asked me, "What was the weather like when you came here from Arcadia?"

"It seemed to be clearing," I replied. "Although there was still a little fog. But I saw some shrimp boats anchored off Indian Point."

Chass became impatient. He gulped his beer down quickly and tossed the can overboard, mashed the transmitter, and said, "This is KDI 252461 here, Chass Parker on the *Portia* over in Elizabeth City. What kind of weather are you having out there? A bunch of us is waiting to go shrimping. We got some bad fog on this end. Can you read me—come back."

There was a silence except for the noisy party on the *Elixir*, and then through the static came a response. "Yeah, I got you over there in Elizabeth City. This is KDI 228137, the *Sally B.* of Tolska, Alabama." Through the eerie hum and meaningless loud static, the voice said clearly, "Weather ain't too bad—most of the fog's died down out here."

Chass was elaborately grateful. "Yessir, here in Elizabeth City I can't see the hand in front of my face," he sang out. His soft voice had a pleasantly musical, chanting quality about it. He said politely, "Thank you kindly now, sure do appreciate that weather report. Would you mind telling us where your position is."

Chicago Sam's voice rasped, "Make it twenty."

And between the rackety static of the radio we heard: "We're off the southeast end of Anderson Channel."

Chass thanked them again with studied courtesy and signed off. When he finished, bearded Wally, who had for the most part been silent and morose on the stern of the *Portia*, hastily drank his beer and rose. "I 'spect I'm going out and catch a few shrimp. What kind of stuff do you need tonight, Jack?"

I rattled off a list. There was another shout of hilarity aboard the *Elixir*.

"I doubt you'll get any octopus," said Wally, ignoring the noise. "Or squid, for that matter. The weather's still too cold. Why, I doubt you'll even get sting rays, but there ought to be a few toadfish or batfish—whatever you call them."

"I'd sure appreciate it if you save me any of that trash. Keep the batfish alive, if you can. Just throw the rest in the fish basket. It's cold enough to where they will keep, unless you get an octopus. Dave here got one last year about this time. And be sure and save all the spadefish you find, all sizes."

Tiny shouted out triumphantly, "Sorry, Sam, a full house beats a straight. Ain't that right, George?"

Wally turned to the *Elixir*, and making a megaphone out of his hands by cupping them over his mouth, he bellowed almost loud enough for the boats out in the bay to hear him, "*Hey, Preacher, move your barge and quit cheating that poor stupid Yankee. Let's go shrimping.*"

This broke everybody up. Danny and Jimmy were laughing so hard that they sank to the deck helplessly. Dave Clark, a big strong man, had a fit of giggles, and every time he thought he had control, he would break down again. Chass's beer went down the wrong way and he was laughing and choking at the same time, and I was doubled up. Wally was tremendously

1. *The sea hare,* Aplysia willcoxi, *is a snail with a tiny vestigial shell. It swims through the water in a lazy undulating motion, gracefully opening and folding its wings. Like its relatives the squid and octopus, it discharges a purple ink that numbs the senses of its enemies.*

2. *The harmless horseshoe crab,* Limulus polyphemus, *tossed up on the shore by the high tide. Its long, daggerlike telson is not used as a weapon, but purely as a levering device to right itself when thrown up on its back.*

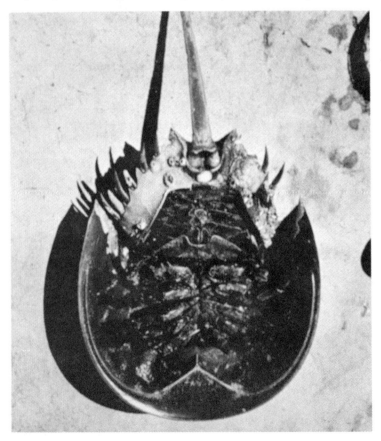

3. *An Atlantic loggerhead sea turtle,* Caretta caretta caretta, *caught in a shrimp net. It is ill at ease on land, moving clumsily over the sand, but in the ocean it is a graceful swimmer. The flat, round barnacles,* Chelonibia testudinaria, *on the turtle's carapace are commensal and live exclusively on sea turtles.*

4. *The male sea horse,* Hippocampus hudsonius punctulatus, *uses its prehensile tail to hold itself steady on a perch—in this case, a finger. The female deposits her eggs on the male's pelvic fins. After fertilization his pelvic fins develop into a modified brood pouch. Upon maturity of the embryo, the male undergoes contractions similar to birth spasms and ejects hundreds of strange-looking little fry into the sea.*

5. *The snake eel,* Ophichthys, *is nocturnal and sleeps during the day and at night wanders out in search of food on the muddy bottoms, where it is occasionally swooped up in a shrimp net. Its numerous sharp fangs can inflict a nasty bite.*

6. *After a hurricane, many interesting invertebrates are torn from their holdfasts or washed from their burrows in the sand and cast up on the high beach. In Florida, the sunray clam,* Macrocallista nimbosa, *is among the many victims frequently seen after a severe storm.*

7. *The common octopus,* Octopus vulgaris, *is one of the most intelligent of invertebrates. However, it is also very delicate, and unless it is handled with knowledge and skill it will soon go into shock and die, as the specimen above did.*

8. *The spider crab,* Libinia, *looks ominous but is a very sluggish and harmless creature. It prefers to hide among the mud and eelgrass feasting on carrion. It depends upon camouflage for protection. This specimen was found in a commercial crab trap.*

9. *The sand starfish*, Luidia clathrata, *makes an impression in the sand at low tide. It is difficult to capture a complete specimen because of its neurotic habit of snapping off its arms at the slightest disturbance.*

10.

*The slipper lobster, Scyllarius americanus, is one of the weirdest-looking crustaceans to be found anywhere. Because these lobsters plow so rapidly into the sand, the fishermen call them "bulldozers." In spite of their horny, sandpaper-textured exoskeleton, they have tender, delicious white meat if you can find a heavy-duty nutcracker.*

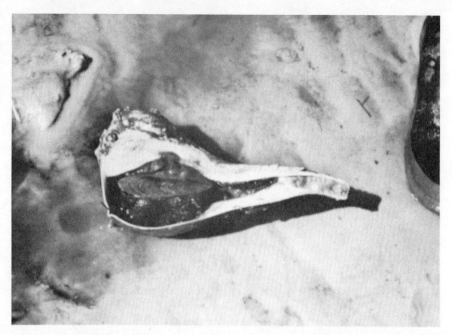

11. Busycon contrarium, *the predatory whelk, is abundant on the tidal flats around oyster reefs. It feeds largely on other conchs, clams, or oysters. Every year commercial collectors gather hundreds of large whelks for invertebrate-zoology classes.*

12. *Just a glimpse of a sand eel burrowing swiftly into the sand. To distinguish and capture one requires a trained eye and a fast shovel.*

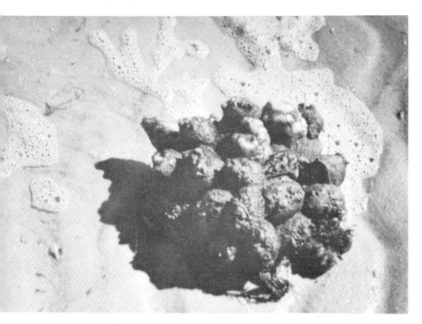

13. *A cluster of solitary sea squirts exposed by the receding tide. The large, lumpy, rough-skinned balls are* Molgula occidentalis, *and the two smooth-skinned ones on the top left are* Styelia plicata. *Both species were gathered for a researcher studying the biochemical properties of their blood.*

14. *It took an extremely low, wind-blown tide to expose this benthonic community of mushy sea pork,* Ascidia, *and the branching, horny sea whips,* Leptogorgia virgulata, *all growing on a rock pile. Rich areas like this are few and far between in the northeastern Gulf and are treasured by the collector of marine specimens and seashore naturalist.*

*15. This is a sample of what can be found in a single strike of a shrimp trawl: the mantis shrimp, Squilla empusa; Texas skate, Raja texana; three commercial shrimp, Penaeus duorarium; a bonnethead shark, Sphyrna tuburo; a sting ray, Dasyatis; and two Gulf squid, Lolliguncula brevis.*

16. [Top] *Fishermen beaching a seine. Fish are trapped by the half-mile-long walls of webbing, which shrink as more and more of the net is pulled toward shore and piled up on the beach.*

17. [Bottom] *A shrimper pulls in the lazy line, which is attached to the weighted doors that sink and spread the net. The man on the left locks the winch after it has lifted the net out of the sea.*

18. *A fisherman getting his oyster tongs ready to rake up the large, fat oysters from the muddy bottoms in North Florida. Oystering is one of Florida's largest fishing industries.*

*19.  Mending a seine is a difficult art that takes experience, a steady, strong hand, and infinite patience.*

20. *With a jerk of the bag rope, thousands of shrimp, fish, squid, and crabs pile out on the deck. Gilled in the webbing of the net are tonguefish, cusk eels, and soles.*

21. *Here a shrimper lowers a webbed basket into the fish hold, where the catch is stored until the shrimpers dock and unload their catch at the fish and shrimp companies.*

22. *This is a handsome catch of commercial·shrimp,* Penaeus setiferus, *after the catch had been culled out from the mound of fish and invertebrates. Although these shrimp undoubtedly ended on the dinner table, commercial shrimp make excellent experimental animals and hardy aquarium pets.*

23. *Sea cucumbers,* Thyonella gemmata. *Three are preserved with their tentacles expanded, as if they were in their natural feeding position. The specimen on the extreme right was preserved in a contracted state.*

24.  *The sting ray, Dasyatis, is a beautiful swimmer. Normally it is not an aggressive animal, but if it is stepped on it will protect itself by lashing its whiplike tail, armed with a venomous barbed stinger.*

25. Physalia physalia, *the Portuguese man-of-war, is one of the most beautiful jellyfish—its brilliant colors range from deep pinks, purples, and blues to bright oranges and reds. But this denizen of the deep has powerful nematocysts and can sting severely.*

pleased with himself and with his success. His eyes twinkled behind his bushy red beard. This latest sally would be talked about for months to come.

We could hear the three rascals being ever so solicitous to-ward Chicago Sam. Tiny was saying, "Ah, that Wally belongs in a crazy house! You can ask anyone. Don't pay him no mind. You'd better drive carefully in that fog. You come see us, hear?"

George too urged him to be careful, and Preacher walked Sam back to his car. They had to cross Wally's boat, the *Wanderer*, to the *Portia*, and from there to the dock. I watched Preacher open the creamy-white Cadillac door while Sam got in. "Don't worry about a thing, Sam. You'll win it all back the next time. You know you can't win every game." And he said again cheerfully, "Y'all come back and see us, hear? Get down to the dock one morning and I'll save you a mess of shrimp."

When Preacher got back to the *Portia*, there was murder in his eyes. Wally, imitating Preacher, had turned his eyes up heavenward with an expression of angelic innocence. But he didn't reckon with the swiftness of Preacher's retribution. All in one motion, Preacher lowered Chass's deck bucket, drew it up, and sloshed the icy-cold water all over Wally. Dripping and furious, Wally yelled with rage, but before he could retaliate, Preacher had leaped from the *Portia* over the *Wanderer* to his own boat. He cast off, and in a moment the *Elixir* was chugging rapidly out into the river.

With the excitement over, everybody returned to his own boat. Tiny was already on his boat, the *Maggie L.*, and George was on his tired old *Xenophon*. I fancied I could see him carefully counting his ill-gotten gains.

The captains had charged up their engines, and some of the smaller boats had already pulled out behind Preacher's *Elixir*.

Chass called cheerfully to me above the throbbing engines,

"Come on, Jack. Let's catch a few shrimp before this fog sets in again."

Suddenly Chass changed his mind. He snapped his fingers as if he had just remembered something important—something urgent that had to be attended to immediately. "Oh yeah, I most forgot, I got to go down to Ronny's Bar and get a beer. Be back in fifteen minutes." His fifteen minutes stretched into a half hour, then an hour. After two hours of waiting, and after all the boats except the *Portia* had left the boat basin, I went to fetch him out of Ronny's Bar.

Two hours later we both left Ronny's Bar in a mellow mood. It was almost night when the solitary *Portia* chugged out of the deserted boat basin into the Elizabeth River and then into Elizabeth Sound. The sound was full of treacherous sand bars and reefs marked with blinking red buoys and mournful bells, but it was excellent shrimping grounds, not over five fathoms, with few rocks and a substratum of sandy mud that shrimp love. But it took skill to navigate a boat in Elizabeth Sound without running it aground or tearing up a shrimp net.

On the distant shore of the little sleeping town of Elizabeth, red and green neon lights of the tiny cafés colored the misty air around them. Frosty-looking stars sprinkled the pale, darkening sky. It looked like it was going to be a beautiful night. Far ahead of us, scattered in the ghostly darkness of the bay, were our fellow shrimpers, who were already pulling up their nets. Their deck lights were like bright yellow fires with an aura of mist around them floating like fantastic elves on the horizon. I switched on our deck lights and waited.

When we had traveled far enough out into the sound, Chass cut the engine down to an idle: we were ready to drop the net. We had to work quickly. I unwound the rope that kept the net hanging from the mast and the net heaped up on the deck. While the captain kept the *Portia* turning in a lazy circle, I dropped it over the side, taking care to see that the webbing didn't tangle with the propeller wheel. Quickly I shook off the clumps of sea squirts and matted bryozoa that clung to the ticker chain. Chass had neglected to clean up last night's debris.

He speeded up, pulling the net along the surface in a straight course to clean out some of yesterday's fish that were still stuck in the webbing, and the elongated bag straightened out like an immense nylon sock.

The *Portia* slowed again. Chass released the lock on the winch, and the massive iron-clad boards attached to the net, the ticker chain, and the lazy line sank down into the black water. The great cone-shaped net dragged down behind it. The winches, like giant spools of thread, fed out two hundred feet of steel cable through the davits until Chass slammed on the lock.

I centered the cables by hooking them through a huge chain and pulled them up to the top of the hoisting mast. It was a complicated process—there were ropes and chains and halyards hanging everywhere, and everything had to be hooked up properly or the net would become tangled. Chass sped up, and the cables became taut and spread into a V formation, indicating that the nets were dragging at the proper angle.

"I reckon that's done it," Chass said, lighting up a cigarette and offering me one.

"How long are we going to drag?"

He looked at his watch. "About two hours, I reckon. Look here, Jack. I want you to look out for them goddam crab pots. If we catch up a net full of them we'll really be screwed. Ever try getting a crab pot out of a shrimp net?"

I nodded. "George caught up a half-dozen one night and they tore the hell out of his net. I'll watch out." I sat on the bow bundled up in my heavy shrimping jacket and by the light of our deck lamps watched the calm black waters for the white cork buoys of the crab traps.

There was a perpetual feud between the Shiawassee shrimpers and the Arcadia crabbers. Once, while the shrimpers were working in open waters off the crabbing village of Arcadia, they caught up several strings of crab baskets. The crabbers called the sheriff and the shrimpers were arrested and fined, which resulted in fist fights. Thus began the feud, and soon some shrimpers carried guns in case the sheriff tried to board their boats. The dispute was resolved legally, if not in the minds of the shrimpers and crabbers, in a court battle—the shrimpers won, because the crabbers had illegally set their pots in open navigational waters.

The crabbers and shrimpers of Elizabeth City and Shiawassee, however, were on good terms, since most of them were kinfolk. Generally the Elizabeth City crabbers considerately set their traps away from areas where shrimpers worked, and if the shrimpers did catch a crab pot or two from time to time, there was no ill feeling. The shrimpers kept the crabbers supplied with bait, and bait was the lifeline of the crabbing industry.

It wasn't long before I saw a white cork buoy bobbing along the surface. "Crab pot on starboard!" I called.

Chass peered out through the darkness and turned a big beaming spotlight on the water. "Sure enough is," he said, and steered the *Portia* away from that area. Shrimping is half hard labor, feeding out nets and culling the catch, and half waiting for the nets to come up with the catch. Often, as I sat on the deck waiting hour after hour, I wondered what the nets were catching. What was happening down there in those black waters?

Sitting on the bow under the stars, I imagined what was happening. The cone-shaped net sinks to the bottom and the cables attached to the two iron-clad boards are so adjusted that their resistance to the water makes the forty-foot mouth of the net spread wide apart. The weighted boards serve as a frame

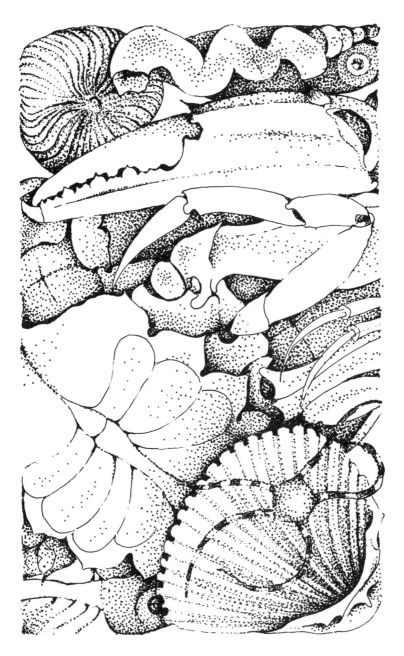

*The net glides on, engulfing starfish, jellyfish,*
*blue crabs, and wandering hermit crabs.*

and balance for the net, and it glides over the bottom like a massive kite.

The ticker chain hangs loosely between the two boards, stirring up the mud and kicking up the shrimp, who are busy feeding and swimming on the bottom. When they dart up, the net swoops them in. Predators from all over, attracted by the frantic shrimp's action, plunge hungrily into the net after them.

Small, hungry fish gobble up the shrimp, larger fish gobble up the smaller ones, and so on. The net glides on, engulfing starfish, jellyfish, blue crabs, and wandering hermit crabs, breaking off sponges and big glistening colonial ascidians, uprooting gorgonians and sometimes corals. And the net catches up the sluggish tonguefish, flounders, and soles, the lazy skates, the rays and scavenging spiny catfish, and the beautifully spotted cusk eels. The net moves so slowly that it causes little stir, and the animals are not aware of their danger until it is too late.

Hundreds of grunts and pigfish, with their mouths full of shrimp and anchovies, are pushed back into the webbing. As more and more individual creatures crowd into the bag, panic sets in. The resistance of the moving net forces them back into the tail of the bag, where they fight against the small meshes. Soles and grunts and cusk eels squeeze halfway through only to be hung up by their gill coverings.

Perhaps there is a large sea turtle or sand shark that enters through the wide mouth and begins greedily snapping up all the fish—until it realizes its own predicament and vainly lunges against the webbed prison. It smashes into the black webbing, but the water pressure and the crowds of tossing, turning fish soon suffocate it. Sharks often die with fish in their jaws, and air-breathing sea turtles sometimes drown.

But we on the deck do not know what is happening. We can only guess. Can it be a big sea turtle the net has just swooped up, or perhaps two hundred pounds of hateful, spiny catfish,

*But we on the deck do not know what is happening. We can only guess. Can it be a big sea turtle the net has just swooped up, or perhaps two hundred pounds of hateful spiny catfish or a great slimy mass of stinging jellyfish?*

or a great slimy mass of stinging jellyfish? Are there any shrimp? Sometimes the shrimp will show up seemingly out of nowhere and load down the net. Other times the net may drag for hours over sterile bottom and not so much as a starfish will come up.

This waiting is a restless, dreary, and often anxious period. As I sat on the bow watching for crab pots, I had the illusion that we were not moving, that no progress was being made while the boat strained forward pulling its heavy load. We found ourselves among several other shrimp boats, some with their deck lights burning bright, others with their tiny red running lights and decks in darkness.

A small trawler drifted past us, deck lights blazing in the thick black night. Two men were culling the catch and shoveling off trash. And then darkness again. It was getting chilly, and the moist air condensed on the deck. Chass said we were out of crab-pot territory, so I switched off the deck lights, went into the cabin, and crawled into a bunk and slept.

The captain shook me awake. I thought I had just closed my eyes, but one look at the clock convinced me it was two hours later, well past midnight. I thrust on my shrimping boots, and Chass put the engine out of gear and flicked on the glaring deck lights. I waited until the tension slacked off the cables, lowered them from the hoisting boom, and released them from the levering chain. Chass jerked the levers that started the winch winding in the steel cables. The spools wound round and round, and the straining, powerful machinery screamed and protested when metal rubbed against metal.

This was another anxious period. Wet cable kept coming up from the sea, and after five long, long minutes the weighted boards rose to the surface, jerked out of the water with a crash, and dangled from the davit arm. Chass raced the boat so the net would be pulled rapidly behind, rinsing it of mud and sand before it was lifted up on the deck.

Hurriedly I pulled the ticker chain and shook it hard to free it from the clumps of wiry bryozoans that clung tenaciously. The captain grabbed the lazy line that was hooked to the tail of the bag and pulled it up to the hoisting boom, threaded it through a halyard, and wound it around the revolving brass niggerhead.

The black net emerged from the sea and hung from the mast. Water gushed out of the bag and showered on the decks. Under our blazing deck lights, the swinging bag looked like a gigantic webbed sock filled with gold and silvery bodies of fish, pink shrimp, and purple sea pansies with cold blue spots of luminescence. Now and then a head, tail, or fin distinguished itself, or a yellow starfish protruded through the black webbing. I could smell the sharp acrid odor of living things from the sea.

Captain Chass Parker jerked the bag rope, and the swaying net disgorged its contents with a flat, squishing sound. Thousands upon thousands of compressed, shaken, exhausted creatures spilled out and heaped up into a living pyramid of struggling, frantic marine life. Aggressive blue crabs scuttled sideways away from everything, their pinching claws raised, like a boxer warding off blows. A large angry speckled moray eel slithered out of the pile with its mouth agape. Silver-gold fish appropriately called gruntfish were grunting, pale-pink shrimp jackknifed and danced, skates pounded their wings on deck, and bonnethead sharks furiously lashed about.

There were mounds of fish, all kinds, too many to describe. Only the large creatures, the colorful ones, and the ones that were conspicuous caught the eye. There were so many, many animals, there was no time to look. Quickly we threw the net overboard and pulled it along the boat, washing it clean of any life still remaining in the webbing.

Then Chass looked over the pile critically and with his boot scuffled through some of the shrimp and fish. "Don't look like there's much shrimp here," he said. He looked out over the bay. "Just look at those lights on shore—it's fixing to fog up directly, and then it will start raining, just like I told them it would. I don't guess we ought to make another strike. Those other boats will come in right behind us. I want to get back before Ronny's Bar closes."

I picked up a lively shrimp and examined it. "We got about twenty-five pounds here," I said, judging from the size of the animals. "That right?"

"Yeah," he said hesitantly, "they might come out to that in the rough. Come on, let's pull up the net and haul ass."

After we pulled in the boards and heaped the net on deck, Chass scrutinized the pile and kicked out a shark remora. "Any stuff you can use in there?"

I picked up a weird-looking batfish from the top of the mound. It flipped its muscular rough-skinned tail from side to side, trying to jerk out of my hands. I dropped it into a collecting container filled with seawater. "I got what I need."

But I had to rush. I wanted to get as many creatures out of the pile as possible before we got back to shore. Ominous sheets of lightning revealed heavy rain clouds covering the stars. The chilling wind stiffened, and the mist penetrated my clothing. It was typical of the Gulf to have beautiful weather one moment and turn stormy the next.

I raked the moray eel into the deck bucket and then dumped it in my large collecting container to keep it alive. Hurriedly I gathered four more batfish, and they joined the eel. The batfish were quite lively; they began awkwardly to paddle about the container with their strange seal-like flippers. Occasionally a batfish would vigorously jerk its muscular tail with cumbersome strokes like those of a beginning swimmer and make its way to the top of the bucket, only to sink down again. As the wind increased, the boat rocked and the water splashed out of the buckets, so I had to secure them to the rail and cover them.

There was so much to do that I had to stop and organize my thoughts. The live animals must be attended to first, and the delicate parasitic forms had to be given second consideration. In the mass of gleaming golden and silvery bodies, several small bonnethead sharks were most conspicuous, some with their tails protruding out, others lying at the top gasping, giving surprising bursts of activity, and then subsiding.

I jerked half a dozen sharks out of the pile and slit their body cavities open. Chass had gone back to the wheel to bring the boat to port, but he came back to watch me briefly. "What in the hell are you doing to those sharks?" he asked.

My hands were covered with blood, and in the heavy damp air the odor of uric acid from the sharks mingled with the Diesel fumes from the boat. "I'm dissecting out their stomachs and intestines to get the tapeworms. These things are generally loaded with parasites."

Chass laughed. "How come you can't just pack them on ice and cut them up when you get home? It seems like it'd be a whole lot easier for you."

I jabbed my knife into the fourth bonnethead, gripping its neck to keep it from biting me, and began ripping open its stomach. "The tapeworms are delicate," I told him. "Soon as these things are dead, the digestive juices make the worms rot and explode." I pulled the gut out and sliced it above the stomach. Then I handed Chass a jar from my styrofoam box of collecting gear. "Mind getting me some fresh water?"

When I had the water, I mixed up a volume of seawater and fresh water isotonic to the parasites—that is, similar to conditions of the shark's normal saline blood—and dropped the guts in. Chass shook his head. "That's the darnedest thing I've ever seen. What do those worms do to the shark?"

"I don't really know," I said as I packed the jars in my ice chest. "No one really knows. Maybe it makes them hungry."

"Something makes them hungry. I swear, a shark's got a

straight gut—they'll eat any goddam thing! By the way," he added, raking through the pile with his boot, "I been meaning to ask you but always forget—what in the hell is this thing?" He kicked out a large green colonial ascidian.

I looked over my shoulder. "Oh, that's sea pork." I had finished the sharks and started dissecting the skates.

"I call it sea gristle," Chass said. "What's it do?"

"Nothing much," I replied. "Just grows on the bottom like a sponge and pumps food out of the water."

"Crazy damn things—so much of them. You'd think they could be used for something—food or fertilizer. Something!"

I shrugged. "I wouldn't eat them." Actually, at one time I had felt the same way—such protoplasm in such abundance should serve as food—but I had found them watery and tasting like an unpleasant fishy mush. Indirectly, however, ascidians and their relatives could be of great industrial importance. They seem to be the only animal that stores up and concentrates vanadium, a rare chemical element, in their blood cells. Vanadium is used in steel alloys and in the production of aniline black and other dyeing materials. In seawater it occurs in almost undetectable amounts, yet some ascidians are able to extract astonishing quantities of it.

Chass kicked the chunk of sea pork through a deck hole. "You got a crazy damn business, I swear," he said good-naturedly. He returned to the cabin to hold the wheel.

I took a routine sample of parasites from twenty-five shrimp, removing their guts and preserving them in Bouin's fluid, then put aside two pounds of "jumbos" for supper. These were the first shrimp of the season, and I hadn't eaten shrimp in months. I also culled out some choice flounders, mackerel, and white trout for my freezer.

I crouched beside the pile and with a short wooden cull board singled out the shrimp and tossed them into a wire basket. The cull board kept my hands from being cut, slashed, stung, or jabbed from poisonous catfish spines, or the whipping spiked tails of the mantis shrimp, or the vicious pinching claws of the ubiquitous blue crabs.

I glanced at the live bucket. The batfish were swimming anxiously at the surface, indicating that the oxygen in the water was getting low. I ran the deck hose in for a few seconds. They seemed more content, so I went back to my culling.

Most of the catch was alive, and I was glad to see the pigfish and grunts swim off as I shoveled and culled trash off the deck. In the cool weather most of the fish were returned to the sea alive. They floated on their sides above the choppy waters for a moment, then recovered and swam down into their dark abyss. During the warm summer, most of the fish would die on deck. When we shoveled off the trash, the waters would be littered with floating corpses, and the sharks, porpoises, and sea gulls would feast.

Whenever I shrimped, I felt obliged to return the unwanted creatures to the sea. Often when I saw a fish hopelessly gasping its life away in this alien world, I was struck by the thought that the power of saving its life was entrusted to me. Why let it die? All that was required was a little extra bit of effort, to snatch up this fish and in the same motion toss it over the rail so that it might go on living. And then I went back to my culling, putting living and dead shrimp into the fish baskets, which were now just so much food.

There were almost as many *Squilla empusa*, the unpleasant mantis shrimp, as there were commercial penaeid shrimp. And in a short time I had raked up the necessary two hundred specimens to meet an overdue order from a biological supply company and packed them in a can of formalin. But I selected six living *Squilla*, with their handsome green-stalked eyes and opalescent colors, and put them in the live buckets for a medical school. I had learned a special method of picking up the nasty creatures, which had almost no fleshy parts

and could flex and slash and jab in any direction. As they
flexed, I grabbed them and compressed them into a U so they
were helpless. But if I made one slip, I could receive a long
deep painful slash across my palm.

My back ached from crouching on the rocking boat, and I
was soaked with icy salt spray and mist. I thought I had done
rather well, as I continued culling and shoveling off trash. I
had several midshipmen, small golden fish with luminous pho-
tophores, but the year before about this time one drag would
have produced the hundred specimens I required. On that
night, out of the dozen or so specimens that I found in the
catch, only three were large enough to sell.

The culling was finished, and I began shoveling the unwanted trash overboard, stopping every now and then to pick
up a beautiful spotted calico crab or a rare conch. Chass left
the wheel and looked at the quarter-filled basket of shrimp and
nodded approvingly. "You sure did learn to cull." He scrutinized the remaining piles of culled trash. "Got all the shrimp
out too. Good job."

"You want me to break them?"

"I'd be obliged if you would. Then I can carry them off to
the fish house when the sun gets up." He looked at his watch.
"It's two o'clock. We'll be back pretty quick."

I continued the hard work of shoveling off the trash. The
great white jellies, *Rhopilema verrilli*, were quite a problem.
Some of them were so large that I had to chop them up with a
shovel to get them over the side. At last the deck was clear and
I swept the shreds of *Bugula*, bits of parchment-worm cas-
ings, and tonguefish into a pile and shoveled it through the
deck hole.

The deck was hosed down until it gleamed wetly white
under the hazy lights, and then I tilted the basket of pale-pink
shrimp on the clean deck and pinched their heads off between
my thumb and forefinger. The edible tails piled up on the

deck. The shrimp decreased in bulk considerably, but heading them doubled their market value. The severed heads were shoveled over the side, and the deck was washed down again. The acid from the shrimp's body makes fingers itch terribly, and this same acid can rot wooden decks. Both must be kept washed.

With the cessation of all that activity, there seemed to be one of those hanging pauses, an arrest in time. All was gone! After all that wriggling and gasping of marine creatures on the deck only an hour before, it seemed like a dream as the white, wet decks gleamed under the hazy lights. All the evidence was tucked away behind the winch: the specimens, the shrimp, and the edible fish.

At last we moved into the Elizabeth River and down to the boat basin. Then the rains started to come. Chass had been right after all—it really was raining, and the other boats were trailing us. In no time the other trawlers had maneuvered into the boat basin and tied up side by side.

The rain was coming down harder, and I was soaked to the skin as I jumped from the *Portia* to the slippery decks of the *Wanderer*, climbed over the *Elysium Queen* and the *Ocean Vista*, and then over the stately *Miss Melanie.* "How many did you get?" I called to Preacher on the *Elixir*.

"About a hundred pounds," Preacher said, lowering his baskets of shrimp into the fish hold. "Here, help me get this hatch cover on."

When the hatch cover was secured, he said, "I left some specimens over there for you. There's a pile of shovel-nose sharks, a few skates, and a mess of sea livers. And there's a few eels in that deck bucket too. Damn the weather!"

Danny Yates hopped aboard, shielding his face from the rain, and handed me two large dead sea horses. "Can you use these?" I thanked him and returned to the *Portia.*

Chass helped me load the two heavy twenty-gallon buckets

of seawater and living specimens into my station wagon.
"You're welcome to sleep on the boat tonight," he said. "No
call to go driving back in this hateful weather. You'll catch
pneumonia."

"Thanks, but I've got to. If those fish die I'll be losing
money."

I packed the parasites down with ice from the fish hold, took
leave of Chass and the other shrimpers, and began the long,
long drive through the blinding rain back to my laboratory. It
was three o'clock in the morning and only the beginning of a
long sleepless period of preserving and packaging specimens
for delivery to the airport.

The continued fog and rain over the next few days gave me
the time I needed to make up a mailing list and send out a
thousand catalogues, then wait hopefully for results. But finally
the waiting for spring ended, the last week in March. The
nights were cool out in the bay, sometimes even cold, and we
had to wear heavy jackets, but the shrimping grew more pleasant. With the warming air, more and more shrimp were
coming into the bay, and the catches were averaging four
hundred pounds a night. I was out shrimping every night with
Captain Chass Parker, building up my stockpiles and filling the
empty drums.

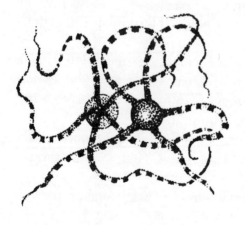

# 10 Quests and Requests

The *Portia* moved into the Elizabeth River, and the cool daylight revealed the sea life in a less dramatic way—quite drab compared to how it looked in the night under the blazing deck lights. The ubiquitous sea pansies looked like wilted pieces of liver, the golden midshipmen seemed like ordinary pale-yellow fish, and the slithering speckled moray eel on top of the mound did not look quite so fierce. The once struggling pyramid of fish looked disappointing, like the Fulton Fish Market on a Monday morning. I always feel somewhat disillusioned in daylight, even though I know these golden and silver creatures are beautiful at night. They fade with the rising sun.

We were culling the last load and saving a few boxes of bait fish for the crabbers. The air was frantic with hundreds of sea gulls, flapping and screaming and diving for the fish that we did not save. Porpoises bobbed up and down, blowing "phwoof" as they snatched up the living and dead fishes as fast as we shoveled them. The closer we came to the docks, the more eager, playful, and anxious the porpoises became as they

tried to keep up with the boat and get the food while the getting was good. Some were clowning and leaping high up out
of the water; their bodies would come down with a mighty
splash.

Chass, his new deck hand Eddie, and I couldn't help watching their glorious exploits, their acrobatic leaps, and they
seemed to know it. They were heralds of spring and warm
weather, because porpoises cannot endure icy waters and freezing air. It was a fine morning, a jolly morning; the porpoises
felt good and so did we. I had a large catch of specimens that
I could readily sell, and Chass and Eddie had five hundred
pounds of good-sized shrimp, and the markets were still paying
high prices. We all felt very good indeed, because we all had
earned our money.

When the shrimping picked up, trawlers from all over Shiawassee and the eastern Gulf crowded into the Elizabeth River
and packed the boat basin. With all these boats in, this was the
time to build up a big stock of specimens that I had already
listed in my catalogue. I came with big twenty-gallon plastic
pails jammed inside each other, all loaded into my station
wagon. I also carried sample specimens with me so there
would be no misunderstanding, and I passed the pails around to
all the deck hands and captains and explained what I wanted.
"Just these small pink jellyfish—not the big clear ones."

"Oh them—you mean stinging nettles."

"And these are heart urchins. I'll buy all you get."

"We call 'em goose eggs."

And so on.

I asked George Williams, "Do you think you can load this
pail with sea livers for me? It's worth five dollars."

"Make it six and I'll do it," he said shrewdly.

"All right, but they'll have to be big. It's hard to sell the
little ones." I knew his net dragged heavier than anyone else's
and he would get more sea pansies.

"I'll do what I can—I'll drag sea-liver hole."

Sea-liver hole was a deep dropoff and a muddy bottom, and it abounded with sea pansies. Most shrimpers avoided it, but George Williams would go anywhere to get shrimp or to make an extra dollar.

The spring of the year was always a busy time for me. Researchers in their laboratories wanted to experiment with this particular crab or that particular snail. I would go out on the shrimp trawlers not only to fill the requests but to restock sting rays and small bonnethead and hammerhead sharks, which I could not keep in stock. No sooner would they harden in formaldehyde than they were packed in a drum and put on a truck. And this year there had been an unusual demand for preserved sea pansies, *Renilla mulleri*. Chemists wanted them frozen, instructors in zoology classes wanted them to demonstrate bioluminescence, and the biological supply houses wanted them in volumes along with coral, jellyfish, and bryozoans.

Since I had mailed out my catalogues, I wanted to be prepared not only to maintain stocks but to fill requests on special order. Some of the requests were peculiar. Squid nerves, perhaps, which had to be carefully dissected out on a shrimp boat and preserved in a fixative so special that the scientist had to concoct a solution for me so that I could fix the giant axon aboard the boat. Or it was fifteen pounds of frozen tentacles of a stinging jellyfish, wanted for studying the toxins of the stinging cells. Or there was a request for two pounds of frozen shrimp eyes for an important experiment dealing with hormones that control light adaptations—these experiments are more successfully conducted in invertebrates and fish because the organisms have specific anatomical and chemical systems that are easier to control and work with in the laboratory.

I was intrigued by these research programs. A zoologist in New York was measuring the quantities of nucleic acids in different members of the animal kingdom. His findings were astounding and promised to shed light on the genetics of evolution. He found the more primitive fishes had higher concentrations of nucleic acid in their blood. Sharks and rays had double the concentration of the more evolved fishes. I became so absorbed in his exciting work that not a single fish, eel, gar, or reptile I found escaped being bled by me. Moreover, he discovered that the tunicate sperms had a weaker concentration of nucleic acids than any other group of invertebrates. The tunicate was always particularly interesting to me, because its tadpole larva starts out with a notochord—a promise of a backbone—and then settles on the bottom, reabsorbs its notochord, and lives a spongelike existence. It appears from this researcher's work that if an animal has undergone any form of evolution the nucleic-acid content decreases.

As I slit open a batfish and drew out half a cubic centimeter of blood and squirted it into the zoologist's special fixative, I wondered what he would discover from this odd fish that looks like it was ready to crawl out of the sea and walk on land, but instead contents itself with walking along the bottom of the ocean. Many scientists think that the batfish represents the most highly evolved form of fishes.

The deck was finally cleared and hosed down, and the disappointed and angry sea gulls flew after us screaming maledictions and curses as we turned into the boat basin. Some flew over us and splattered the deck with their droppings, seemingly from spite. We would have liked to have wrung their necks, but helplessly we washed the deck down again.

Many shrimp boats had already docked, and Captain Chass cautiously and skillfully maneuvered the *Portia* alongside another trawler. I tossed the stern line to one of the shrimpers, who fastened it to his tie post. I could hear snatches of cheerful conversations—"Hey, Preacher, come here a minute." "What'd you get last night, Jim?" "Believe we got twenty-six thirty." "Twenty pounds of flounder . . ." "Got to adjust my boards, we're catching too much trash." "Hey, Junior, help me cull off." And more of the same. Captain Wally on the *Wanderer* had made a big pot of fresh coffee, and we all took a break and sat on the stern of the big shrimp boat rehashing the night's events—which all of us knew very well, because we had already talked about what we were catching on the radio during the night.

But we soon went back to work, because everybody wanted to go home and sleep. The net was hoisted to the mast and tied off. We shook it hard to free it from the cusk eels, soles, grunts, and tonguefish that were always gilled in the webbing. Often shaking was not enough, so we had to pluck them out one by one. Crab fishermen were waiting to buy bait from us. The crabbers baited their traps with grunts, cusk eels, and pigfish— almost every morsel that would appeal to a crab. They cut the tough skates and sharks into small pieces so they would fit in the bait cages of the traps. The crab fishing was getting better and better.

Crabbing skiffs with their powerful inboard and outboard motors churned up the basin's calm waters as they moved from boat to boat loading boxes of fish. They were glad to pay two dollars for a hundred pounds of fish, since the fish houses would charge six, and it was an extra bonus to the deck hands too, because the fish would have been discarded anyway.

I made the rounds of all the shrimp boats that had come in, collecting the specimens I had asked them to save the night before. I paid each deck hand or captain by check when he finished helping me lug the heavy pails over the decks from one boat to another, lifting them over the rails, sloshing seawater, and finally getting them onto the dock and into my station wagon. One shrimper had caught two live octopuses, which would delight some instructor. I had featured a shrimp-trawl assortment in my catalogue—it was a potluck order that sometimes proved very exciting and different. I was already getting two or three of these orders a week.

The *Elysium Queen* was one of the last boats to come into the basin. I had been waiting for her and for the *Xenophon*. To my surprise, she had ended my quests of quests: a large sea turtle was lying on its back, waving its flippers impotently. I leaped over the railing of the *Wanderer* onto the deck of the *Mary Ann* and caught the bowline Danny Yates tossed to me and tied it off. "We're fixing to have turtle stew tonight," he said cheerfully. "Come and get your guts, eyeballs, blow holes, blood, and whatnots. You're gonna have more guts than you can carry. Better get your stuff—I'm fixing to butcher her right now."

I had had an order for several months from a biochemist who was working with the kinetic properties of a particular enzyme and needed a large quantity of turtle liver, intestines, and blood. Big sea turtles were sporadic in the Gulf. During some years they were abundant, and I have seen the shrimpers bring in as many as fifteen in a single night. But in the last few years they had become more and more scarce, and this season not one had been brought in. I had put out an all-points bulletin with the fishermen that I wanted one, but no one had answered my request, and just yesterday I had apologetically answered an insistent inquiry from the biochemist.

I boarded the *Elysium Queen* with two ice chests and plastic bags and waited, with mixed feelings, for the butchering to begin. I always hated to see sea turtles killed. They are the largest surviving reptiles of an ancient era. And when the fishermen were butchering these hapless beasts, I felt the furthest removed from them.

Danny and his deck hand, Jimmy, straddled the unfortunate loggerhead sea turtle and began to cut its throat. Blood spurted out of an artery and a gory river ran on the deck. In seconds a gallon of blood gushed into my containers. Then the bloody and horrible butchering continued. The poor turtle lurched forward, and Danny and Jimmy jumped back. The awkward, heavy animal paused, trying vainly to gather enough strength to lift its three hundred pounds and escape. During the turtle's pauses the shrimpers proceeded in the throat cutting. The turtle repeated its lurching four or five times, but the shrimpers persisted in slicing away at its thick throat. It seemed like a long agonizing time, but actually it is one of the fastest ways of butchering a turtle. The creature made hideous gasping sounds as it lurched all over the deck, until finally they cut through its windpipe. The big sea turtle fluttered its great flippers convulsively as the fishermen twisted its head around in a gruesome fashion. I was glad when the head was finally off.

The first time I witnessed a turtle butchering, I became sick and quickly left the scene, and I didn't come back shrimping for three days. Perhaps I was particularly sensitive about turtles anyway. I had raised baby turtles as a hobby when I was a boy, and they grew over the years from the tiny green turtles that you buy in the five-and-ten-cent stores to big lumbering sliders. They learned to recognize me and would clamber up the sides of the glass aquarium whenever I entered the room, demanding food. Eventually I presented them to the Staten Island Zoo. I received a beautiful official letter of appreciation, bearing a gold seal—and the stupid zookeepers put my beautiful turtles in the same pen with the alligators, which promptly devoured them.

I never forgave the zoo, and perhaps that is why I was repelled by the butchering of sea turtles. At first I was angry at the shrimpers, but then I realized that it was an irrational feeling, that these shrimpers were not heartless, they were decent men, and the turtle to them was like any other edible creature in the sea. They were good men doing a bad thing, and I would have to accept it.

The white deck of the *Elysium Queen* was drenched with

bright-red blood, and Danny himself looked like a bloody exe-
cutioner as he quickly and vigorously sawed around the dead
turtle's plastron. Danny was surprisingly agile and strong for
his slender build; he moved as swiftly and softly as a cat. The
plastron was removed, and it was sickening to see the animal's
heart and lungs still working—the heart was pumping and the
lungs were contracting and expanding futilely. Most unfortunate of all, it was a female with hundreds of ripening eggs. We
removed yards and yards of intestines and the massive liver,
sliced through membranes, and carefully placed the internal
organs in my large plastic bags. Jimmy held the bags open as
we maneuvered the guts in.

When the digestive organs and four quarts of blood were
packed in my ice chest, I helped them remove the edible
muscle. Most of the meat on the turtle comes from its limbs, so
the flippers and their associated muscles were cut from the
shell—or hull, as the fishermen called it—and tossed into a wire
basket. Danny and his deck hand were sawing and slicing the
meat away, one holding the flipper taut while the other cut it
free. Flies buzzed around and settled on the blood-splattered
deck and on the meat.

I kept the turtle's head. It must have weighed ten or twelve
pounds. When I opened the jaws and looked down the throat,
I found a dozen small ivory-white barnacles that I had been
hoping to find. During my last visit to Harvard, a zoologist
who specialized in barnacles had showed me a line drawing of
*Stomatolepas*, a barnacle that lives in a turtle's gullet. The yel-
lowed line drawing was in an ancient leather-bound volume
written by a nineteenth-century naturalist. The zoologist had
told me to be on the lookout for this particular barnacle, because it had never been reported from the Gulf of Mexico. It
was even possible that if one did occur in this region, it might
prove to be a new species. *Stomatolepas* poses certain vexing
problems: are these barnacles commensals or parasites? One

wonders if there is sufficient water circulating in and out of the turtle's mouth to keep the barnacles fed on chance bits of plankton, or if they feed on the fish and crustacea that the turtle swallows, thus making it somewhat parasitic. I was hoping to help solve this puzzle by supplying the specimens, adding them to Harvard's museum collection.

Later that year I was able to get the Caribbean Conservation Corporation, an organization set up for the purpose of protecting the green turtle from total extinction, to authorize me to pay fishermen for any sea turtle caught so I could punch a numbered tag on its flipper and set it free. Zoologists at the University of Florida have been working extensively on this turtle-migration project, and by tagging turtles in my vicinity, keeping records of when the turtles were caught and their location, size, and sex, I was helping in my small way. Biology, or more specifically ocean zoogeography, is still a young and growing science, and there is no telling when seemingly unrelated bits of information can be put together and put to practical use. Perhaps such data as scientists are gathering may someday lead to a widespread turtle-farming industry, and the sea turtle can be raised rather than wiped out.

After twenty minutes of butchering, the job was done. Danny and Jimmy helped me pry the many large white barnacles off the turtle's carapace. When we finished, Danny asked, "Do you want to save this hull, Sugar?"

"No. I've got no sale for it."

"What do you mean, no sale for it?" demanded Jimmy, the deck hand. "Tourists buy those things all the time. I bet if you was to dry and cure it, put a coat of varnish on, why you could get maybe twenty-five dollars for it."

"I don't sell stuff to tourists," I replied. "Scientific and educational institutions only, like it says on my permit."

"You oughtn't to be so damned uppity," said Danny. "You wouldn't be driving around in that old beaten-up station wagon if you were so special." He turned to Jimmy and said, laughing, "You ought to see his place. He's got a sign up saying, 'Specimen Company—No Exhibits.' Lives like a damned hermit."

"I don't want to fool with tourists," I explained. "I'd never get any work done."

The empty, bloody hull was tossed overboard with a great splash, and the blood was washed off with a deck hose. Except for the meat that was left and the trappings I had gathered and the turtle's head, there was little to indicate that the butchering had taken place. Tiny fish swarmed up to the surface, biting at the bits of meat and congealed blood, as the turtle's shell sank down into the depths.

Everything was loaded in my station wagon, and all I had to do was wait for George Williams. The *Xenophon* was late, and I knew just as sure as if I were out on her that it would be something trivial, something that required a tinkering or tightening, that kept her from coming in. The *Xenophon* was my initiation boat, and there had always been something breaking or falling apart on her. George had inherited the sponge fishing boat from his father twenty years before and converted the *Xenophon* into a shrimp boat. George's distinction lay in being the only Greek descendant who became a shrimper. All of his relatives in Shiawassee, of which there were many, remained traditionally sponge divers.

Captain George Williams was my mentor and teacher, and he had the proverbial heart of gold. I remember when I was awarded my first important contract to supply the Seattle World's Fair with sixty to a hundred live horseshoe crabs at a dollar a crab, every month for six whole months. I was eager to show that I could supply and I was reliable.

However, the weather was still cool, and horseshoe crabs were scarce. Day after day I combed the beaches searching, finding only one or two specimens and spending more on gasoline than I was earning from specimens. I worked nightly on George's shabby old shrimp boat, and we only caught about three *Limulus*—horseshoe crabs—a night in his trawls.

The deadline for my first shipment was fast approaching and I had only eight miserable horseshoe crabs. I was desperate. This was my first big order, and I couldn't fill it. I poured my troubles out to George as we sat with the other shrimpers on the dock. He read my telegram silently and passed it around to the others, then held a round-table conference. Each one thought they had been catching three or more horseshoe crabs every night, but they hadn't paid much attention. They all agreed to save them for me.

That night every shrimp boat in the area, local boats and boats from Louisiana, big double-riggers from Texas, Alabama, and North Carolina, fishing inshore and offshore, working to the east and to the west—probably the greatest combined effort for a single objective that the shrimpers ever made—saved horseshoe crabs. And on the radio on George's boat I heard not only about the shrimp, but I frequently heard, "Are you getting that boy any of those horseshoe crabs? Come on."

Perhaps it was my youth that moved them, or perhaps it was their natural kindness and their wish to see me succeed. The next morning when the boats came in, I would have needed a big Diesel truck to haul off the tons of *Limulus* which they tossed up on the hill. I selected a hundred of the largest monster-sized females and sent the rest back alive to the sea. I met my commitments with glory and went on to get other important contracts.

The boats had been in the basin over an hour, and many of the captains and their crews had loaded the shrimp on their trucks to be sold at the fish house and gone on home to sleep. At last George's tired old barge, the *Xenophon*, came chugging in, black smoke pouring out of her exhaust funnel. As she moved into the dock, George's deck hand, Martin, threw a rope to me, and I moored the boat.

Among the last to leave were Preacher and Chass. Chass was giving Preacher a ride back to Shiawassee. When they saw the *Xenophon,* Chass switched his ignition off.

"How come you're so late, George?" yelled Preacher with a sneer. "Engine screw up on you? I didn't hear you on the radio last night."

"Yeah," George answered, coming out of the cabin covered with black grease; his graying hair and pink chubby face ere streaked with it. He looked disgustedly at the pile of t. and shrimp, which had not yet been culled. "The damn eng e threw a shaft again and we had to wait until daylight to h t. I guess I'll have to buy a shaft for it one of these days.

Preac r viewed George's boat with good-natured contempt, n that he was captain of the Yates Brothers' handsome *Elixi* "Can't expect nothing from that nigger rig," he sneered.

Chass laugh 'heartedly. "Hell, that ain't no nigger rig. A nigger wouldn't ave a rig like that. That's a Greek rig!"

"At least I ow it," George replied, looking pointedly at Preacher. Then he 'ooked at Martin, who was busy culling rapidly. He called t me, "Hey, Yankee. We got your sea livers. Come help us c 'l off."

I stepped down onto is deck and willingly grabbed a cull board. I also wanted to see if there was anything of interest to me.

Preacher climbed out of the truck and called out, "We'll give you a hand, George."

"Naw, go on. There isn't but a little bit left. The three of us'll get it."

Chass said, "Are you sure, George?"

"Yeah, go on. I'll see you this evening."

We culled rapidly, with George urging us to hurry. Culling the trash fish into the river was against the city ordinances and strictly illegal. Most of the boats culled off before they came into the river, circling out into the bay until their decks were clear. "And keep an eye out for that old crocodile"—the sheriff. "Like as not he'll come sneaking around."

Watching Martin shoveling the fish through the deck hole, George asked, "Didn't you get no order for a bait box?" George was always concerned about his young deck hands making enough money. The bait-box money belonged to the deck hand; if he sold three or four boxes, it was quite a bonanza for him.

"Naw. Jimmy got an order from the Russian. I didn't get no orders last night."

"What happened to Saunders and the Frenchman?" demanded George.

While helping cull I had found a basket sponge, and oozing over its surface was a peculiar black-and-white-striped flat-worm, very exotic. I was trying to ease the delicate worm into a vial of seawater for my shrimp-trawl assortment.

Martin was saying to George, "I don't know what happened to the Frenchman or Saunders. I heard they quit crabbing."

"The Jew said he wanted two boxes the other day. You should have spoken to him," George persisted.

Actually the Russian was not a Russian, nor was the Jew a Jew or the Frenchman French. George called a crabber from Virginia "the Russian" because he was so big and ugly. "The Jew" could actually trace his ancestry back to England more than three hundred years ago when prisoners were sent into Georgia. He was called "the Jew" because he was stingy. No one knew why "the Frenchman" was so named.

George and Martin were so absorbed in the discussion of bait and I in coaxing the little worm that we forgot to keep a sharp lookout. Suddenly we heard a gruff voice. "George!"

We all shivered and looked up. There was the sheriff, ordinarily six feet four inches tall, and now looking over ten feet tall in his tan uniform.

He glared down at us with his cold blue eyes, his arms folded across his chest. Even though Robert Youngblood was an elderly man, he was still intimidating. And George was caught—caught with the cull board in hand, right in the middle of heaving trash fish into the Elizabeth River off a city dock. He turned slowly around and smiled weakly. "Hello, Robert," he said.

The sheriff nodded and continued staring at him.

"Want a mess of crabs?" said George brightly, looking around the deck at the large blue crabs scurrying around the trash pile and hidden in the piled-up net. They were part of the trash we were discarding. "We caught some real big ones. Come, get you a mess, they make good eating."

"I don't want no crabs," rumbled old Sheriff Youngblood, looking at George narrowly.

George grinned weakly and looked around the deck. "How'd you like some nice fat ground mullet? We just got them in the last trawl. Martin, get Robert up a big mess of them."

"I don't want no ground mullet." Robert Youngblood took a step closer and looked down at the basket of shrimp.

George wet his lips and reached into a basket of fish and produced a large flounder. "Here's you a flounder, Robert. Come get him. We caught him on the last trawl too."

Youngblood just shook his head.

George looked despairing. "Well, come get you a mess of shrimp."

Robert nodded and climbed down onto the boat and pulled out a double-lined paper sack from his back pocket. "Thanks, George," he said, grabbing the shrimp up in his huge hand

and cramming them into the bag. "I believe we'll have a shrimp dinner tonight."

George didn't look pleased as the sheriff helped himself liberally. He tightened his lips and grumbled to himself. Shrimp brought eighty cents a pound, he muttered, and that old greedy-guts was putting away a good twenty pounds. Actually Sheriff Youngblood was taking only about five pounds, which was still a lot, but the more George watched him stuff the shrimp into the bag, the more the amount grew in George's mind. It was a good exchange, however, because he was avoiding a fifty-dollar fine.

"We'll see you," said the sheriff, looking pleased as he lumbered out of the boat.

When he was out of sight George turned on Martin and me with a fury. "That fat, sourbelly hog took twenty-five pounds of my biggest shrimp at ninety cents a pound! First I have to pay that hog off for Goofus here"—he jerked his head at Martin—"running the school zone last week, and if it weren't for your damn sea livers and me working sea-liver hole for you I wouldn't be in such a fix, you damn Yankee!"

I couldn't see how the sea pansies had anything to do with culling off the trash in the river, but when George was in such a passion I couldn't reason with him. He paused and said, "And you, you were supposed to look out for that ox. What were you doing?"

I couldn't resist it. I held up the little vial with the striped flatworm in it, knowing full well what would happen, and said, "Isn't that pretty? I was busy getting it off a sponge and I forgot about him."

Later people said they heard George hollering a mile up the river, and the cussing I got reminded me of the good old days.

# 11　Live Shark—Do Not Delay!

I had received an order for two live sharks from the University of Wisconsin. Investigators in the department of biochemistry were isolating and mapping out the molecular properties of a protein that was found only in the nervous system of lower chordates. The order was marked rush delivery.

I was delighted—the orders that had come in such abundance at first were already dropping off as the season advanced and the researchers were off to Woods Hole, Massachusetts, for the summer. I felt anxious; from past experience I had reason to dread the coming of the midsummer doldrums when the flats are sterile and beachcombing is impossible. Often even skin diving is out of the question when the sea becomes hot, cloudy, and dangerous, because I would not be able to see a foot in front of me and would have no idea of what I might bump into.

The shrimp will move on and so will the shrimp boats, and those people who do not follow the shrimp will become despondent and irritable, hating each other, the heat, and the biting insects. It is a time of the year when I usually attempt to go elsewhere, but I had no alternative this year except to endure it, since all my surplus capital had gone into publishing and mailing the catalogues and buying much-needed new equipment.

I was worried. Every order, no matter how difficult or small, was treasured. I wanted to establish a reputation as a reliable collector of live marine animals as well as survive the summer doldrums until the fall school orders came in. There were many biological suppliers, but none who delivered live marine animals from the East Coast except the Marine Biological Laboratory in Woods Hole, a nonprofit corporation. Other orders had come in for live sea anemones, sea hares, and fiddler crabs, but the sharks posed a problem.

How do you take an active shark out of the sea, confine it to a packing container, and send it far inland, halfway across the continent? This was my first live shark shipment, and I was very anxious to have it succeed. One of the curators at the New York Aquarium had given me a demonstration of how it should be done, but sharks, in spite of their ferocity and strength in the sea, are delicate animals and are more susceptible to severe shock than any other fish. Severe shock is an irreversible process: there is complete constriction of the blood vessels followed by massive clotting and death. The more active the animal, the more it is prone to shock. The excitable, roving hammerhead shark expires within minutes on the deck, while the sluggish nurse shark ships very well and can be maintained in an aquarium for years.

That night as I stood on the deck of the *Elysium Queen*, I watched anxiously the long, black shrimp net emerge from the ghostly, dark waters. My anxiety had spread to Danny Yates and his deck hand, Jimmy, and they too were hoping that I would get small live sharks on the fourth and last strike, even though they had every reason to hate sharks. Soon the net hung from the boon and the immense gorged bag swayed slightly over the deck. This was the moment of suspense, waiting to see if the net had any live sharks in it.

During the night I had watched the trawl come up three times, only to be disappointed. The first strike brought up hundreds of fish and shrimp and other little creatures of the sea, but not a single shark. When we raked through the pile, Danny, seeing my disappointment, said, "We'll catch some, I know we will. We've been catching them most every night—no reason why we shouldn't this evening."

The second strike had brought up half a dozen small sharks. There were three bonnetheads, one small hammerhead, and two sand sharks. All but one were dead, suffocated by the crush of fish in the dragging net. One of the bonnetheads had a twitch of life in it, but try as I might to revive it, putting it in seawater and even bubbling oxygenated seawater through its gills, it died within five minutes.

The third strike brought up more sharks. Some were barely alive and even swam feebly around my collecting container. However, even with the most careful attention—pushing them around in the bucket so the water would circulate through their gills—they too turned belly-up and died.

Jimmy watched me while I dejectedly removed the dead specimens from the bucket and threw them into my ice chest. "Danny says he's going to make a shorter strike, only ninety minutes, 'cause we've got to get back. The sun will be up soon. I believe them sharks will live on the last strike."

At the very hint of dawn the nocturnal pink shrimp mysteriously disappear. This is one of the strange phenomena of the sea. One moment a net can be pulling through a sea packed with shrimp, and the next moment, with the first ray of light, they vanish like fairy gold and burrow deep into the mud. With nightfall the shrimp return to feed.

"The sharks will have to live, Jimmy," I said. "It's simply

too much trouble and expense for me to go out night after night for a single order."

"If worst comes to worst," Jimmy said kindly, "come on over to Shiawassee Saturday morning and we'll go hook-and-line fishing for them from the dock. That way they don't get drug around in the net and will last better."

"I might do that," I replied gloomily, looking down into the black waters. "But the weekend is no good. Flights up north are impossible, and if the sharks get held over somewhere, they'll die for sure."

The night went on, and we waited. It was four in the morning and I had not allowed myself two hours' sleep. If I did get the sharks, it was going to be a rough drive to the airport to catch the morning flight.

I thought about my customer. The order stipulated that he wanted *Sphyrna tuburo*, the bonnethead shark, and *Mustelus norrisi*, the smooth dogfish, and he wanted them both in the same shipment. But this year I had seen only a few specimens far offshore, not in the shallow bays. However, any shark would do, if only I could bring it back alive. But to simplify matters I hoped it would be a bonnethead, because there would be no trouble with tricky taxonomy and keying out or classifying the specimen. I wasn't about to measure the angle of the teeth (the proper way to identify sharks) of a live carcharhinid shark (sand shark), because conceivably it might bite me, or die in the process of identification, since I had to keep it out of the water until I counted its teeth. The importance of having the correct identity on experimental animals cannot be overemphasized, particularly in biochemistry, for two closely related species may have entirely different enzyme structures and kinetic properties.

I couldn't help being amused at my swift change in attitude toward sharks. Aboard the shrimp trawler I had no fear of them. True, at night, when I culled fish over and saw the flurry of dorsal fins splashing and the appearances of dark forms in the illuminated water, as the fish disappeared down their gullets, I had to shudder and move away from the railing.

Ordinarily on board I was master and the sharks were just so much fish. But a few days before when I had been collecting sea anemones and was in the water with the sharks on equal terms, I could not help drawing an analogy to the "Lobster Quadrille" in *Alice in Wonderland:*

> When the sands are all dry, he is as gay as a lark
> And will talk in contemptuous tones of the shark:
> But when the tide rises and the sharks are around,
> His voice has a timid and tremulous sound.

It started out as a beautiful clear day, but not a good tide. The sand bars where the anemones dwelt were covered by three to five feet of warm, muggy water, but I had no time to wait for the low tides, which were not due for several days.

I waded out into three feet of water, wearing my mask, fins, and snorkel, and crouched down in the shallow, murky water and peered through the glass plate of the mask for the telltale stubby gray tentacles of *Bunodactis stelloides.*

All I could see were a few obvious worm tubes sticking up. I had to play it by feeling with my fingers over the bottom sand. Hunting sea anemones, my hand crept along. I could feel the contours, and dead floating seaweed washing about that sooner or later would pile up on the beach. Now and then I felt the spiny round forms of the sand dollars, and sometimes my fingers were stung by their cilia. Then I felt something firm and fleshy holding a cluster of shells together. When my fingers moved over it, I could feel a contraction of muscle and flesh in the center of the shell ring, which swiftly began to suck down into the sand. This was the sea anemone *Bunodactis stelloides*. Minute sucker disks on its outer body wall gather bits of shell, perhaps as some sort of protective measure.

My fingers were just as swift as the anemone. I dug around and undermined the sand with a stranglehold on the slippery creature. My other hand brushed the sand and water away until the slime-exuding anemone was free, and I pulled it up. In this hunting by braille I had to be swifter than the anemone's responses, because it could contract far down its burrow and out of reach.

I had already collected six anemones when my legs were suddenly pelleted by fleeing mullets. I jumped up and saw dozens of frantic fish leaping out of the water all around me. I knew something was chasing them to make them so frenzied. An instant later a shark appeared on the scene. It was not a very large shark; judging from the distance between its dorsal and caudal fin, it couldn't have been more than two or three feet long. One small shark didn't worry me, but it is best to be cautious at all times.

I went on with my work and found a seventh anemone. While I was putting it in my diving sack, I was startled by another rush of mullets which slammed into me and then twisted aside. I looked up again, and this time there were two larger sharks. But I was determined to get my anemone quota despite the unpleasant intruders. I didn't want to make a futile thirty-miles round trip. They were after mullets, they wouldn't bother me, I told myself as I searched for the eighth anemone. But somehow I wasn't positive: somehow I felt uneasy. One of the stupid sharks might, in that murky water, mistake my leg or arm for a mullet.

Sharks always seem to spoil things for the biological collector. In the Indian Ocean I have been down in the most exotic coral reefs, seeing the most beautiful fish, lustrous sea anemones and gorgeous sea fans, a complex, crowded community of sea life competing in sizes, shapes, and bizarre colors—a collector's dream. And suddenly a large shark appears and it becomes more and more difficult to concentrate on these wonders of the sea. It's always in the back of your mind—what will this monster of low intelligence and greedy appetite do next?

But these sharks on Indian Point were not big enough to worry about, I assumed. There didn't seem to be that many. By the time I had successfully wrenched the eighth anemone from its burrows, the waters were getting rough and dark and there was a stiff wind. I was still being pelleted by terrified mullet, so before searching for a ninth anemone I decided I had better look around and evaluate the shark situation.

Now I understood why the mullets were panicked. There were sharks everywhere, all sizes, converging on the shallows to attack the school of mullet, which had run shoreward for protection. The sharks were flying in from all directions, attacking and feeding voraciously, and from the look of all the fins, the splashes of tails in the sea, the appearance and disappearance of dark forms below the surface, they were on the verge of a feeding frenzy. During a feeding frenzy sharks have been known to bite wooden sticks and boat bottoms, even rend and tear each other to pieces. My stubborn determination to collect the anemones dissipated, and I fled to the safe dry beach.

Then a very unnerving thing happened. Just where I had fled from an instant before I saw a huge shark, bigger than the rest. Its fins sliced through the water and I could see it must have been all of twelve feet long. Its whole back and dorsal fin rose up distinctly as a sailboat. Then the shark became uncomfortable in the shallows and moved out to stuff itself on more conveniently located mullet.

Finally I realized the rush order would have to wait for another day. The weather was getting stormy, and more and more sharks were rushing in. I waited half an hour, watching the sharks, but the wind blew the waves up harder on the beach and the tide was rising. I conceded that the anemone search was impossible.

The sharks had caused me a delay and considerable expense, since I would have to take the long drive back to the same area the following day. In the collecting business, delays must be accepted, telegrams and rush orders regardless, but as I drove back to my laboratory with only a third of the anemone quota, I had a helpless feeing of anger toward the sharks, and I cursed them all the way home. But my attitude toward any animal was usually governed by the scientists' requests. And now here I was, just two days later, waiting anxiously aboard the *Elysium Queen* for sharks, hoping to catch some and tenderly keep them alive.

I wasn't too hopeful as the winch began to wind around and the cable was pulled up from the sea. After a night of failure, it is hard to have a sudden burst of optimism, but as the fishermen say, "When you're disgusted and just about to give out, that's when you run into the real luck."

And that is what happened. Danny opened the bag and great piles of fish squished out on the deck—and right in the middle of the pyramid of marine creatures were two thrashing bonnethead sharks. "You got two sharks," Danny said excitedly. He pounced and grabbed them at the back of their flattened heads. He held them firmly, keeping them from twisting from his grip. "They got a lot of spunk, too. I believe they'll make it."

He quickly stepped around the pile and threw the sharks into the container of seawater, then attended to the net. I soon noticed that one shark seemed a bit more sluggish than the other. Jimmy handed me the oxygen cylinder and we put the tubing into the seawater and turned on the valve. Oxygen bubbled through the water and the sharks settled contentedly to the bottom. I was still concerned over the second shark: it was a shade less lively, and in the water it seemed slightly sick. I put the tube of oxygen close to it, giving it more pressure. I wondered if the shark would make it.

This was the last strike. There would not be another chance. The sharks had to be given every opportunity to survive, and they had priority over any other animal in the catch. Although Jimmy had pressing duties, hanging out the net and getting the boards on deck so we could go into dock, he helped me give the sharks that opportunity.

Jimmy and Danny were fishermen, and they hated sharks more than anyone. They had seen schools of sharks rip a valuable net to shreds, seen them slice a grouper off the snapper boat's fishing line just before the fish was pulled up from the water, and yet they felt this same concern that I had felt.

I had to pack the sharks, and the sooner the better. Jimmy assisted me by holding open the mouth of the plastic bag. I lowered the deck bucket over the side and drew up fresh seawater.

I poured the fresh, clear seawater into the plastic bag, then grabbed a live bonnethead shark by the back of its neck. The animal was only two feet long, but if I made one slip, it could inflict a very nasty bite. It fitted perfectly into the wide bag and had plenty of room in which to swim. Jimmy put the oxygen tube down into the water and I collapsed the bag around the tube. I signaled him with a nod, and he increased pressure. Oxygen bubbled energetically through the water, charging it with life-giving air, and soon inflated the bag. I jerked the air tube out and quickly tied a knot in the inflated bag to lock in the oxygen. Then we held it up, proudly watching the shark swim contentedly around.

We packed the other shark, and we both noticed that it was failing rapidly. "I don't believe he's gonna make it," commented Jimmy, probing the bag to make the shark move about. It responded feebly, respiring with great difficulty. "It's a pity, too," he added.

"I'll try to get him to revive when I get home. I wonder if adrenalin would help."

"How much are those sharks worth to you?" Danny asked suddenly behind us. He always moved softly and swiftly.

"Twenty-five dollars apiece."

"Damn, that's good money for a night's work. I sure hope you get them to live. When you two finish with them, let's cull this mess off. We're heading for the dock. I'll circle until we get cleared off."

Danny cut the engine down to an idle and began to cull out the shrimp. Jimmy and I left the sharks and helped him with the catch.

"We can't cull off at the dock no more," Danny said, throwing two handfuls of shrimp into a wire basket at his side.

"No? Why not?"

"They got a new law in Elizabeth City where you ain't allowed to throw no trash into the river," he replied, raking through the catch with his cull board. He snatched up a speckled moray eel that was still feebly alive and tossed it in front of me. "Need that?"

I nodded, pushed the eel off to one side, and went on with the discussion. "It seems to me that that rule was in effect quite a few years ago."

"They got some teeth in it now," Danny said angrily. He wrenched a big dead sand shark out of the pyramid of fish and showed it to me. When I shook my head he tossed it overboard. "Fifty-dollar fine every time they catch you."

"They fined several shrimpers the other day," Jimmy added, cursing.

"It's getting so there's more damn rules and regulations in

this day and age that a fellow just can't keep up with them. Now you take the State Board of Conservation," Danny said bitterly. It was a favorite topic of conversation. "If you're a tourist and come down sports fishing, they'll kiss your butt on a Sunday morning, tell you the best place to fish, where the best restaurants are, and practically bait your line for you. But if you're a fisherman trying to make an honest living, they'll put you through more hell than a body can stand!"

Fishermen are among the remaining individualists in our society. Unlike people who have salaried jobs and routinely punch a clock, the fishermen find it difficult to put up with any regulations. They consider them infringements on their freedom.

"Same goes for the Highway Patrol," said Jimmy indignantly. "If you're a tourist and you're speeding, drunk, blind, and crazy, driving on the wrong side of the road, they'll stop you—if they do stop you—and say, 'Welcome to Florida, but we don't drive thataway on the beautiful Sunshine State highways.' The most they'll do is give the sonofabitch a warning ticket, buy him an ice cream, and show him a map to help him get where he's going. But if I go ten miles over the limit, there goes a thirty-five-dollar fine."

I nodded. "Thirty-five dollars? Is that all?" For all his indignation Jimmy was a maniac behind the wheel. "I think a hundred-dollar fine would be more fitting."

Danny added, "Throw in a good thirty days of hard labor with bread and water to boot. One of these days they are going to be picking up little pieces of Jimmy all over the highway."

Jimmy grinned self-consciously. "You ain't no angel either, Danny. What about the time you got fined for drunken driving?"

Danny frowned. "That wasn't fair. You know damn good and well I wasn't drunk. That old crocodile in Elizabeth City couldn't meet the payment on his new Chevy so he grabbed me just because I was drinking a beer at Ronny's Bar. They're getting just as crooked there as the State Board of Conservation officers."

Jimmy chuckled. "Hey, Jack. Did you hear what happened to old Admiral when you was away in Africa?" He pushed a load of trash fish through the deck hole and I waited impatiently. Everybody disliked this Conservation warden. He had served time in the Navy and he was nicknamed the Admiral by the fishermen because he was so officious. Admiral had made himself thoroughly disliked in the two years he had been here; he was ambitious and in his very first week in Shiawassee he passed an edict that made him famous over three counties. He commanded all fishermen to restrain themselves until the boat docked before they went to the bathroom, or carry a suitable receptacle so they wouldn't pollute the oysters and fish.

He also made himself a thorough nuisance by his constant surveillance of fishing boats. With a ruler in hand he boarded shrimp boats at all odd hours, even when the fishermen were asleep in their bunks. It was in December when he boarded the *Portia*, while she was anchored out in the bay, and beamed a searchlight into Chass's face. The captain, after too many beers and no shrimp, had been sleeping it off in his bunk. Admiral demanded to inspect the shrimp. Chass, furious, made short work of the undersized warden and hurled him into the icy sea.

Admiral levied fines indiscriminately. Nor had he endeared himself to me when he searched frantically for a reason to arrest me too. He was even more distraught when he could not find any regulations against specimen collecting. My permits were in order.

"Well, what happened, Jimmy? Did he break his leg?" I asked hopefully.

Danny stopped heading the shrimp and laughed. "No, it's better than that. He fined Delmar twice in the same day. The first time he made him cull out his whole catch and found enough small oysters. Delmar called him a son of a bitch. Two hours later Admiral met Delmar on the hill, made him cull all through the catch again, and fined him another fifty dollars. That did it! Delmar grabbed him by the scruff of his neck, rubbed his nose in the oysters, and then kicked his ass. Another warden, Bob Trammel, jumped Delmar, then two other boys weighing their catch piled in on Bob. Bob drew his revolver and told them he'd shoot the piss out of them. He said he didn't want to hurt anybody, but if they took another step he would."

Jimmy cautiously scooped up a dark, gray-spotted electric ray with his cull board as if he were scooping up an egg out of a frying pan. "Do you want this shock fish?"

I nodded and threw the electric ray into my ice chest and continued culling. It felt good to be on a shrimp boat again and catching up on all the local gossip. But even while I was laughing, I had an inner feeling of guilt; it was like a throbbing nerve. I could not analyze this feeling at the time. Here I was, enjoying myself, and it seemed wrong, all wrong. I should be in school and getting my degrees. I should not be among fishermen, I should not be concerned about Admiral, culling shrimp, and earning money by filling orders for scientists and becoming a businessman.

It was the word "businessman" that always caused me to contract like an invertebrate blob in alcohol and caused the guilt nerve to throb painfully. Earning money by selling! What contempt I had for that dull clod the businessman. He was fat, uncultured, and greedy—as if the businessman had a monopoly on being all three. Where I got this notion I did not know. It may have been hammered into me while I was in academia or during my childhood. For a long time I felt it was my duty to return to the academic world, become a Ph.D., go in for research and teaching as all my friends did, urging me to do the same. By now I should be well into graduate school.

At the time I could not concede that business could be every bit a creative, intellectual, philosophical, and challenging endeavor, with the advantage that it supports itself comfortably. Supporting myself comfortably was fast becoming my goal. Anyway, I liked the challenge and the independence of mind that business and free enterprise offered. But at the time I could not see it, and the guilt nerve kept throbbing.

We culled off the last of the trash fish, and the deck of the *Elysium Queen* was clean in little more than half an hour. The sun was up in the sky and it was getting hot, so I left my work and thoughtfully threw a few handfuls of ice on top of my shark bags. They were still alive, and the vigorous specimen was still vigorous, but the other was losing ground fast. It persisted in lying on its back and making sporadic gasps. Sadly I made plans not to include it in the shipment. Probably it would die before I got back to my laboratory.

Usually I stayed behind and helped put the boat to sleep for the day. The nets had to be hung, the catch unloaded on deck, weighed, and sold, but today I had to run. I backed the station wagon down to the entrance of the fish house, and Danny and Jimmy dropped their work to help me load my specimens and collecting gear. Then we carried the sharks in large plastic buckets covered with ice.

When I reached Arcadia the sick shark had died. I put in a long-distance call to the air-freight office in the city and told the freight agent about my delicate cargo that would be arriving shortly. "You're cutting it mighty thin," Edwards said. "Better make out your own waybill to save time, and get here no later than ten o'clock. The plane leaves at ten twenty."

It was nine twenty-five by the time I had packed the shark in a specially insulated carton partitioned with ice, taking care that the ice did not touch the shark's bag, which might make the water cold enough to kill the shark, and then I crated it.

At the little, sleepy air terminal, I unloaded the crate and hauled it into the freight office.

"You sure are cutting it thin today. The plane's out on the runway right now getting ready to load passengers."

"Sorry about that, Edwards," I said. "I just left the shrimp boat a little while ago."

He nodded and quickly loaded several parcels on the motorized push cart, hastily scribbled the weight on my waybill, and pasted an Air Express envelope on the crate. The label read: "Contents, One Live Shark," "Keep Out of Sun," "Not Good If Delayed," "Living Specimens—RUSH!!!"

"They may very well listen to that," Edwards said hopefully.

"Just to make sure," I said, opening the crate, "I want you to see that it's in good condition before we send it off." The bonnethead shark was enjoying the darkness and lying sluggishly on the bottom of the plastic bag, as sharks are apt to do when the water is cool, for they are sluggish animals and really don't move around much unless they are feeding. I probed the shark and it swam in wild gyrations around the bag, thrusting its ugly, flattened head up out of the water with its mouth agape, displaying its multitude of small sharp teeth, its tail beating the water into a turmoil. It gave a most convincing display of being very much alive.

Edwards was impressed. "There's no reason why he shouldn't make it. Mean-looking stinker, isn't he! He's got plenty of life, I'll swear to it."

I knew the airport employees quite well. I delivered live and frozen specimens to the airport two or three times a week, and during a busy season, I drove to the airport every day with my perishable cargo. They cooperated with me in rushing my specimens from the sea to the laboratory.

Edwards was a surprising person. Inside the air terminal he

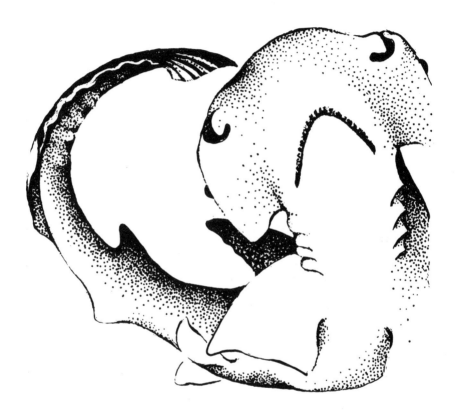

*I probed the shark and it swam in wild gyrations around the bag, thrusting its ugly flattened head out of the water with its mouth agape, displaying its multitudes of sharp teeth, its tail beating the water into a turmoil.*

was clerk, ticket man, baggage and freight agent, and diplomat, bookkeeper, liaison officer, and what-not. Outside on the air field he was an aeromechanic, dressed in white coveralls, adjust-

ing the jet engines and controls. Dressed in dark-blue full
uniform he signaled planes in, greeted passengers, supervised
the loading and unloading of baggage and freight, and signaled
the pilot on departure. I often had the feeling that if a dignitary
came from Eastern Tasmania, Edwards would rise to the occasion, greet the official in his own native language, and thoughtfully direct him to a hotel. In between times he would diagnose
my old station wagon's ailments and give me advice on how to
fix it, and his diagnoses were surprisingly accurate.

Edwards loaded the shark on the motorized cart, packed it
into the airplane, and sent it on its way to the University of
Wisconsin. Suddenly the lack of sleep, the night's work, and
the long hard drive all caught up with me, and I felt exhausted.
Wearily I called Western Union and had a telegram sent on
ahead informing the biochemist of the scheduled time of arrival
and the waybill number—all standard procedure. It was all
over for me.

Later I learned that it was not over for Edwards. For him,
transporting the shark had just begun. He felt that from my
wild appearance, exhausted as I was, unshaved, splattered with
fish scales, smelling strongly of a shrimp boat, and yawning,
that the order was something extra-special and that I would be
most miserable if I had to come back in a few days with another shark. He wanted to make certain that the shark arrived
alive. It was just sheer luck—almost uncanny—that there was
going to be a perfect connection in Washington, D.C., from
National Airlines to Northwestern that would fly the shark
directly into Madison, Wisconsin.

There was only one hitch: the connection in Washington
was only one all-too-brief hour. In the gigantic Washington
Air Terminal it would be tough enough for a passenger to race
from one plane to another. What chance did my shark have?
Edwards was determined to give it a chance. As soon as the
plane left the runway, he called Jacksonville and put them on

the alert for the coming of the shark. "And don't put your finger in the bag," he cautioned humorously. "It bites." Jacksonville notified Northwestern in Washington—"A shark is coming, urgent. Must meet connection," flashed over the teletype.

Edwards also teletyped Washington directly, and the message was relayed to Madison. At six p.m. the plane landed in Washington and the freight agent was right there and grabbed the shark crate.

As a rule the airlines did not go to all that trouble for my shipments. A crate of sea urchins, a carton of sea anemones or crabs or sea squirts, may or may not make good connections. If the shipment was held over, most of the time the animals survived, and if they didn't, I would philosophically duplicate the order. These sea creatures do not seem very important to someone who is not concerned with them, because they are too sluggish to be considered more alive than vegetables. Few marine animals are as spectacular as a live shark.

As I sat at the laboratory table in Arcadia, pouring the narcotizing fluid into the pans of sea pansies, the shark was still on my mind. I wondered if it was still alive, or whether it was a dead shark being flown into Wisconsin.

Fortunately for my peace of mind, I didn't have to wait too long to find out. Early the next morning, while I was still on my first cup of coffee, the phone rang. It was the biochemist. I held my breath. He was cordial, but instead of telling me immediately about the shark, he discussed a special catalyst that had to be prepared in order to isolate the nerve protein, and it would take time for them to make up more. He had a very limited supply on hand and it would be at least a week before he would have more made up.

While the professor was discussing his problems so casually, I was in a sweat. I could hardly wait to get in a word. When he paused I asked him timorously, "How's the shark?"

"Oh, he's fine," he replied nonchalantly. "He's still in the plastic bag, swimming around. We've got enough catalyst to start working on its nerves this morning. What do you use to anesthetize elasmobranchs?"

I was breathing easily now and rattled off the standard anesthetic that ichthyologists use.

"Good, we'll use it. By the way, we're so pleased with the way the shark arrived that we'd like to get a series of other lower chordates from you in the fall." He asked me to hold up on the second shark until they had enough catalyst, and told me that he had checked my catalogue and would be wanting tunicates, amphioxi, sting rays, electric rays, and more sharks.

To send my first live shark halfway across the continent successfully was most gratifying. Skill and knowledge was involved, but luck had a big part to play in it—as luck does in all phases of collecting. And most important was the splendid cooperation of the shrimpers, Danny and Jimmy, and of Edwards and all the other freight agents. It is moments like these that make the profession of biological collector so satisfying.

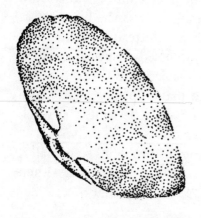

# 12 Lean Pickings

The *Elysium Queen* moved into place and her hull banged gently into the dock, knocking off the little brown river snails that had crawled up on the pilings. I had an urgent request on special order for two live octopi from an instructor in a small Georgia college who wanted the animals for an interesting and exciting summer classroom experiment. The order was marked "rush," because he had only two weeks left for his project.

Jimmy held the ice hose and waited. Suddenly a great roar came from the ice house and the hose began to vibrate, and soon the chattering crushed ice spat violently out of the hose into a great cold misty white pile. There were four compartments in the fish hold, and each had to be filled. We were taking on a thousand pounds for a three-day trip.

While the hold was being filled, I sat lazily on the bow sucking a big piece of ice and watching the river traffic. By being with fishermen and knowing their superstitions, I had picked up a few of my own. I was a little apprehensive about taking on so much ice, because it seems that when you go collecting or fishing just a trifle unprepared, that is when you get the most. Too much ice or too many collecting containers, preservatives, oxygen, vials, or whatever, and there are never enough fish or specimens caught to justify it all. And I was overloaded with equipment, including my large oxygen cylinder, instead of the small one that I used for short hops. But in the course of this planned voyage, I hoped to get those two live octopi and use every bit of equipment I had to keep them alive.

I watched a speedboat churning up the blue waters of the calm river. It traveled at a tremendous speed, and when it came near I saw it was Wally with a helper, a tall, lanky boy sitting on the bow. Wally cut the throttle of his outboard and moved up to our boat. He was still bearded and looked more than ever like Captain Castro.

He pulled up alongside and cut his motor off. "You going along with them to work, or to goof off?" he yelled to me.

"I imagine a little of both."

"Hell, you ought to give up on that sorry crew and come with us. This morning I caught a thousand pounds of those little white bait shrimp and sold them to one of those out-of-state fish trucks." His dark eyes flashed gleefully; they seemed faintly maniacal.

"Out of season, aren't they?"

"Why sure. But I'll tell you, you can't hardly steal shrimp no more. Those conservation wardens got bigger boats this year, and a poor man just can't outrun them." He looked woeful. "Now if you was to come along with us using that scientific permit . . ."

"No!"

"Why?"

"I like that permit," I said emphatically. "I want to keep it."

"How in the hell are you going to get rich if you don't use your permit?"

"I'll use it on jellyfish and bugs. Not on stolen shrimp. Did you happen to get any octopus out there?"

"No, you know better than that. You don't get no octopus inside the bay this time of year. They're all offshore in deep water. We did get a mess of those electric rays, but I didn't know you was in town or I'd've saved them for you. Pea-Picker said you was paying fifty cents for every one you got."

Danny walked over to the port side. "Hey, Castro. You do any good?"

"Made a hundred and ten dollars. You ought to strike some of them little bait shrimp too, and make old Jack here show them his science permit."

"Over my dead body," I said, laughing.

"If you're making that kind of money, Wally, I believe we can arrange to do it over his dead body," Danny said with a thoughtful air, his eyes twinkling.

"Sure, just tell them wardens you're getting shrimp guts or something," said Wally.

After all these years, Wally still remembered my order for shrimp guts, and if I live to be a hundred I won't forget it either. I had stepped aboard Wally's shrimp boat, young and quivering and expectant, with my neat case of precise polished, chrome-plated dissecting instruments. I had needlenose forceps, thumb forceps, clamps, tiny dissecting scissors, dissecting needles, and sterile paper towels inside a plastic sheath. I had rubber gloves, automatic pick-up tweezers, and neat black-capped specimen bottles filled with yellow Bouin's solution in a handsome leather carrying case.

I had been commissioned to take samples of gregarian parasites that lived in the intestines of shrimp. The researcher who had loaded me down with all this shiny new equipment was investigating the three species of commercial Gulf shrimp, and it was very important that I identify the species correctly. I was quite impressed with the importance and responsibility of this commission.

I had studied all the literature on the parasites, and I had a briefing session with the scientist and was given a taxonomic key to the three different species of commercial shrimp, which were white shrimp, *Penaeus setiferius;* brown shrimp, *P. aztecus;* and pink shrimp, *P. duorarum.* To the untrained eye they all looked like shrimp. And this week the scientist had requested brown shrimp particularly, because he was positive from reports in the fisheries bulletin that they had migrated into the Shiawassee Bay. Since shrimp grow very quickly, he wanted to take a population sample of the parasites from particular locations at this time of year.

So I loftily and authoritatively informed Wally, who had been shrimping in the bay ever since he was an infant in his father's arms, that brown shrimp, locally called hobos, were in the bay at present and we should catch plenty of them. Wally and his deck hand, Eddie, stared at me for a moment and then burst into wild laughter, deriding me, the stupid scientists, and the State Board of Conservation's fisheries bulletin.

"You tell those scientists they're crazy as hell. There won't be no hobos in the bay until the first of June." It was then early in April. "There ain't nothing but pink shrimp—hoppers—in the bay right now."

Wally was a hired captain of a fish-company trawler. He was a much-sought-after captain, because no one knew the reefs, sand bars, channels, and bottoms better than he. After we had been out towing, Wally looked at me seriously with his deep brown eyes. "Do you know what a hobo looks like?" he demanded.

"Not really," I confessed, "but the fisheries bulletin says it's a clear colorless shrimp with a groove in the last abdominal segment."

Wally was clean-shaven in those days, but he looked wild as

he shook his thick head of hair and thrust a shrimp under my nose. "This shrimp is a hopper. See that spot? No hobo has that!"

It did look oddly like the pink shrimp I had been catching with George and Preacher in Elizabeth Harbor twenty-two miles to the east, but I repeated what the researcher had said to me. "That spot doesn't necessarily mean anything. Under certain conditions even pink shrimp lose their spots. Anyway, I don't intend to argue about it. I'll bring some specimens in for identification. That way I'll be sure."

Of course Wally was right. If I had known him a little better, I wouldn't have been so snooty with him. He yelled at me at the top of his lungs, "They're hoppers, goddammit! *Hoppers!* Not hobos! Let's knock the sonofabitch on the head and throw him overboard, Eddie." We glared at each other, and Eddie laughed and went back to the wheel.

Wally and I sat opposite each other culling, and he was shouting his instructions on how to cull: "Not that way, you bullheaded jackass. You spread the stuff out with the cull board. Yeah, and with both hands pick out the shrimp. Now, throw them in the basket and push that trash behind you and make sure you pick out every damn one of them shrimp. That's right . . . Now, if you go at it ten times as fast we'll make a deck hand out of you yet."

When the culling was finished, I began dissecting the fifty shrimp I had laid aside. Wally watched me for a few moments. "Are you going to take all night cuttin' them up, or do you want some help?"

"I don't have any extra instruments," I said a little snobbishly, carefully removing the intestines from the fleshy tail with a pair of forceps, "but thanks for the offer."

I snipped the gut off with a pair of small scissors, dissected out the rectum, and dropped it into the yellow Bouin's fixative.

"I don't need no damn instru-ments or whatever you call

'em." Wally immediately went to work with his small, razor-sharp pocket knife, as skillfully as an expert surgeon removing an appendix. He dissected out the rectums and intestinal tracts, and put them into separate bottles of preservative. It was amazing to observe his speed and dexterity. I felt like a fool with five thumbs and my nice shining useless instruments. The shrimp were dissected, and Wally returned nonchalantly to his task of breaking off the shrimp heads.

When the *Elysium Queen* had finished taking on ice, Wally waved farewell and roared off, and Danny steered the trawler gently out into the river. The drawbridge was closed, and cars were speeding over the bridge. Danny cut the engine to a crawl and blew his foghorn to notify the bridgekeeper to open the bridge. He blew three times, and nothing happened. He put the horn to his mouth and gave three louder toots. He laughed and said, "I wish I had one of them horns those tugboats have—I'd creep up on him, get right under that bridgehouse, and vibrate his butt so loud the windows would shake."

Jimmy said, "He sure has an easy job, doesn't he? You'd think he would at least turn that bridge when he sees a boat coming."

"Naw, he's sleeping. That sorry thing just sits up there. Has a radio and electric fan going and gets drunk. He sleeps most of the time. I'd sure like to have a horn that would blast his ass."

I don't think there has been a single time that Danny has not said all this when he passed under the bridge. All the fishermen get along fine with the bridgekeeper—they have to, because if they get too persistent he'll take twice as long to get the bridge to swing open. But Danny had had a friendly running feud for many years. He put the *Elysium Queen* into reverse so she wouldn't get caught in the current and bang into the bridge, tooted the horn some more, and cursed.

"He's not up there all the time, is he?" I asked.

"Hell no," Danny answered. "They got two shifts. One fools around up there all day, and the other loafer takes over at night. I was up there with him the other day. We polished off two bottles of whiskey. He called me up and said he was lonesome."

"I wonder how that poor scoundrel goes to the bathroom?" Jimmy mused.

"I don't know—never thought about that." Danny laughed. "I guess he walks all the way to the edge of the bridge. They don't have no bathroom up there." We all laughed. "I'd hate to be some poor critter going under that bridge in a skiff some night when he has a bladderful."

At last the bridge's warning bell rang, the barricades came down and stopped the traffic, and the bridge swung open. I took the wheel for an hour, steering the *Elysium Queen*, keeping her right on course between the brightly colored buoys in the channel. Most of Shiawassee Bay was very shallow, and if the boat went even slightly off course it would run aground. The sun was warm, the bay hot, and the waters were just as calm as if they had been an inland lake in early morning. The bright-yellow afternoon sun blazed a golden reflection that made me squint through my sunglasses.

But the bay was alive with shrimp boats going out to sea—the *Miss Lillian*, the *Catcher*, the *Loner*, the *Night Shadow*, the *Celia*, and the *Portia*. Behind them were other boats I couldn't recognize; double-riggers spread out their outriggings like giant bats ready for flight. We were all traveling fast, all racing over the calm waters and out into the Gulf in search of shrimp or butterfish, which had been coming into the bay and outer Gulf in large schools.

There is something exciting, something electrical in the air when a fleet of shrimp boats are running out to sea. Side by side we traveled, over the clumps of floating hyacinths that had drifted out of the river into the bay. I held the wheel while

Jimmy and Danny worked on the nets, which had to be let down from the boom, piled up on deck, and straightened. All possible knots and trouble had to be ironed out in advance. You never can tell—there might be a huge school of butterfish and you're on top of it before you know it. It pays to be ready.

But that afternoon and night the efforts of preparation were in vain. It was a night of lean pickings. Not once did we find enough shrimp or fish with the try net to make it worthwhile to lower the big trawl.

The try net is identical to the big shrimp trawl in every way except size. It generally is less than sixteen feet long, and it is used to make short, quick samplings of the bottom population to determine what the big net would be catching, or whether there are enough shrimp to bother putting the big net down at all. Generally the try net bites into the bottom much harder and gives a different benthonic sampling—that is, sampling of the benthos, or ocean bottom. It may fill up with sea pansies, and the big net will skip over them. The fishermen count the number of shrimp in a try-net tow to give them some idea of what the big net would be catching.

We moved on into the great fiery orange sunset, dropping the try net down and pulling it up every fifteen minutes. The catches usually contained a few pink shrimp, some mantis shrimp, a cluster or two of *Pennaria* hydroids, perhaps one or two sea pansies, a number of grunts and catfish, perhaps a sting ray, cusk eels, and tonguefish—nothing worth bothering about.

Just at dusk we pulled the net in again, and Danny said without even glancing at the black webbing, "I can tell you what's in it before you open it: two lousy, chicken-assed, knockkneed, crosseyed, bucktoothed hoppers and a bunch of junk." I opened the bag and he was right; there were exactly two pink shrimp.

We put the net over for the fourteenth time and started dragging. Suddenly the towing cable began shaking and pulling violently. Danny ran to the winch and started pulling the net up. He looked worried as he worked the winch lever. The winding cables overpowered the fighting net and pulled it up from the bottom.

"I hope whatever the hell it is don't tear my try net all to hell," Danny said anxiously. There was a tense moment on board, because we expected some huge fish or sea monster or something to be hauled up on deck, but when the net came up, the chains were twisted, the boards jumbled, and nothing was in it except one large sea cucumber that was hanging on the boards. We were puzzled. I remembered that while we were pulling the net up I had seen porpoises bobbing around the boat and splashing playfully. Perhaps we had run into a porpoise, but that was unlikely, because they skillfully avoid trawls.

"Do you think we ran over a porpoise?" I asked Danny.

"I doubt it seriously. They're too quick and smart; they usually stay away from the net."

"I sure wish we had caught one," I said wistfully. "I need a live porpoise to ship off."

"Once in a while you catch one on a seine boat," said Danny. "I've been out with my uncle and caught them in his purse-seiner. They'll jump like crazy when you're pulling them in, tear up a net when they can, but as soon as you lay hands on them they go limp. I guess they hope you'll roll them out of the net—most people will. And if you keep them on the boat, they begin a high-pitched whimpering and screaming. You can almost hear them say 'Please let me go . . . please let me go!' " he mimicked in a high squeaky voice.

"If I caught one that said all that I wouldn't let him go no-how," Jimmy said emphatically. "I wouldn't care how he hollered. I'd cart his tail off to that Marineland near St. Augustine and sell him for a fortune. Why, a porpoise like that would be worth millions."

"I could just see that," Danny chuckled. "You rush him down there, bring him in, tell them people you got a talking porpoise, and say that when you caught him he asked you to let him go. So they're waiting around the table to hear him talk. He won't talk. Then as the men in the white coats drag you off to the little wagon with bars on the windows you'd be hollering, 'He talked, goddammit, he talked!' "

We tried to guess what could have become tangled with the try net. From its effects on the net we all agreed that whatever it was, it was big and alive. I suggested a sea turtle, Jimmy a shark, and Danny said it could have been either or neither. "But since we have no idea," he said dreamily, "it could have been a mermaid. A nice slim pretty one with long yellah hair."

Perhaps it is a good thing that our try net came up empty, shrouded in mystery, for man still wants something magical and mysterious in his life. A shark, a porpoise, or a turtle is a real thing, but it has no mystery about it. We want flying saucers in the sky and sea monsters in the ocean. And above all we want to see the beautiful maid with the fish's tail. I have often heard the shrimpers talk of catching a mermaid. Perhaps every man that strains against a net in freezing weather or under an unrelenting sun wants to believe mermaids exist. It is thought that life began in the sea; the sea is the mother and the father of all living things. The Greeks believed that Aphrodite, the goddess of love and procreation, sprang from the foam of the sea.

I have heard the myth of the goddess of the sea in the coastal villages of Madagascar. She is also well known in the Red Sea and the North Sea. She has been described by Portuguese sailors and by Englishmen. The fact that scientists can cold-bloodedly explain her as the grotesque manatee or dugong, a sea mammal that swims holding its young to its breasts like a human, does not mean that the ancient sailor or fisherman at sea did not see a beautiful woman with a fish's tail swimming in the calm, or that when he heard the smashing waves on the treacherous rocks and the high-pitched wind whipping the oceans to a fury it was not her seductive singing. The sea is deep and mystical—"the divine for which all men long," as the *Odyssey* puts it—and it has so many phenomena that are difficult to explain.

All we were catching aboard the *Elysium Queen* was a pitiful little pile of trash fish and one or two shrimp. Out of all our strikes I had salvaged a hermit crab carrying two reddish-orange commensal sea anemones on a moon-snail shell, some good clusters of hydroids, six large horseshoe crabs, which were covered with crawling commensal flatworms, and an assortment of fish. But even for me it was lean pickings.

We hadn't pulled up a single pound of shrimp, and Danny finally became discouraged. Because of our unrelenting bad luck we headed back to an offshore island reef and dropped anchor. We talked on the radio with the other boats in the bay and learned that it was lean pickings all over--no one was catching anything. Perhaps we would get some shrimp later on in the evening if we continued fishing, but there was no sense in burning fuel on that scant hope. None of us liked to quit, but there was nothing else to do. With a flick of the switch the engine died, and there was silence out in the calm, dark Gulf.

I was brooding over my failure to find the octopi. The instructor and his freshman students wanted so much to study the parasitic mesozoans in the octopus's kidneys. Mesozoans are peculiar ciliated wormlike creatures, and many scientists think they are the missing link between the protozoans, or single-celled animals, and the metazoans, or many-celled animals, which include man. If I did not find the octopi within a week, the order would be canceled. I hoped that I would be luckier the next day.

It was stuffy in the cabin, where we all sat in a dead silence reading the ancient magazines. On deck it was pitch-dark, and the only noise came from the gentle waves lapping against the boat. Toward shore the red lights of the radar tower and a few lights of shrimp boats doggedly working the bays could be seen, but faintly. It was lonely under the calm. The stars were brilliant overhead, and the lighthouse cast a long rotary beam over the stillness of the night.

In the endless nebula of bright stars a shooting star left a streak of blue fire behind it as it plunged through the sky. It was cool on deck and a little damp, but I found it the best place to sleep on this night of failure. A roach crawled along the wheel-room wall, and the quiet waves lapped on.

Danny and Jimmy talked quietly in hoarse voices below in the cabin. Soon the lights went off. It was past midnight, and the *Elysium Queen* was plunged into darkness.

# 13 Sea Wasps

I awoke, feeling stiff, cramped, and chilled from sleeping on a cork life preserver. My clothes felt damp, and the decks were wet with dew. Off in the distance I could see shrimp trawlers anchored up after a discouraging night of searching and dragging for shrimp and not finding any. I wanted a cup of hot coffee, but I didn't want to clatter around brewing a pot in the galley while Danny and Jimmy were still sleeping.

But now was as good a time as any to ease the flatworms off the horseshoe crabs. Flatworms were always a good-selling item, and if I could get up a sufficient quantity of them it would make up for the night's lean pickings.

I turned a large horseshoe crab on its back and noted that it was heavily infested with the triclad flatworm, *Bdelloura candida*. While the crab futilely attempted to run upside down, churning its legs and folding its body into a sharp angle, I picked off the small flatworms with forceps and dropped them into a vial of seawater. They had to be removed just right—too much pressure and the forceps would squash or tear them, too little and they would slip out of its grasp. The yellowish-white flatworm oozes and slides over the crab as it seeks its food.

No one really knows if *Bdelloura candida* is a true parasite or a commensal on the horseshoe crab. All flatworms are carnivorous—many of them eat small bristle worms. But if *Bdelloura* is isolated and raised in an aquarium, the worm will starve and shrink, slowly digesting itself. Any number of marine

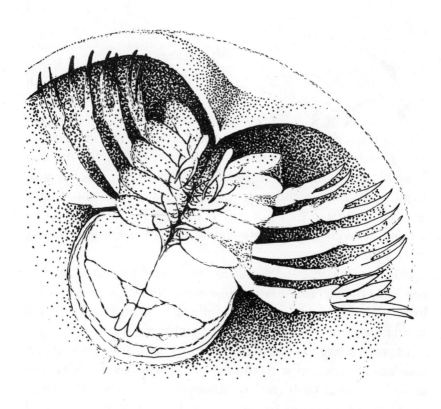

*I turned a large horseshoe crab on its back and noted it was heavily infested with the triclad flatworm,* Bdelloura candida.

animals, like sea anemones, ribbon worms, and nudibranchs, will do the same when there is no food, but when they are fed again, they soon regain their size. But even when food is offered to *Bdelloura candida*, it will not eat and continues to shrink. So it is suspected to be a true parasite taking its food from the crab itself. However, it does not disturb its host or injure it in any apparent way.

Down in the cabin I heard the blaring ring of the alarm clock, Jimmy's hoarse protests and groans, Danny's grumbling and coughing. Moments later there was a clattering of pots and pans, and then Danny's sleepy unshaven face, with a morning's cigarette between his lips, looked at me, relieved because I was still aboard. "Oh—you're still here," he said. It was absurd, and yet I understood that as captain he was responsible for all hands. We both laughed, and he popped back into the cabin.

The morning sun rose higher. The smells of freshly brewed coffee and frying ham and eggs were irresistible. Jimmy had cooked a magnificent breakfast. The eggs were fluffy and perfect, the ham was fried tenderly, and the grits were smooth and creamy. We ate, sitting on the bunks with the plates on our laps. After breakfast, I washed up while Jimmy and Danny went on deck. The engine spluttered and choked and caught with a roar, *chumm-chumm-chumm*, and we were off again, full speed, looking for butterfish.

I returned to my worm picking. The horseshoe crabs were making it difficult. As I tried to grasp the slippery worm, the crab scrabbled, bent its abdomen sharply, flexed its telson, and just when I thought I had the worm cornered the crab's ineffective pincers managed to push my forceps away. It is a time-consuming business to collect five hundred of these flatworms. And now that my time was so much more valuable, I had to make good use of my leisure moments. I thought of my carefree days when I could sit on deck with nothing to do but enjoy the view. That was when I had first turned my back on pursuing a formal education and being a laboratory assistant. When I began my career in earnest, I had no more free time, because there was so much I had to learn—not only about collecting and preserving biological specimens, but also about business practices.

Two large biological supply houses had issued want lists with accompanying prices which they would pay for specimens. Certain jellyfish might be worth twenty-five cents apiece. *Blaberus cranifer*, the common Southern black cockroach, fetched a dime each, if anybody wanted to collect the large ugly insect. Parasitic tapeworms from dog's guts and flukes from sheep liver were all worth something. And also the supply houses wanted sharks, sting rays, midshipmen, and moray eels.

I had been in business for two months and had also been sending live horseshoe crabs to the Seattle World's Fair. But nobody had paid me for my service. What was wrong? I had done my part—the shipments had arrived in good condition. Why didn't those people pay me?

I was making a bare living by going shrimping with Captain George Williams and Preacher. George was paying me a penny a pound on the shrimp and two and a half cents a pound on fish as an apprentice deck hand to Preacher (by courtesy only), and all the trash fish for specimens were mine. At first they were very decent about it, even though in the beginning I was worthless as a deck hand. Sometimes I earned as much as five dollars a night, which paid for the rent on my trailer and for my gasoline. I lived on a steady diet of fish and shrimp, which cost me nothing.

But this could not go on forever, because I was taking a percentage of Preacher's earnings, and the boat would have functioned just as well without me as with me. Fishermen are notoriously clannish, and it is doubtful that I would ever have become a part of their community if it had not been for the lanky Preacher's tender heart.

Preacher made me part of his family. He took me home to his wife for dinner and we drove into the north Florida backwoods to visit his folks. I found them to be the most warmhearted, generous people I have ever encountered. Aside from giving me a delicious Southern dinner of fried chicken, hot biscuits, heaping platters of fresh-cooked vegetables, salad, and pickled watermelon, they loaded my car down with ears of fresh corn, garden vegetables, watermelon, and pears and peaches, and their children helped me fill an order for one hundred green tree frogs and fireflies.

My first month on George's boat, aside from worrying about being paid for specimens, was the most carefree and happy time of my life. Since I had left the university under rather unhappy circumstances, I was nursing a lot of resentments. But night after night under the fiery white stars in the black skies out in the bay, pulling in the black webbing and the mounds of silvery fish, all my grievances seemed to shrink and recede into a dim nothingness.

The university's dean, a pompous, self-important man with a narrow, limited idea of what education should be and who should be in education, had once loomed so large on my horizon that I was completely discouraged. But now he shrunk into his place, and I could scarcely remember him. Why think of such a trivial man when the net had just come up loaded with shrimp and electric rays? And electric rays fetched a dollar and a half each. There were twenty-five in the net, and I would be richer by thirty-seven dollars and fifty cents—if the supply house paid me.

"Did you get your money for any of this junk yet?" asked George Williams for the fifth time that month. I had borrowed ten dollars from him twice.

"No," I said, suddenly feeling depressed. "I wish they would pay me. I'm sick of eating fish."

George looked at me shrewdly. "You sent them a bill like I told you to, didn't you?"

It would be just like George to send somebody a bill. Preacher always had to haggle with George over his share of the fish. So I said, somewhat embarrassed, "Oh, no, they'll be honest about it. They'll pay. I can't be that rude."

George shot me a look of exasperation and utter disgust. He turned to Preacher. "He's no good," he roared. "I never saw anybody so dumb. Why don't we cut him up and sell him for crab bait?" Then he bellowed at me, "Dammit, you dumb Yankee, if you ever want to get your money out of them, send them a bill!"

I looked at Preacher for help, but he looked confused and shrugged his shoulders. Apparently bills meant the same thing to him that they did to me. They were something you received through the mail from utility companies, garages, and other unpleasant money-grubbing businesses. Surely scientific companies and universities didn't go in for such crass, rude practices. The university had always politely paid me in salary checks. I did my part and they theirs. But I could hardly explain such delicate matters to George. We let the subject drop.

Then one day I received a letter from a supply house: "Received specimens in good condition, but we have not been billed. Please send us an itemized invoice." Then and then only did I realize that there was more to my profession than memorizing scientific names and determining the sex of a shark. And so the Gulf Specimen Company was officially born. I acquired stationery with letterheads, invoices, a typewriter, and later, as the checks came rolling in, a ledger.

Five years had passed since then. I still had not achieved a Dun and Bradstreet rating, but with the catalogue out I was hoping that the company's growth would be more rapid, especially when schools opened in the fall. I needed more capital and sooner or later I would have to hire employees.

The *Elysium Queen* was racing westward, and I chucked the last big horseshoe crab overboard. We were off Cape Mudhole, and Danny cut the engine down and dropped the try net.

Fifteen minutes later we recovered it with a most interesting catch. Two highly speckled portunid crabs, *Aerencus crabarius*; one *Calappa flamma*, the box crab; and numerous small sand dollars, *Encope michelini*, which the shrimpers called poker chips because of their small and uniform size. There were many interesting creatures in this catch, and they were different from the animals we had been catching the night before. Two large pinkish jellyfish, *Dactylometrea quinquecirrha*, with masses of fine reddish stinging tentacles and seventeen radial lines like spokes of a wheel, pulsed and quivered next to the speckled sea cucumber, *Theelothuria princeps*. Croakers, small butterfish, little flounders, and other fish flopped hopelessly, opening and shutting their gills, as the oxygen was starved out of them. Jimmy quickly scooped these up and tossed them back into the sea. The gulls swooped down and caught a few of them before they had a chance to swim down to the life-giving sea, but some escaped. The sea cucumbers were already in the process of exploding their sticky viscera over everything.

I have only mentioned a few of the animals present. If I mentioned all the species of bryozoans, the tunicates that were encrusting the shells, the minute hermit crabs, I would have a list that would go on and on and would be of little interest to anyone except a marine biologist.

Having traveled twenty-five miles westward, we left the shallow bay sand, muddy brackish estuaries behind us and encountered a different type of bottom community, animals that live in higher saline conditions with a firm, sandy bottom. Although some animals flourish in both habitats, other species are rigidly zoned and are not encountered in the marsh or flat-shelf areas. *Aerencus crabarius*, the speckled crab, and *Theelothuria princeps*, the sea cucumber, are two examples.

When we rounded Cape Mudhole and moved into Elizabeth Bay, we made several strikes with the try net and started catching more and more large butterfish. The butterfish, *Leiostomus xanthurus*, looks much like a gruntfish, and one might be tempted to write it off as one of the smaller inedible bony fish. I did in the beginning, until I tasted it and found it to be one of the most delicious creatures in the sea.

Danny was encouraged with our last strike of three large butterfish. Other shrimpers had struck butterfish in this same location just a few days before—they had caught tons of them, and he said we might too. We continued towing toward the beach with the try net, and soon the highway came into sight, with cars flowing back and forth. We could see bathers on the beach. I often wondered if the bathers, especially the pretty girls, realized how much they were under inspection. There was no better way of spending time than observing the beauties with a pair of binoculars, making appropriate comments, of course. But we had no time now that we were pulling our nets with a purpose and a blossoming hope that the aimless striking here and there would be over.

The *Elysium Queen* had moved away from the beach and continued westward. Off in the distance I saw other shrimp boats following us. Then we made another strike in fifteen feet of water and the net came up with eighteen large butterfish and two peculiar-looking bell-shaped jellyfish. All the hit-and-run fishing had come to an end.

"Let's get the big net over," shouted Danny, his voice jubilant. We had struck fish.

Jimmy and I worked feverishly, feeding the webbing over the side, while Danny fed out the ticker chain. Time counted, every minute of it. We had to strike the fish and strike quickly before the school moved on.

The huge weighted boards lying on deck were jerked off and suspended from the starboard davit with a flick of the winch lever. Then the lock was released and they splashed into the water. The big net sank down behind them. After we levered and fastened the cables, the towing process began, and so did the anxiety of waiting. Danny puffed on his cigarette at the wheel while Jimmy and I threw the try-net butterfish into a wire basket.

I had never seen those peculiar-looking jellyfish before. Casually, I picked one up. Through my formaldehyde-thickened fingers I received so painful a sting that I dropped the jellyfish as quickly as if it had been a piece of burning coal. The sting was almost as painful as a wasp's.

When I got over my shock, I remembered that I had seen these jellyfish before. It was during a briefing session just before I left for Madagascar at the Smithsonian Oceanographic Sorting Center in Washington. I was shown pictures of dangerous marine animals of the Indian Ocean that I might encounter. The most dreaded animals next to the sharks were the cubomedusans, commonly called sea wasps.

I looked at my two specimens in the live bucket. They were the most active and most rapidly pulsating of any jellyfish I had ever seen. Both had been eating—one had a whole minnow in its gastric cavity, and the other had a partially digested one.

I realized that my quest for knowledge could never end, that I must forever be learning. For here was a new life form for me to learn about, just one of the many strange life forms in the sea and along the beaches. So I would send these specimens to the Smithsonian Institution to learn the exact identity of this cubomedusan, its known points of distribution, and its history.

The cubomedusans that I had been warned about were the Indo-Pacific species, which administered such a venomous sting that victims were known to die within three to five minutes. I have seen microphotographs in a medical journal of the muscle in a Polynesian's arm, deeply penetrated by the thread-like stinging cells. The Australian sea wasp, *Chironex fleckeri*, can be considered the most dangerous animal in the sea, for it is believed to have claimed far more lives than sharks. Although most victims experience severe agony at their sting, not all of them die. The nature of the sea wasp's poison is unknown, and there is no known antidote.

Most of the deaths reported from cubomedusans have come from Australian waters. There is a related cubomedusan, *Chiropsalmus quadrigatus*, which is suspected of causing fatalities in Malaysia and the Philippines. The species we had on deck might have been *Chiropsalmus quadrigatus*, because it had the bell-shaped umbrella and four branching tentacles. Fortunately, it was not; if it had been, all three of us aboard the *Elysium Queen* would have been dead from the splattering stinging cells.

As the great net with its wide mouth and long bag pulled over the sandy bottom, I could not help wondering how many cubomedusans we might catch. Danny and Jimmy were only concerned about butterfish, and I didn't want to cause any unnecessary alarm. Two specimens were nothing to worry about.

I strongly suspect that about ten years before I was the victim of some form of sea wasp. I was wading in the shallow Gulf flat with a friend, catching scallops for the family dinner in waist-deep water. Suddenly I felt a searing pain across my thigh just below my bathing trunks. I yelled with pain and searched frantically for whatever had done this to me, but saw nothing. My friend also looked but found nothing. Within a few minutes I doubled up with cramps. My friend helped me into the skiff, although he was skeptical about my sudden pain and disability. By the time we reached shore I was having difficulty breathing and was suffering ghastly abdominal cramps, which caused me to double up and contort. A large red welt had formed across my thigh.

None of the local fishermen could imagine what kind of an animal had stung me. There were no Portuguese man-of-war reported in the bay, and it certainly was not a sting-ray wound. The fishermen's remedies were applied—they were quite ghastly. I was fed tobacco snuff, vinegar, and hot coffee until the doctor came with his injections.

In spite of all medication, the spasms continued for two hours. My pulse, before the tobacco and coffee, was rapid and weak, and each breath was labored and horribly painful. For days afterward I felt as if each muscle in my body had been torn from its ligaments. From what I now know of the stinging animals that inhabit the Gulf, I think I must have been stung by some species of cubomedusae. The symptoms I suffered are similar to those described by Australians who survived sea-wasp stings. And, similarly, the sea wasp is almost never seen by its victim.

When the try net came up the next time there were six sea wasps in it. Just getting them out of the webbing cost me and Jimmy several jolting stings.

"Have you ever seen these before?" I asked Danny.

"I never pay any attention," Danny said, looking at one of the peculiar bell-shaped animals, with long tentacles extending from its four corners. He shook his head. "Before you came out with us, I never paid them no attention. Sometimes we get a mess of jelly that stings like hell. But it's all jelly to me. I hate the stuff."

The next try net brought in eighteen cubomedusans. We handled them very carefully, picking them up by the bell and taking great care not to touch the tentacles. I dropped them into seawater and formalin solution.

I remembered that the textbook said that some deadly sea wasps travel individually, others in great shoals. Cubomedusans

vibrate very rapidly, one hundred and fifty pulsations a minute. This movement is deadly as the sea wasps cut through a
school of anchovies with their venomous tentacles. The same
silent glass-clear swiftness can converge in the shallows where
bathers are wading. Probably their screams ring a dinner bell
with the natives of the Philippines or in the Gilbert Islands—
sea wasps pickled in vinegar are a highly prized delicacy in the
markets.

The second try net brought up eighteen more, and every one
had eaten—there were little fish in all stages of being digested.

"Danny," I said apprehensively, "let's pick up the big net
and get out of here. If we get a deckload of these jellies they're
liable to kill us."

"I can't, Sugar," said Danny stubbornly. "We've had jelly
on board before. We're really hitting the butterfish now.
That's our living out there."

And there certainly were butterfish. The try net was bringing up thirty and forty at a time, all big ones too. Danny told
his brother-in-law Jerry over the radio, in code, that he was
catching butterfish. But somehow all the shrimpers found out,
and just as the birds flocked to us, double-riggers from all over
pulled up their nets, spread their wings, and headed at full
speed to converge on the spot we had struck.

In the blue waters, great trails of mud arose where the boards
were stirring up the bottom. There was excitement in the air.
We could see schools of butterfish break the calm water with
their ripples, stirring the surface with flashes of their silvery-
gold bodies in the hot afternoon. The sea was loaded with fish.
Sea gulls flocked to the scene, flapping their wings, screaming
their encouragement and impatience. Danny's brother-in-law
on the *Supreme Lady* was the first to come, but after him were
a dozen other boats.

On the *Elysium Queen* the anticipation of a big catch over-
rode any concern over stinging jellyfish. Danny and Jimmy

nervously puffed on their cigarettes as we moved in for the kill like a school of hungry sharks. All over St. Joe Bay big double-riggers were pulling their heavy nets filled with fish; the boats rocked from side to side under the strain of the loaded nets.

I looked out over the muddied waters astern of us. Within the scope of the V-shape of the steel cables that reached down to the trawling net a large black fin cleaved the surface. Sharks! More fins appeared—they always do when you get a big catch of fish. And sharks were something else to worry about. They could get into a feeding frenzy and tear the net to shreds as they swam around madly snatching mouthfuls of fish out of the webbing. Sometimes a net will come up with the entire bag chewed off. All we could do was hope that it wouldn't happen this time.

A large black shark swam alongside the *Elysium Queen*. As much as I hated the creature I couldn't help seeing the resemblance, the kinship of the predators—the screaming flocks of birds, the shrimpers, and the sharks all attacking the frantic schools of yellow butterfish.

We had made a two-hour tow and the big net was coming up. The winches wound round and round, as yard after yard of dripping cable came in. It seemed to me that it was an eternity of waiting. I had mixed feelings of dread and hope. What would the net bring up? Would it be a rewarding catch, or would it be the frightful cubomedusans? Finally the boards rose from the green sea and hung on the davit. Moments later we had hooked the net to the niggerhead, and as it started rising from the sea, we could see it was filled.

When the net was opened, piles and piles of butterfish poured out, along with a baby manta ray, sharks, sting rays, and more sea wasps, forming a gigantic mound on deck. The fish pounded their tails, slapped their bodies, grunted and gasped. The commotion they made sounded like a thunderous clapping of hands in a huge auditorium. The beating tails and fins and jumping bodies sent the stinging sea-wasp tentacles splattering everywhere. Our shirtless bodies were sprinkled with nematocysts, and red welts appeared on our skin. My skin felt on fire. Danny turned the deck hose on us—it might have made Danny feel better nursing us, but we were just as bad off as before. Nothing helped! We tried to continue the culling, but several times we had to back off. Over the radio we could hear the other fishermen complaining and cursing.

Danny had retied the big net and sent it splashing back into the sea. When the fish became less active, dying, we were able to sit and cull. Stubbornly through our discomfort we culled and culled fast—there were one thousand pounds of fish on board. And I was loading yesterday's empty collecting buckets with all different kinds of jellyfish. Never had I seen such a variety of jellies. There were *Dactylometra*, the rubbery *Stomolophis meleagris*, cubomedusans, *Aurelia aurita*, and a mass of ctenephores, comb jellies. The last were too torn and battered to be used as specimens.

Just as there are traditional fishermen who won't handle flatworms, we have the traditional instructor who will demonstrate only the traditional *Aurelia aurita* of the North Atlantic. But as with the burrowing sea anemone *Bunodactis stelloides*, perhaps a market for other jellyfish could be created.

In no time I had used up all my collecting buckets with jellies and had to borrow an old fish box from Danny for my other animals. With deep regret, I had to discard the baby manta ray. I lifted it up by the folds of its earlike flaps and heaved it overboard. The black body made a huge splash and sank beneath the surface. I liked to pride myself on being an independent collector, but at times like this I realized how limited an independent collector was. Had I been a part of a government or a university expedition collecting specimens aboard a research vessel, that baby manta ray would have been preserved regardless of expense. But the quantity of preservatives and the special handling required to make the small manta ray a museum specimen made it impractical for an independent collector. And there are few museums, if any, that can boast of having a perfect, complete manta ray.

As I sat there culling, I jerked sand shark after sand shark from the pile and tossed them over the rail. The hammerheads and shovelnoses went into the borrowed fish box. Squatting over the pile facing Danny and Jimmy, all of us culling swiftly, I had turned to throw the undersized butterfish back when all of a sudden a great cloud appeared in the blue sea and rose to the surface. And there, for just a breathtaking instant, the biggest manta ray I had ever seen leaped clear of the sea and high, high into the air. For a moment it glided like a kite in slow motion. It was huge, almost as big as the *Elysium Queen*, and if it had been taken aboard, I'm sure its wingspread would easily have overlapped the sides.

Before I could shout or say anything to attract Danny's and Jimmy's attention, the ray had completed its leap and crashed heavily back into the sea. The calm exploded with a geyser of water leaping high up, and I was left with my finger pointing and my mouth soundlessly open.

Danny and Jimmy quickly turned around. "What in the hell was that?" asked Danny, astonished.

"That was a manta ray," I said a little breathlessly. "Just like the one we caught, only this beast must have weighed a ton."

Under the hot afternoon sun we culled all the smaller butterfish overboard, because they would lower the price and reduce the fishermen's profit. There were many other forms of life that had to be discarded, such as male catfish, who had been carrying their young in their mouths and had spewed them out in their death struggle. Almost as unpleasant to handle as the jellyfish were the sea cucumbers. The net had scooped up hundreds of *Theelothuria princeps*, and true to form they expelled their sticky, messy viscera, which clung like melted marshmallow to the fish and to our fingers and smelled like an unpleasant oil. We sat there, most uncomfortable, covered with jellyfish stings, fish scales, and sea-cucumber guts, culling as swiftly as possible, wanting to get the nasty job done before the big net came up.

The deck was hosed down and we hardly had five minutes' pause when it was time to haul up the big net. The cables were winding in rather slower than usual and the drums behaved as if they were under an extra strain; the taut cables did not have their usual merry spinning sound. Danny frowned. "That could be a lot of fish, but somehow, I don't think it is."

When the boards swung up, a thick coating of jellyfish slid off and plopped into the sea, and more of them were twined around and wedged in the links of the chain. Danny turned to me with a look of hopeless disgust. "Sugar, do you want some jellyfish?"

"No," I said. "I've got more than enough."

"That's too bad. Somebody ought to get some good out of it," he said angrily. "Because we're fixing to take on a couple tons of it."

We all felt sick. If this were so, it would be the end of our fishing trip. As long as there are fish or shrimp to catch a fisherman will suffer any hazard—stinging jellies, bad weather, vicious moray eels, spiny catfish, sharks, it doesn't matter. As Danny said, "That's our living out there." But when the jellyfish invade, swarm in by the countless millions, the net becomes gorged, packed and weighted down with the jellies, preventing fish and shrimp from getting in the bag.

But even worse than the loss of the shrimp and fish is the damage the massed weight of the jellies does to the net. The jellyfish is 99 per cent water held together by protein, minerals, and salts. And water weight sixty-five pounds per cubic foot.

And a socklike net packed with all that protoplasm-contained water can burst.

I knew one shrimper on the Atlantic coast who took on a deckful of moon jellies in a rough sea on a stormy night. The

*The jellyfish is 99 per cent water held together by protein, minerals, and salts.*

boat rocking in the wind slid the jellies into the winch. With all that slime, the lock skidded and slipped and the cable's drums whirled insanely, screaming, while the net went splashing into the sea. The shrimper tried to slam on the brakes, but they wouldn't hold with the slick jellies coating them. And every bit of cable spun off, whizzed through the halyard, back-lashed over the rail, and went down to the bottom of the sea, carrying the net with it, lost forever—every bit of four hundred dollars' worth.

Danny threaded the lazy line through the pulley, taking the precaution of looping the lazy line four times around the re-volving niggerhead. There was a tortured strain laid upon the lazy line, the rigging, and the machinery by the weight of the jellies in the net. The net came up painfully slowly, creeping up inch by inch. We held our breaths as the net swayed heavy and cumbersome over the deck.

Danny spoke sharply, commandingly. "Get back, get back." The swollen net swayed. I had never seen a bag loom so filled and large with nothing. There were some clear transparent colors, pinks and browns, in the big nothingness. The silence was marked. Danny jerked the bag rope and sprang back quick as a cat. It seemed like the ocean came gushing out in waves. Jellies hit the deck with a regurgitating sound and ran in tor-rents all over the deck. Soon we were wading in jellyfish up over our boots, and the fiery stings hit our legs. There were a few fish, but we didn't care. We opened the deck holes and shoveled and shoveled and shoveled. And we could not stop, no matter how tired we felt.

Hours later, we joined the fleet of disgusted shrimpers. With them we were in full retreat back to Shiawassee. "Do you reckon you did any good with this mess?" Danny asked.

"I didn't get any octopus, and that's what I came out for. But I'll be able to sell some of this stuff, I'm sure."

"Well, I'm glad you got something out of this trip. We

would have been in the money if that jelly hadn't showed up. There's no shrimp here. I'm heading for Mississippi in the morning. I hear they're catching six hundred pounds of shrimp a night over there."

I was sorry to hear this. I liked shrimping with Danny.

"Cheer up, Jack. You get down here in the morning and you'll catch one of those big boats that will be working off to the east. They'll probably catch an octopus or two out there. I'll see you in the fall when I get back, unless you want to come and join me."

We cleared the decks and hosed it down. I could not go to Mississippi with Danny, because the fauna there was too impoverished. The bottom is nothing but soft oozing mud. The bell buoy clanged mournfully as we entered the pass of Shiawassee Bay and headed back to the dock.

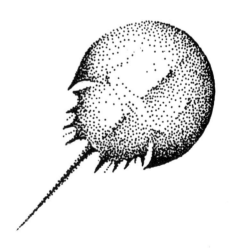

# 14  The Octopus Search

Danny Yates had gone to Mississippi, and so had Chass Parker, Cully, Wally, and Preacher and his new deck hand, Little Joe. In fact, just about all Shiawassee's fishermen had emptied into Mississippi and Alabama, following the shrimp. As I drove over the long bridge into town, I saw only a few shrimp boats left where once the river seemed choked with them as they tied up side by side at the docks and wharfs.

The boats that were left were mostly bay jumpers—smaller crafts that seldom ventured out into the open Gulf but worked the sheltered bays and estuaries. I was still searching for octopi, which could be found only in the open Gulf, so I hunted up and down Waterfront Street until I found a big double-rigger.

Fortunately there were a few of these trawlers that were still in. The boats that belonged to the big fish companies were run by hired captains and crews. *Miss Melanie* was one of them. Through a whole series of unfortunate events, this stately craft had lost its crew in Alabama and was now back in Shiawassee for a new crew and some minor repairs on her electrical system.

The former captain of the *Miss Melanie* had committed a heinous crime. Even in one's own home town this is not a wise thing to do. But to cruise into a port of another state, enter a bar, and charm away a local used-car salesman's girl friend is very bad indeed. It is even worse to have an altercation with the lovelorn salesman which leads to the interference of the local police. And what red-blooded, sea-going deck hand can stand idly by and watch his own inebriated captain get man-handled by a couple of rednecked hick cops? And how unfortunate can a body be when the local judge happens to be the car salesman's uncle as well as the brother-in-law of the constable with the swollen, discolored eye? And so the *Miss Melanie* was left tied idly to the dock sans captain and crew. Both, incidently, got thirty days.

So the Shiawassee Fish Company had to come and retrieve its craft. The *Miss Melanie* was a stately sixty-foot double-rigger which slept four. She was built to take the roughest seas, travel anywhere up and down the coast, and stay out for months as long as there were shrimp to chase.

The new captain, Dave Clark, was short-handed and was glad to take me along. Those two huge nets gave promise of catching a lot of fish. The captain and his deck hand, Carrol Thomson, helped me load my gear aboard. And even though I had three big collecting buckets, several smaller ones, three styrofoam ice chests filled with dry ice, bottles of preservatives, an oxygen cylinder, and a box of plastic bags, it all seemed lost on the large boat. Finding space on smaller boats was quite a problem, and often I had to line the bow with buckets. But on the *Miss Melanie* I hardly filled up one corner.

Tonight there would be hard work ahead for me because I had to serve both as crewman and as collector. The *Miss Melanie* would take on another deck hand in a day or two and then travel west to Mississippi. Tonight was just a trial run out in the open Gulf.

"I feel sure you'll get an octopus where we're going," said Dave Clark. "There's a deep hole just south-southeast of El-mor's Cape that near about always has one or two. I believe you'll find a bunch of junk there."

"I need to get some sponges too. Those big red finger-type sponges and the basket-shaped ones. That's why I brought this dry ice. I had to drive clear to Panama to get it this morning."

"Don't worry, we'll drag right through that mess. I believe you'll do all right this evening," he said reassuringly.

We moved down the river, fueled up, took on ice, and went through the drawbridge out into the bay. I took the wheel while the captain and Carrol worked on the rigging, untangling and straightening the nets and letting the outriggers down until they spread out like wings.

Most of the shrimpers I worked with were independent owners of their own boats. But these men were professionals who had shrimped all their lives from boat to boat and port to port, wherever shrimp run. It was a grave responsibility to operate such a big, expensive craft, but they were ready to make any decision. They could repair the motor, patch a badly torn net, and ride out a hurricane. A big boat like the *Miss Melanie* had to catch a lot of shrimp to cover the cost of operating, paying the crew, and sharing the profit. It was expensive to keep her tied to the dock; she had to be working all the time for her keep.

As big as the *Miss Melanie* was, it was a pleasure steering her through the channel. She ran on a magnetic steering system, and her rigging was designed for ease and comfort. I had on occasion worked on boats this size on the southeastern Atlantic coast, but never in the Gulf. A boat so big was bound to catch a lot of fish.

Again I had come well prepared, with thirty pounds of dry ice. Certain sponges were required for biochemical studies, and in order to preserve various enzyme structures, the sponges had to be frozen within a few seconds after capture. Even while animals are still alive in a collecting container or in an aquarium, a degree of physical and chemical deterioration begins to set in. I have often heard physiologists who were measuring respiration rates and oxygen consumption in various snails or electrophysiological responses of the eyes of horseshoe crabs complain that animals kept for several weeks in captivity develop a more sluggish and less responsive metabolism than animals studied within a short time after capture.

Carrol relieved me at the wheel and I made myself comfortable on the bow. Using a life preserver as a pillow I watched the pleasant sunset. Dave climbed up on the rail and pulled a small wooden box off the roof of the cabin. He carried it over to me as if the box were filled with precious jewels. And it might well have been, because when he opened the box, I whistled with admiration. He had a magnificent collection of deepwater sea shells.

"Where did you get these?" I asked in astonishment.

"I don't know where Willie and them got this mess." Willie was the former captain of the *Miss Melanie* and was still serving time in Alabama. "But it looks like the kind of stuff that you find in that deep trench off Biloxi. They sure are pretty. What are their names?"

I picked up a polished, oval shell etched with a checkered pattern. "This is a Scotch-bonnet shell."

"It does look kind of like Scotch plaid," Dave said.

"And this is the Junonia." It was a yellow shell with black leopard spots on it. It was really a superb collection, and the shells were clean, polished, and not odorous, unlike most of the shells the shrimpers saved for me. Usually I was asked the names of these odd shells; the shrimpers expected me to know them all, as a professional biological collector. Visitors to the seashore expected me to rattle off a long list of sea shells, but in a business where the jellyfish, flatworms, crabs, and tunicates are as important as shell-bearing mollusks, it was difficult to know everything, including the names of all the marine fish. But I tried, and with the aid of my library, my identification sufficed. But if I had to make a blood sample of a fish, I did not attempt to key it out myself. Unless it was something like the most ubiquitous, common species of catfish, I had an ichthyologist put a name on my specimen.

I replaced the beautiful shells in the box and said, "Do you think Willie would sell these to me?"

Dave puffed on his cigar and shrugged his shoulders. "I don't know. Willie's funny about his shells. Being he's locked up and all that you might be able to buy them from him pretty cheap. I'm going to visit him in a few days and I'll ask him for you."

"I'll have to know where they came from before I can buy them—otherwise the museums won't want them."

"Don't worry about it. I've been with Willie a lot of times, and that's all he does is mess around with those shells. He'll know where he got every one of them."

It was getting dark. We were now eight miles offshore and all about us was the quiet Gulf and a big, ominous yellow moon reflecting on the rippling black waters. Traveling to the shrimp grounds and waiting for the nets to come up is all part of shrimping. You cannot write about how nice it is to lie on your back on a soft bed in a shrimp-boat cabin with just a slight, cooling breeze blowing through the open windows, watching the glowing lights on deck and listening to the drone of the engine, the crackle and conversation on the radio as the boat goes out to sea, but this is what a goodly portion of shrimping is.

This waiting period is not always so pleasant. In winter you lie on the bunk huddled under covers shivering, with every burner of the gas stove going, or if you're at the wheel you're bundled up with heavy clothing, your breath steaming in the thin, cold air. And getting out in the icy winds while culling the wet catch with numb fingers makes one want to curse the very existence of shrimp. But it was summer now, and I was comfortable and felt extremely lazy.

My loafing was interrupted briefly when Dave cut the speed of the engine and asked me to run the boat while they put the big nets over. "Hold her on a hundred and eighty degrees south," he said, tapping the big illuminated compass. Moments later both big nets splashed down into the sea and arranged themselves on the bottom. Dave returned to the wheel. "Carrol, put the try net over," he said. He turned to me. "We'll be pulling it up in fifteen minutes. You may get some of your stuff then."

It seemed no time at all before Dave said, "Let's get the try net," and left the wheel. Carrol jumped off the lower bunk and I slid off the upper, got into my boots, and followed him out hurriedly. The net wound in easily, and when the boards emerged from the dark waters, the net jingled with shells. They were mostly shells of bivalves, bright-colored scallops and conchs—all fossilized material that makes up much of the bottom in the outer Gulf.

The try net's catch looked encouraging. There were fifteen pink shrimp, several small unusual-looking fish that I saved for the American Museum of Natural History, a few portunid crabs, one stomatopod mantis shrimp, and a thin, frail sea spider that looked unusual. I slit an opening behind each fish's gills and with a small hypodermic needle drew out half a cubic centimeter of blood and squirted it into a vial of buffered formalin for a biochemist who was studying the nucleic acids of blood. There were a few ctenophore comb jellies, which I dropped into a plastic bag and put on dry ice. There were other pieces of formless, broken jellyfish that I could not identify, so I had to discard them.

As I finished culling and preserving, Carrol threw the try net overboard, and under the weight of its boards it sank back to the bottom. Then came the surprise. The second try-net drag produced a beautiful catch—a rash of colorful, vivid creatures. There were ninety pink shrimp with big brown spots on their abdomens. The trash was spectacular. Dozens of small brown portunid crabs scuttled off in all directions. There were rock shrimp, *Syconia typica*, with purple-and-white-striped legs, short pointed antennae, brown tiger-striped backs, and an orange ventral surface. The rock shrimp has a hard chitinous exoskeleton, hence the name "rock" or "hard-backs," and it is as bizarre a creature as any. There were clusters of red and orange sponges, *Axinella*, and yellow *Haliclona* sponges, which looked like a tangle of vines, and white *Geodia* sponges, which resembled little balls. Brown and yellow sponges were covered with tunicates, encrusted with dark-blue sponges, and mixed with mossy encrusting lacy bryozoans. How could so many forms and so much color be concentrated in one catch? Quickly I washed them off under the blasting pressure of the deck hose and packed them into a styrofoam chest with dry ice.

There was a giant red hermit crab, *Petrochirus diogenes*, that looked like a hairy boiled lobster, living in a water-worn Scotch-bonnet shell, and the shell was covered with six large *Calliactis* sea anemones and a patch of *Astrangia* coral. The brown anemone, with a circle of red spots fringed with yellow, was beautiful in its contracted, jellylike glob form. Large gray starfish and mottled yellow and brown ones with cream-colored spines twisted and writhed their arms on deck. There was so much, the deck was so full, so wonderfully full—there were five big fig shells, *Ficus*, with bulging fleshy meat projecting from their paper-thin shells, and orange-striped box crabs, and calico crabs.

And there were skates and grunts, catfish and eels, and a large poisonous scorpion fish with bristling spines. This last specimen I handled very carefully, edging it into the bucket with a shovel and avoiding its spines. Carrol called it a feverfish, because people who have been stuck are said to become delirious. "Be careful," he warned me. "If you get stuck by that, we'll have to carry you back to dock." I was also taking a blood sample from it.

There were even more creatures on deck, more than I can mention. Once in a great while I ran into a bottom community like this, and always I felt miserable because I didn't have hours to go slowly through the catch, taking samples of all the specimens.

I had to select only a few, th : most showy ones, because my space, my preservatives, and r ıy dry ice were so limited. In just a few minutes the net wou ld be coming up again and the decks had to be clear. I had to cull decisively and take only what I could use, the animals I was sure I could dispose of—although everything in the catch would have been of value to a museum for distribution records. Even as I put the specimens into plastic bags and collecting containers, they began to change and lose their luster. The beautiful starfish with the two-foot spread of arms began to twist, contort, and break into pieces.

I was barely through half the pile of specimens when the winch began spinning and pulling up the try net. Quickly I raked through the pile, taking out the big and strange sponges, pieces of coral-like branching bryozoans, bits of real coral—things I couldn't let pass. A cluster of small red gelatinous hydroids, feather-duster worms in a chunk of limestone rock, pink sea anemones on sponge bases. It was unfair, time had slipped away, and Carrol looked a little irritated when I grabbed an attractive calico crab away from his shovel while he was scooping up the trash.

This had been a momentous catch, better than any I had encountered in years. There really isn't much known about bottom communities in the Gulf. We had pulled in quite a bit of the West Indian fauna that found its way up into the

northern Gulf. Essentially the Gulf of Mexico contains two
different faunal communities. The inshore brackish-water animals are generally the same as the Carolinian fauna, and the
creatures taken out in the deep, oceanic waters of the northern
Gulf are generally semitropical or tropical West Indian forms.
There is frequently an overlap of the two faunas.

You never know what you will catch in a shrimp net. Sometimes the net will drag through a very rich area, as was happening tonight aboard the *Miss Melanie*, and just a few miles
away the bottom may be sterile—a couple of starfish, maybe
some shrimp, but not enough to excite a fisherman or even a
collector.

A good analogy would be a collector from another planet
on a spaceship flying a safe thirty thousand feet above the
ground. All that is beneath him are endless blankets of misty
clouds, some resembling white snowbanks, and he would have
no idea of what life existed below him—no more than we have
cruising on top of the water, far up above the communities of
fish and invertebrates that inhabit the bottom.

Just as in the ocean, there are regional differences. The temperate zones are more populated than the semitropical zones.
For a moment, let us suppose that this cosmic collector is interested in making systematic samplings of the life that lives below
while making a flight from Maine to Florida. As he soars over
the clouds and mists, he drops down a huge trawl in New
England and pulls it for a short interval.

He would pull up a peculiar collection of people endemic to
Maine, few in numbers, uttering short, choppy vocal sounds.
As he drags farther south, specimens from each small New
England town will have their own vernacular. But relatively
few will come up in this trawl, and if he were making a
commercial-fisheries report he might say this was not a productive area. Yet he may have missed Boston entirely, or dragged
through it in the middle of the night, and his report would be

unchanged. Should he drag Boston in the daytime, he would say the population is diurnal, productive, and occurs in a great variety. However, the Boston benthos would be similar to New York City's.

There are so many factors to be considered in such benthonic sampling. Suppose the net drags through New York City at twelve midnight, starting on 57th Street and Fifth Avenue and working slowly toward the Lower East Side. The collector in the spacecraft will not be aware that he is not getting a typical catch. He will be deluded into thinking that night people, beatniks, dogs and their owners, Bowery inhabitants, anesthetized winoes, prostitutes, and cops in blue uniforms are the typical and dominant members of the community in New York City.

Of course the morning rush hour would give the collector an overly dense fauna, and he would soon find that he had to shorten the trawling time to a minute or two or the nets would become so gorged that he would not be able to lift it, even with the most powerful winches.

The collector, after passing over Washington, Arlington, Virginia, and Maryland, finds the population decreasing. At North Carolina the population gets thinner and thinner, and when he strikes his net over South Carolina, Georgia, and North Florida, he will find nearly sterile bottom—an assortment of people, horses, dogs, cats, and wild animals, but nothing like what he had found in the more temperate zone. He will find that no matter where he casts his net, the dominant species is *Homo sapiens*. His trip finally ends in Miami with a netful of scantily clad, sunburned vacationers bathing along the beaches, and he will be a most confused student.

The taxonomy of *Homo sapiens* is in an even more confused state than the taxonomy of polychaete worms. For under this single species of *Homo sapiens* there is tremendous individual variation. The study won't be easy, since a great many inhabit machines called automobiles and must be pried out before they can be examined, much the way a collector of marine life must pull a hermit crab out of its snail shell.

Some people will be beautiful, others intelligent, others stupid, ugly, pompous, ignorant, or conceited. There will be different skin colors, and there will be conservatives, radicals, and liberals. All will appear to have an aversion to everyone else and will seem outraged at being caught in the same net.

Of course all these problems may not bother the collector if he is forced to do what members of most scientific expeditions are forced to do. He could simply preserve the whole mess, give the cordinates of where they were collected, the time and the date, and hope for the best. He might even scribble down some quick notes on how they looked and acted when alive. Expeditions and trawling operations are such hurried affairs that you never get a chance to scrutinize the catch properly.

Undoubtedly the collector would have a much better understanding of life below the clouds if he dived down and walked among the communities. He could visit a fishing village in Maine, or sit in a beatnik coffee shop. He could walk along a university campus when the students are hurrying from classroom to classroom. Or he could stand in a South Carolina cotton field and listen to the Negroes picking cotton and watch them carrying bales in the hot sun. Or he could sit in an airconditioned, pink-tiled dentist's office with piped-in music.

But with all the academic pressures, what collector has the time to go down and do all that? Even if a rare individual takes the time, he must be exceedingly careful in making his observations. He cannot jump to conclusions and say, "This is the way it is," but rather, "This is what I have seen at this particular time and can relate only within my own realm of experiences."

Aboard the *Miss Melanie* the second haul of the try net brought a hundred and thirty-seven pink shrimp. They jumped and wriggled, forlornly waving their antennae. At a glance I could see what was new. Among the sundry fish was a foot-long filefish with golden sandpaper skin that scintillated under the deck lights. There was a frogfish, and pink sea urchins, slowly and mechanically moving their short spines. The sponges were again dominant, but there was a live *Tonna* snail with an attractive round shell.

I was glad to see the great heavy-shelled helmet conch, three red squid, each about a foot long, and one scyllaroid lobster, or Mexican crawfish. The fishermen call them bulldozers, which is a more fitting name than the books give them— slipper lobsters. It was hard to say which form was most spectacular. Was it the brick-red sea fan, *Lophogeogia hebes*, with its beautiful interlocking branches? It was like traveling through a garden.

If this try-net catch was a fair sample of what would come up in the big nets, I felt I would go mad. I would be over-whelmed by the huge volume of specimens dumped on deck. However, the try-net catch is not always a good indication of what the big net will bring up. Should I be a magpie and grab anything, stuff and cram things into my buckets, ice chests, and plastic bags? Or should I hunt coldbloodedly for what I knew I could sell? I felt like a bewildered child who is con-fronted with choices of ice creams, cakes, and candies, sits down confused, not knowing what to grab first, and proceeds to have a nervous breakdown.

I knew that I must take generous samples of everything. Methodically I picked up a magnificent red hermit crab and wrenched three big sea anemones off its shell, placed them in a plastic bag, and put them in the dry-ice chest. Then I froze the lobster, one dozen shrimp, two brown basket sponges, and a large red squid.

The squid would be a problem. There were only a few spe-cialists in the United States who regularly classified cephalopods. The one specialist I knew was simply too busy with his own problems to work on the preserved specimens I sent him. So the squid would have to be sent to the biochemist with a collection number. Later I could supply him with the name.

But I wanted to know the name of the red squid for my own satisfaction. Every now and then this same species came into the nets. The annotated fauna checklist of the marine invertebrates put out by the local university listed only one species of squid, *Lolliguncula brevis*, the common small white Gulf squid, which seldom fails to come up in every net haul. They were useless as dissection specimens, but excellent for eating when baked with rice and tomato sauce. In addition to all my other studying, I had to learn how to cook. Along with my collection of zoology books I had accumulated several good seafood cookbooks.

The red squid was a valuable specimen, but it remained unidentified. A professional biological collector must know the scientific and common names of all the large, conspicuous animals that he finds in his vicinity. This in itself is almost a lifetime work, but it must be done. Over the years, as I have been able to put more and more names on creatures that have come up in the nets or been dug out of the sand, I have noticed a slight but perceptible change in my attitude.

The net drags through a bed of sea pansies, and a beautiful greenish sea slug with yellow stripes comes up with every drag. Looking at this animal carefully, I discover from its anatomy that it is a nudibranch. I take delight in how this nudibranch glides over the bottom of my aquarium, and how it munches on the polyps of the sea pansies.

The next step is to narcotize this nudibranch, preserve it fully expanded in a feeding, moving position, and send it to a specialist in Woods Hole to identify it. Sooner or later a name is tagged on it—*Arminia tigrina*. And when I am back on the shrimp boat and the net brings up three of these attractive little

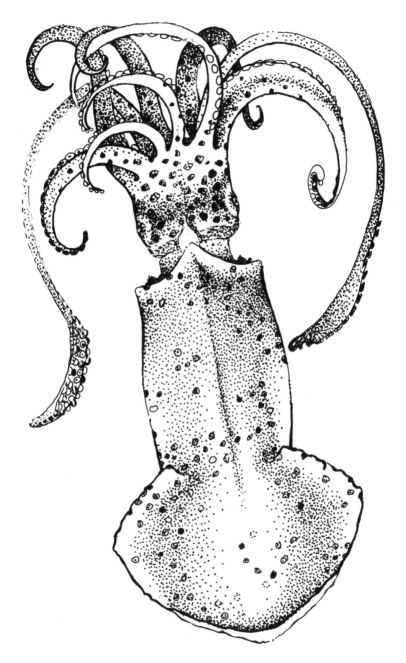

*The squid would be a problem. There were only a few specialists in the United States who regularly classified cephalopods.*

sea slugs, I record, "Three of the small striped nudibranchs, *Arminia tigrina,* appeared in the catch of sea pansies, *Renilla mulleri,* off St. John's Island in six meters." I record it with a feeling of accomplishment and pride.

But the mystery of this beautiful little creature is gone. Somehow when the name is tagged on it a good bit of its splendor disappears.

Aboard the *Miss Melanie,* the try-net catch was truly wondrous to me, because I didn't know the names of half the invertebrates and a good number of the fish. There were many unfamiliar creatures—red sponges, branching sea fans, pale-white sea squirts. It would be a challenge to catalogue them in their proper places. In the meantime I enjoyed the mystery of their exotic strangeness and beauty, even though not knowing their identity left me with a feeling of inadequacy.

Carrol, an efficient deck hand, raked quickly through the pile, culling out the commercial shrimp, now and then finding a large butterfish, a flounder, or a whiting and automatically adding it to the fish basket. He was not impressed by this catch, but all I could do was to sit and slowly examine each and every form, until I inadvertently picked up a glass sponge, *Geodia,* and was compelled to spend the next two hours picking out the glasslike spicules from my fingers.

The night wore on and we continued pulling the two big nets behind the boat. The massive kitelike structures swooped up all the shrimp, fish, and sponges. Wisps of clouds floated past the moon, and sea gulls flew alongside us, beating their wings, effortlessly keeping abreast, diving for fish, and squawking into the blackness like pale-gray phantoms.

Time slipped away. The two hours of dragging seemed a few minutes. The monotonous hum of the engine died down to an idle, and the big nets wound in on their winches with the determined whirring sounds of machinery. Although I considered myself an old hand at this sort of thing, an experienced collector, the rich catch of the try nets had excited me. What would the big nets bring up?

The nets rose slowly. The winding seemed endless, but finally the boards rose from the water and Carrol locked the winch. As the trawls emerged dripping from the sea, I could see at a glance that they were both filled. I always enjoyed the sight of the two nets being opened, one right after the other, and the spilling of fish. Dave jerked the bag rope on one net, then the other, and the deck heaped up with an enormous pyramid of marine life. As the nets emptied the pile grew and grew and grew until it enveloped the whole deck. There was a mountain of trash, fish, and shrimp, and as I looked at it all my excitement evaporated. I despaired at having to cull through it.

There was no splendor in this catch—just an endless faceless mass of millions of creatures, not individuals but undistinguishable trash. It sounded like coal rushing down a chute. It was as if the extraterrestrial collector had dragged over New York City during the rush hour, catching thousands and thousands of human beings, squalling, angry, and bewildered, heaped upon each other. The most beautiful woman or the ugliest little man would be shaken and compressed and lost and never noticed.

As I stood looking at the pile in dismay, Dave said, "There's an octopus. He's alive, too."

I stared blankly at that mammoth pile. "Where is it?" I asked. Dave and Carrol were more accustomed to spotting individual animals in the pile of struggling, pounding, and straining creatures. I thought myself observant too, but when there is so much it is difficult to discern any one particular creature at a glance unless it is exceptionally large and showy. A soft reddish-brown octopus that looks like a lump of decaying meat is almost impossible to see.

Dave pointed to a corner of the pile, and there it was.

*As I stood looking at the pile in dismay, Dave said, "There's an octopus. He's alive, too."*

Blushing red with rage, the large blob with its two malevolent eyes and eight legs covered with sucker disks slid out from under the mass of fish and oozed onto the deck. It moved like quicksilver, like a mass of flowing jelly, in such a spineless manner that I couldn't help feeling a slight revulsion. Yet I had collected and handled hundreds of octopi.

I snatched it up, and the cold, slimy creature wrapped its tentacles around my wrist with a viselike grip, angrily emitting a squirt of ink with an unpleasant squishing sound. Hundreds of its firm sucker disks clung to my hand as it strove desperately to slide out of my grasp and flushed with rage. I held it firmly by its mantle so that it couldn't bite me, then released it in one of the twenty-five-gallon collecting buckets. It shot away with a jet-propulsion movement, clouding the water with ink. I poured the inked water out of the bucket and filled it with fresh seawater from the deck hose. The octopus clouded the water again, and again I changed it. If I had not, it would soon have suffocated in its own ink.

Finally the octopus settled down to the bottom of the bucket and puffed and contracted its mantle, adjusting to the new situation. Its evil-looking little eyes seemed to register hatred and resentment at being captured. I inserted a tube of oxygen into the water and set it bubbling slowly.

While I was caring for the octopus, Dave and Carrol put the big nets over again, and then we started the mountainous task of culling the shrimp, edible fish, and specimens from that gigantic pile. As I sat and culled, the sweat ran down my forehead—culling slow or furiously didn't seem to make a difference. No matter how much shrimp we extracted from the pile, filling basket after basket, it looked as if it had hardly diminished. We squatted at the foot of the mountain and culled and culled and culled. After hours, my back ached and I was exhausted, but I continued to cull and save the specimens. Perhaps it was because I no longer got so much exercise, but years before the strain of a huge catch had not bothered me in the slightest. Or perhaps then it had been exciting and adventuresome, but now it was nothing but hard, backbreaking work.

We wore heavy gloves to protect our fingers, but in no time they were soggy and wet, and the shrimp acid ate into my fingers and made them swell. Slowly, ever so slowly, the pile diminished. There were plenty of specimens. I found a huge *Murex* conch with projecting points, a large collection of brittle stars, and more sea anemones living on sponges. There were thousands of *Siconia typica*, the rock shrimp, and after collecting a few pounds that were required for frozen specimens and five hundred for stock preserved specimens, I put aside fifty pounds for my food freezer.

I don't know why gourmets have never discovered the rock shrimp. Perhaps it is because they inhabit relatively deep water and are hard to clean. They have to be cracked and the meat pried out. But when the rock shrimp is brushed with garlic and melted butter, you have a dish that can be equaled only by fresh Maine lobster. We had more than a hundred pounds of rock shrimp in this drag, and what I could not save was culled overboard, because there was no commercial market for them.

There were also six slipper lobsters, *Scyllarius americanus*, culled from the catch. I dropped them into a bucket of alcohol—which was a pity, because they are delicious.

The deck was barely clear when it was time for the big nets to come up again. Even while the winches were winding in yard after yard of dripping wet cable, I was still shoveling trash fish over the side. It was cool that night, and most of the fish went back into the sea alive, although the sea gulls, porpoises, and sharks that hung around the boat grabbed what they could.

The mounds of fish once again rose on deck, and this time even I saw many octopi oozing out from under the fish. Dave and Carrol helped me grab them up, writhing and squirming, and we kept changing the water until they settled down. I found that they simply would not stay in the collecting buckets, even with a strong lid on. No sooner had I put one in than I would find it had crawled out and slid onto the deck.

It was strange that we hadn't really touched on the octopus population while dragging over the rock piles and sponge beds where they lived. It was only after we had moved a few miles away from the cutting rocks, onto sandy muddy bottom, that we found them. Had they left their shelter to feed, or to mate? Whatever the reason, we had quite a number of specimens aboard.

Only one *Octopus vulgaris* taken from the mound of fish was dead. Others were still in the pile, and we uncovered them as we culled, but these were damaged and dying, and I weeded them out for preservation. The lively individuals that crawled quickly away from the confusion and onto the deck were the ones I wanted to keep alive. At a glance you could tell which were healthy. The active octopi had a rich brown pulsating color. The dying ones were pale and feeble.

From time to time, as I culled, I attended to the octopi as best I could, changing the water every time I noticed black ink in the pails. I used the deck hose to gush in fresh seawater again and again.

At four o'clock in the morning, I had four healthy, active specimens in the collecting buckets. I thought of how pleased the instructor would be to have the octopi for a student demonstration. The octopi anchored themselves to the sides of the buckets, putting as much distance between themselves as possible, and glared savagely at each other. Between Dave and Carrol they received excellent attention, and there seemed to be no reason why they should not survive.

The last drag produced no octopi. Before the sun came up, I transferred the living specimens into plastic bags, charged them with oxygen, sealed them, and placed them in buckets with cushioning seawater to stabilize the temperature. I took every precaution I could think of to keep them alive.

We were just approaching the island pass that led into Shiawassee Bay when I noticed the octopi were swimming about nervously. Fearing that the increasing daylight in the sky was disturbing them—they are nocturnal creatures—I put covers on the buckets. Moments later, as the sun grew higher, I checked the octopi again. To my despair, one of them had turned pasty white and slumped to the bottom of its bag dead.

Within the next two hours they all died. I tried every possible means to rescue them. I ripped open the bags, put in fresh seawater, and lowered the temperature by putting sealed plastic bags of ice in the containers, but the more I tried to do for them, the quicker they died. To this day I don't know the reason why. I had successfully collected and shipped octopi before that night, and I have collected them since, always in the same manner.

As the *Miss Melanie* neared the Shiawassee Bridge I knew it was hopeless, although one or two had a trace of life left in them. I froze their cadavers with the others in the already packed ice chests. I was disappointed about the octopi—and I was exhausted.

# 15 Summer Doldrums

NO. 070790 FOR TWO LIVE OCTOPUS DUE TO YOUR FAILURE TO
MEET SCHEDULED DELIVERY DATE.

I read the telegram twice and then filed it. I was not angry,
merely disgusted with the whole business. All those days
aboard shrimp trawlers, all the time spent persuading the captains and crews of party fishing boats to save me a live octopus,
driving from fishing port to fishing port in the hot sun to make
arrangements. But each time the octopus came back dying or
dead.

The long summer was dragging out, hot, fierce, relentless,
and the orders had thinned out. Many of the professors
had gone on vacation, and the summer schools were closing.
There were back orders I could finish up at my leisure. The
tides were getting low once again, but the collecting was unpleasant, hard, exhausting work, and the flats were not productive, because many life forms either die during the summer
or seek cooler, deeper water.

On this particular morning the weather seemed to be the

hottest it had ever been. There had been scattered light show-
ers in every vicinity except ours. The sun shone through a
dusty haze, the plants were scorched, and the earth was dry,
and it seemed that the flies were biting with a ferocity un-
equaled in other years.

I drove down to the post office and picked up my mail. The
morning crowds looked limp and exhausted. People grunted
their good mornings, and women's unhappy voices were whining more than usual, complaining about the heat, slapping at
the swarming flies, complaining about the falling crab-meat
market. In the mail were bills, a few checks, two new orders,
and a letter from a scientist, an old friend of mine.

Hopefully, I opened one of the orders first, as I always did.
It was a rush order for two dozen live *Glottidea pyramidata*,
the Gulf coast brachiopod. But this order was impossible to fill,
because brachiopods seasonally disappeared from the intertidal
grass flats. In the same sand bars where I had dug hundreds
in the right season, now not a single one could be found, and
it was this way year after year when the grass flats became soft
and mushy and the mud stank from the heat. In October, when
the cold snap came, I would find brachiopods again, but it
would be too late for this researcher. So I answered his letter
with a conventional "We regret."

I opened the letter next—I was too discouraged to read the
second purchase order. Probably it would be just as impossible
as the first; that was the way my luck had been running lately.
The letter read: "Just a little note to ask you if you would be
interested in a position as staff biological collector, helping us
build a museum collection of Pacific Coast marine invertebrates
and fish." The letter went on to describe the delightful climate,
the beautiful beaches, and the lovely tidepools of the Pacific.
Beautiful girls and surfing, and even time to continue my education if I wanted.

And this was not a small, local marine laboratory that I

would be working for. It was one of the largest oceanographic institutions in the world. And just to make it even more tantalizing and harder to refuse, I was offered a staggering salary. I sat sweating over the typewriter in just my shorts, hearing my Airedale panting at my feet, reading the letter again. That salary! And I wouldn't have to put it back into the business, to buy chemicals, glassware, shipping containers, and a new dissecting scope. The salary would be all mine to do with as I pleased. Perhaps I could buy a new car. My old station wagon was dying. Every time I turned the starter it whined hideously before the engine caught. When it finally gave out I planned to buy a practical pick-up truck, not a modern new car. Never had temptation reared so beautiful a head.

It was almost irresistible. But when I returned from Madagascar I had promised myself as well as my regular customers that I would really try to make my business succeed.

I opened the rest of my mail. The bills would be paid with the two checks I had just received. The second order was a new one: a purchase order for six live toadfish with an accompanying letter from a physician in a medical school in Louisiana. I felt considerably better; this was what I considered a gravy order, because I could get all the toadfish I wanted on the mud flats across the street from my laboratory.

I planned my itinerary for the day. Before going on, I checked my live aquaria. I usually performed this task the first thing in the morning. Dead animals had to be removed, and pumps and filters had to be checked to make sure they were working properly. During the slow seasons I kept only one live tank going for my own interest and as an exhibit for friends. The other four tanks were discontinued.

It was a very attractive aquarium, with live red and yellow gorgonians covered with snow-white polyps, pink and white coral, reddish-brown sea cucumbers, purple spiny sea urchins, orange starfish clinging to the glass with their tubed feet, a small speckled moray eel hiding among the rocks, and a number of sea anemones blossoming like flowers. There was a small greedy flounder who doted on mole crabs, and a large handsome sea horse that liked to wrap its tail around the sea whips, and on the clumps of rocks were large round ivory-white barnacles ejecting their feathery legs like jack-in-the-boxes as they swept the water for planktonic life. I usually fed my pets in the evening when I returned from the beach, having collected some extra tidbit like beach hoppers or mole crabs.

During the school seasons nothing stayed very long in my aquaria. One large order from an invertebrate-zoology instructor who was using live animals for demonstration would clear out all the aquarium setups before I had a chance to become too attached to them.

I got my buckets and dip net together and made ready to collect the toadfish and a routine order for a thousand male fiddler crabs, *Uca pugilator*, that were scheduled for delivery within the next few days. These orders and an order from a Connecticut university for ghost crabs and mole crabs would probably be the last of the routine orders of the season.

I drove down to the Arcadia Landing and met my Airedale, who was happily lying in the smelly mud and cool water. She rose and greeted me with a welcoming, wagging tail, bowed before me by putting her forelegs down and her rump up high, and then lost interest in me when a dirty white hound crawled out from under a parked truck to sniff noses with her.

All over the muddy marsh-grass beach lay old wrecks of water-worn skiffs grown over with scummy green algae and filled with water, and piles of last year's rusty crab traps that had been pulled in, never to be used again. Logs and lumber scraps covered with barnacles and oysters lay half sunk into the mud. An old refrigerator and a rusted engine block completed the atmosphere of the Arcadia flats.

I liked Arcadia the way it was. True, sometimes the odor of

cooked crabs and dead fish permeated the air for miles, but places like this little fishing village are getting scarce along the coastlines of the United States. Once they bring civilization in and incorporate the town, there will be a policeman. Taxes will be instituted to pay the law officer's salary. And that will only be the beginning. A policeman will need a jail, which will require more taxes; law and order will encourage Northerners to colonize, which will mean another policeman, streetlights, garbage collection—and the next thing you know, there will be paved roads and sidewalks. Then there will be no stopping the encroaching civilization; there will be a city hall and even a schoolhouse.

I probably would not object to these innovations, but the real-estate men will turn Arcadia into just another Florida resort area with ugly motels, honky-tonk restaurants, flashing neon lights—the cancerous growths of resort and amusement areas.

Few people in Arcadia suffered from the diseases of modern civilization. Ulcers and heart ailments were rare, for most people led a simple life of fishing day after day on the lazy Gulf, and time slipped by about as slowly and peacefully as a fig whelk sliding over the mud.

I pushed into my boots and started walking over the exposed flats and oyster bars. Linda left the hound and followed me. Herds of fiddler crabs scattered at our approach with the sound of fall leaves rustling in the wind. I would get those later.

The boat landing made a fine collecting ground. I could always count on finding plenty of scavengers that came to eat the wastes of the crab houses. There was no better place anywhere to find mud shrimp, *Upogebia affinis*, which burrowed in the stinking mud. Hapless spider crabs and small dead stone crabs lay rotting in the mud with dead toadfish and hermit crabs. They had wandered into the crab traps, and since they were of no commercial value, they were tossed out to die.

The flats smelled powerfully of decaying fish. Flocks of angry, screaming sea gulls dived after live foraging minnows and splattered white droppings over the docks and skiffs. In this wonderful ecological habitat, great black eels, *Anguilla*, lived under the pier and found plenty to eat side by side with the pugnacious toadfish and foraging catfish. Sharks too hung around the docks, gutting down more than their share. Thousands of large and small black sea roaches—isopods—scuttled up and down the wharfs.

These residents could always count on lots of food, because every afternoon thousands and thousands of crabs were brought into the crab houses and dumped into immense pots of boiling water. After they turned a bright orange and were thoroughly cooked, they were dumped on long tables, where women wearing sterile white uniforms picked out all the edible crab meat with skilled fingers. Much of the waste was piped out into the bay.

On the high tide grapsoid crabs, *Sesarma reticulatum*, dart out from under the debris and tear at the rotting flesh of the dead fish. But nature has other ways of keeping her beaches clean. Vast quantities of pigmy whelks, *Nassarius*, scour the flats, eating anything dead. Fig whelks, *Busycon*, are common, and *Melongena*, the crown conch, slides over the oyster bars feeding voraciously on living conchs and oysters as well as crab debris.

There were lots of hermit crabs. Some wore *Busycon* shells, others carried crown-conch shells covered with mossy dead barnacles. They fed on the dead fish. Alewives that had been discarded by fishermen lay rotting on the flats, their soft flesh sunken and their thin bones sticking out.

There were many animals I could collect here in cooler weather. When I needed live conchs, I had merely to walk down to the water with a collecting bucket at low tide and pick up all I needed. But even more surprising, just below the

low-tide level among the submerged rocks and oyster shells
there were rich growths of pink and white star coral, *Astrangia
astraeiformis*. Properly preserved with the soft pink polyps expanded out of their limestone cups, this coral was highly valued
as a laboratory-demonstration specimen. Throughout the winter I often went diving off the boat landing for them. At the
same time I also collected long red, yellow, and purple sea
whips which sprang up from the rocks, with yellow boring
sponges, clusters of sea pork, and luxuriant growths of hydroids. But that was in winter. Until October the bay would be
a hot, smelly sewer.

Often when I was on the flats I walked past any number of
toadfish, never giving them a second thought, while I searched
for conchs or dipped up comb jellies. A naturalist who gathers
specimens for a living gets to know a good deal about the animals he is after. He learns where they live, whether they come
out during the day or night, what they feed on, and when to
capture them. I had learned that toadfish live in garbage. They
prefer a rusty tin can, a sewer pipe, or a waterlogged board to
any natural oyster reef or mud-flat burrow. In fact, the toadfish is one of the few marine animals that benefit from man's
turning the ocean into a garbage dump.

I lifted a rotten barnacle- and algae-covered board lying in
the mud and saw a splash and a whirl in the muddy brown
water. That was a toadfish, and I scooped my net down and
brought up a handsome specimen. *Opsanus beta*, our local
form, has a wide squat head and mouth lined with nasty teeth.

The toadfish is very capable of giving an ugly bite. It generally has an offensive odor, possibly from the garbage it eats,
and it lets out angry grunting sounds when disturbed. One
might wonder what would anyone want with such an unpleasant creature. But it is a very popular experimental animal, and
a great deal of work has been done on its neuromuscular system, brain, heart, blood, and visual responses. Researchers insert

delicate electrodes into its nerve cells and the impulses are recorded on oscilloscopes. The electrical responses can then be measured, helping the researchers learn how the central nervous system controls muscular responses and how the regu-

*The toadfish is very capable of giving an ugly bite. It generally has an offensive odor, possibly from the garbage it eats, and lets out angry grunting sounds when disturbed.*

lating centers in the brain and spinal cord work. More than a few researchers have been bitten, but this fact is selflessly withheld in their research findings.

A great deal of research is conducted on simple marine animals. For certain experimental work, an animal like a toadfish, jellyfish, or sea urchin is more useful than a cat or a dog.

For example, these more primitive forms are frequently employed in neurophysiology because their nerve functionings are similar to those of higher animals, yet their nerve fibers and nerve-cell bodies are more accessible to dissection and more simply organized.

There are many reasons why a toadfish or some other marine animal becomes popular for experiments. Perhaps the most endearing characteristic of the toadfish is that it is available and is readily collected almost anywhere along the American Atlantic coast. If a scientist can obtain a large supply of specimens whenever he needs them, he has solved one of the basic problems in preparing for his research program. A fish or invertebrate that shows up after a rough storm or is only occasionally dredged up is useless in a large-scale research program, where quantities of the same species are required routinely over a period of months or years.

The Marine Biological Laboratory in Woods Hole, Massachusetts, is one of the world's leading research centers on the life forms in the sea. Their supply department keeps volumes of toadfish in large tanks for their visiting scientists, who come from universities and medical centers throughout the United States and from institutions in several European and Asian countries to work on the specimens. During the summer, when the laboratories are packed with visiting scientists, a staff of biological collectors from the supply department run their boats day and night getting up toadfish, squid, sea urchins, clams, and other animals used in various research programs.

They trawl over the sea bottoms for this creature or that and rush their catch up to the laboratories, where physiologists study the division of sea-urchin eggs, pigment changes in crabs, and the working mechanisms of the simple toadfish brain, nervous system, and hormone-regulation centers. Hundreds of toadfish are kept in great vats of seawater. Powerful pumps suck up the sea and stream it into the tanks and aquaria,

and the seawater splashes out and runs over the floor into the
drain and gushes out into the sea again. As soon as the supply
of specimens dwindles, the collectors are out dredging and
trawling for more.

I too got my share of toadfish orders. The requests came
from a medical school where a physician was studying organ
transplantation and wanted to see if the toadfish was suitable
for his research. From the work of other scientists he had
learned that in certain types of fishes, mostly sculpins and
angler fish, the islet cells of the pancreas are anatomically sepa-
rated from the enzyme-producing cells, making them particularly suitable for research in transplantation. Previously I had
written this physician that neither the angler fish or the sculpin
occurred anywhere in the Gulf of Mexico. Woods Hole could
not ship them down to Louisiana alive. Would the more
abundant toadfish serve the same purpose? I would first have
to collect the specimens, then the physician would know
whether or not they were suitable for his research.

When I emptied out a section of oyster-grown sewerpipe,
another large angry grunting toadfish spilled out on the mud
and began thrashing about. I edged it into the net and dropped
it into the bucket with enough muddy seawater to cover it. I
have seen toadfish thrown up on the beach by crabbers that
tenaciously survived for most of the day in the hot sun, grunting and jumping about when they were touched. It takes a lot
of punishment to kill one. Consequently they ship well and
survive well under aquarium conditions.

It was miserably hot on the flats, so I kept the toadfish covered, even though they could probably take the heat better
than I could. Flies bit me as I rummaged through the debris.
They pestered Linda, who snapped at them viciously. But I
kept on looking.

Soon I had the required six toadfish, but some of them were
small, and the order called for large animals. I continued look-

ing under debris, under pieces of rotten canvas, getting bigger specimens and letting the smaller ones go. Sweat was dripping down my neck. The summer doldrums were upon me—everybody suffers from them. Feuds break out. One shrimper in a fit of temper had signed up with a big shrimping company to work off South America and hadn't returned yet. He remained under a rigid contract. Other shrimpers get into fights with the police and spend the summer in jail. I usually wanted to go North. Just the word sounds cool, although I know it was no cooler than Florida—in fact, much hotter. But now I wanted to go West, just to see what it was like there, I told myself, thinking of the job offer.

The afternoon was wearing on, and crabbing skiffs were beginning to come into the landing. The tide was dropping, leaving more oyster bars and debris exposed. The crabbers were beaching their boats, looking disgruntled, yet their skiffs were piled high with fish boxes packed with crabs. There was Ramsy with a stubby growth of reddish hair on his face. Old Andy was tying up at the dock with William and, of course, C. D. Pearson, who failed to give me his usual toothless smile.

They all looked rather grim, and I wondered idly whether it was the flies or the heat that was bothering them. But it couldn't be just the flies or the heat, because I had seen them stand out in the bay unloading boxes of fish and ignoring the voraciously feeding yellow flies and mosquitoes.

Ramsy backed his decrepit rusted-out pick-up truck down to his skiff. His brother Bubba helped him load the heavy boxes one after another into the truck.

I greeted them according to custom and said cheerfully, "Giving the crabs hell, huh?"

Ramsy looked at me dismally, slapped at a fly, and said, "We're the ones who are catching hell. The market's gone down to the lowest I've ever seen. We're getting three cents a pound. We have to work twice as hard and get near about double the crabs to make any money, and the crab houses won't take over a thousand pounds from each boat."

"Well," I said, after making the appropriate sympathetic noises, "this looks like a good time for me to buy a bunch of good-sized blue crabs from you for preserving. I'll give you five dollars a box if you bring them up to my lab."

Ramsy looked more cheerful. "Yeah, I guess so—it's two dollars more than the crab house pays. Two dollars is two dollars." He looked in my bucket. "What have you got there?"

"Toadfish."

"Oh, those things." He grimaced. "We call 'em dogfish. Where did you get so many of them?"

I told him and he said, "Well, I'll be dogged. I've been fishing here all my life and I didn't know they live under all that junk. You gotta watch those dogfish—they'll bite the living fire out of you."

"Yes, I know," I said. "Once in a while I get careless and they bite me. I have to get some fiddler crabs now, so if you want to bring those boxes of blue crabs down to my lab, I'll write you a check later."

"You still selling them fiddler crabs?" There was a note of surprise in his voice. "If you're paying what you were, I'll get rich in just five minutes," he said, looking at the herds of fiddler crabs all over the beach.

"Why should I pay you when I am just as capable of herding them as you are? And I can use the exercise too."

"That's okay," said Ramsy, "we'll give you a hand. Me and Bubba's been sitting in a boat all day pulling up traps. It wouldn't hurt us none if we were to limber up our legs some."

We had a special strategy that bait dealers use for gathering fiddlers. The fiddlers on this beach are accustomed to fishermen stomping all over the landing. When a fisherman walks down the beach, the heard of fiddler crabs gets up and moves, and when they do, it looks like the beach gets up and runs—there is no other way to describe it. It is a simultaneous movement and all in one direction, away from the stomping feet that might carelessly step on them.

We tried to walk up on them as if we were perfectly indifferent, just walking normally. They had been browsing quietly, feeding on diatoms, when we approached. A wave of panic swept through them and they dashed as a unit toward the protective marsh, almost as if they had guessed our intentions.

We raced ahead of them and cut them off from their retreat to their burrows. Stamping our feet, we turned the herd back toward the water and started a wide circling trot. We pretended we were herding cattle, shouting, "Get 'em up—move 'em out! Yah, yah, wahoo—sue-it, crab, move, crab, come on, crab—" Of course the crabs didn't hear us, but the yelling made us feel good. The multitudes of fiddler crabs tried to get away from the inexorable stomping feet until they were forced to run in a circle. Little by little, shouting as we went, we narrowed the circle, and the frantic crabs began piling up on each other. Again the noise of all those crab bodies reminded me of the wind stirring up autumn leaves into a vortex.

The climactic moment had almost arrived when we would wade into the confused mass of piled-up crabs and pack them into our buckets when Linda charged across the flats and pounced among the crabs, snapping and biting at them, scattering them helter-skelter, thinking she was a great help. Yelling at Linda when she was excited was about as useful as yelling at the crabs, so I reached in and grabbed her by the collar and marched her in our circle.

When the crabs were piled high into a mound we scooped them up in our buckets. I tossed Linda into the water, and by the time she came tearing out, Ramsy and Bubba had their buckets filled and Linda had to content herself with chasing and snapping at a few stragglers.

We were all slightly dizzy. I had a distinct sensation that some of the pine trees and oaks that bordered the bay were whirling about me. "I could do with a nice cold beer when I quit spinning," I said. "How about you?"

Ramsy said, "That sounds real good. You get us a sixpack from Miss Hopkins while we go sell our catch."

So a little later we drank beer while we sat on fish boxes and sexed the fiddler crabs. The order required a thousand male *Uca pugilator*. We sorted out the males and let the females go. The males are easy to distinguish, because they have one large claw which they use to threaten and bluff one another and to attract the female. They wave their enlarged pincer claw like a maestro playing the violin, hence the name "fiddler."

Ramsy finished his beer and crushed the empty can, wiped his lips on his sleeve, and said, "You know, you ought to be making a big business out of this specimen stuff."

"I'm working at it," I told him, throwing handfuls of male fiddlers into the bucket. But, I thought, perhaps I was not working at it, not doing all I could possibly do to increase my business. Perhaps I did not spend enough time drumming up trade and increasing sales. So far I was just making a meager income for myself, and nothing more. I was not taking chances, the gambles that other businessmen take. I had not tried to incorporate or sell stocks. Perhaps underneath it all I was afraid to take chances, run deep into debt to expand. I was afraid of failure.

Bubba was complaining, "Them little nasty so and so's!" He disengaged a crab's claw from his finger and started cursing again. "It's got two claws on it—how come?"

I looked over at his crab and shook my head. "Throw it away. That's a rock crab." It was a grapsoid crab, *Sesarma re-*

*ticulatum*, that had somehow wandered into the fiddler herd. Fiddlers are capable of giving almost as nasty a pinch.

Ramsy was still worrying about enlarging my business. "I'll bet," he said, "that you don't get near the orders you could. It stands to reason that there's schools all over this country, and all of 'em use this junk, don't they?"

"That's right," I said absentmindedly, prying a pinching fiddler crab off my thumb. "How many crabs do you have?"

"Three hundred and nineteen." Ramsy picked fast.

"I got two-eleven. What about you, Bubba?"

"I think I got two-ninety. I can't keep my mind on them with you all talking."

"Let's pick three hundred more and let the rest in the bucket go." I opened three beers and passed them around.

Once Ramsy got on a subject, he was as bad as a terrier on the trail of an armadillo. "Shoo, without too much trouble you could be taking in a thousand dollars a week, maybe more, maybe even two thousand, and you could put us all to work. Then we could tell the crabbing business to go to hell."

The three of us got misty-eyed and dreamy. I had visions of a huge gleaming white laboratory building filled with technicians making microscope slides, mounting hydroids and jellyfish in plastic blocks and beautiful museum jars. Large trucks lettered with the name of my specimen company would be pulling up, loading and unloading barrels of every kind of specimen: dogfish sharks with their veins and arteries shot full of colored latex, barrels of squid and sea anemones from the New England coast, tropical corals from Key West. Scientists would be coming from all over the country, all over the world, to conduct their research on Gulf specimens in my beautifully equipped modern laboratory. And no matter what specimen they needed, we would supply it.

Ramsy spoke dreamily of investing money in the company and eventually opening up a subsidiary fish, oyster, and shrimp company, having shining new trucks, picking up specimens, operating an ocean-going double-rigged company shrimp boat, and making a fortune. Bubba would be his deck hand. At this Bubba became indignant and flatly refused. He wanted his own boat, he wanted to be his own boss and have his own crew and not have to take orders from anybody. Then he would marry one of those classy city girls who worked for the State Department.

I thought Bubba had a point there—he wanted independence and he was willing to take the risks that go with independence. Supposing I took this once-in-a-lifetime offer on the Pacific Coast? What would it really be like? Definitely I would have to surrender my independence and work in cooperation with many scientists, graduate students, and technicians, and submerge my individuality. This might be a small price to pay for my security and comfort, and I would still be doing the work I loved to do, collecting—not counting or sorting preserved materials that somebody else caught—and I would get a continuous fat salary for doing the work I liked.

I was not sure. Perhaps it was the summer doldrums talking, I thought, slapping futilely at a biting fly.

Ramsy was saying, "Why, we can put old Roscoe to work, and we can get him to sell his land, because we're going to need all of it to put up more buildings. A company like ours is going to need maintenance buildings, freezer plants, garages, wood shops, storage sheds, and whatnots."

And so we sat on the fish boxes under the water oaks, slapping at the flies and sexing and counting the fiddler crabs. It would be so nice to be rich—I would be the boss and nobody could tell me what to do either. And Ramsy said softly, "Hell, yeah, I'll even put my old lady to work and we'll be richer yet." We had these dreams, especially when the summer doldrums were upon us.

"Can she type?" I asked, businesslike, crushing a yellow fly.

"Why do they just want boy fiddlers? Why can't they take gal crabs too?" asked Bubba.

"I don't know," I told him. "I've been wondering about that myself. But someday I'll find out and I'll tell you. I'm going for some Spanish moss to pack them in."

I emptied all the male fiddler crabs into one bucket and said, "I'll see you at the lab, I guess." And still brooding and dreaming I went back to my station wagon with Linda.

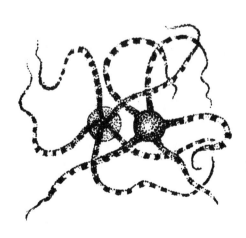

# 16 No Rest for the Weary

Being a one-man operation had its drawbacks. When I wanted to have some sort of a social life, a date with a girl, I had to plan ahead of time. With the toadfish and the fiddler crabs I had an airline delivery that night, and ghost crabs and mole crabs were scheduled for the next day. But I thought that with a little intelligent planning, I could get all my work done and have all of the next evening free. Before I left to gather the Spanish moss, I called my girl and made a dinner date with her for the following evening, to dine at the most expensive restaurant—I felt entitled to a decent steak and relaxation at least once in a while—and take in a movie.

Fortunately, my girl was free, and I asked her to buy the theater tickets for me in advance so that there wouldn't be a last-minute hitch. I was really looking forward to my night out on the town, and I went back to work with more than my customary zeal. Nothing, I promised myself, was going to interfere with my date.

The oak woods around Arcadia were draped with beards and festoons of gray Spanish moss. With a rake I pulled down enough to fill a bushel basket. I considered Spanish moss indispensable for shipping many marine animals that did not have to be in water. It had better drainage than seaweed and was less likely to decompose and build up heat, which was so detrimental to the animals. By soaking the moss thoroughly in seawater, I kept the fiddler crabs sufficiently dampened and insulated. All this packing, by this time, was a matter of routine—it had to be done with every live shipment to make certain the animals arrived in a healthy condition. They had to have extra care and caution because of the nationwide hot weather, and because I could not depend on the express company's consideration. I always packed the animals to withstand the worst possible shipping conditions.

Once a shipment of shrimp-trawl assortment containing jellyfish, mantis shrimp, holothurians, and other delicate marine forms destined for an invertebrate-zoology class in Chicago got mislaid for three days and still arrived in good condition. However now and then, a shipment was not so lucky and I would get a telegram informing me that everything had arrived dead and foul-smelling, in the last stages of decomposition. In a case like that, it was obvious even to the express company that they were at fault, and they paid the claim.

But money in this case was poor compensation, because by the time I learned what had happened, the tides had shifted, or the water would be too murky for skin diving, or the shrimp boats were not working in the bay, or, as in the case of the octopi, school was out and the specimens could no longer be used—and my reputation as a reliable collector suffered.

Although the toadfish is a sluggish animal and requires less oxygen, I gave my specimens the same care that the more delicate spadefish or sting ray would receive. I put them in plastic bags before placing them in a styrofoam box. I could not help but admire what ugly creatures they were, with their wide, gaping, whitish mouths, bulldog-like heads with bushy whiskers, and small cruel-looking yellow eyes. I put two plastic bags of ice with the fish to keep them cool and slow down their metabolism, thereby lowering their oxygen consumption. With these precautions the express company could lose the toadfish for a week and they would probably still arrive in good shape.

I checked the flight schedules and found that the toadfish would have to sit in the airport overnight anyway. But at 11:02 p.m. there was a northern flight for the fiddler crabs, which was perfectly fine—it would enable me to send the ghost crabs and the mole crabs off to the university in Connecticut at the same time.

Linda and I had an early supper of leftovers and canned goods. I put the gasoline lantern, the long-handled dip net, six buckets, and a box screen and shovel in the station wagon and we drove to the outer beaches with plenty of daylight to spare. I drove down the long, sandy road to the beach. There was only one car, with a Georgia license parked there. Most of the bathers and picnickers had left. It is easier to collect when there are fewer people. I can let Linda run freely without worrying about nervous people who are afraid of dogs. Nor do I have to answer questions about what I am doing and why I am doing it.

There were only three people on the beach—two middle-aged men in the water playfully splashing each other, laughing and yelling, acting like two small boys, and one thin, unhappy-looking woman in a bathing suit standing on the sand, near a stretched-out blanket. She called to the men in a plaintive voice, "Come on, you all! The flies are biting me something fierce." But she may as well have been talking to the beach birds for all the attention she got from them. She was no longer young; her thin face was weatherbeaten, dried, wrinkled, and bright red from too much sun and wind.

The only one who gave her any attention was Linda, who ran up to the woman and sniffed her bony legs. The woman gasped and jumped with fright. I snapped my fingers and Linda returned to me.

"Come on, you all," the woman called again. There was a hint of anger in her voice. "Them flies are eatin' me up."

One man shouted back, "Just a minute. We're having some fun."

I couldn't help feeling sorry for the woman as I went to screen my mole crabs. I was wearing a long-sleeved shirt, buttoned up to my chin, long trousers, and boots, and the exposed skin of my face and hands was covered with insect repellant. Even Linda had been thoroughly sprayed before we went out.

The story of the unfortunate woman and her two friends was obvious to anyone who cared to see it. They had probably met her in a beer joint in Atlanta the night before and decided to have a holiday in Florida. Strings of beer cans had been strewn over the highway and left in the motel room where they had spent the night; a mound of beer cans rose beside the blanket they had been lying on. Now they were no longer interested in her and were having fun, splashing in the sea. And there she was, ignored, and tortured by flies in her flimsy little bathing suit.

I began screening the mole crabs, *Emerita talpoida*. The sweeping surf dislodges thousands upon thousands of these creatures, pale, almost as white as the sand they swim through. And as each wave recedes their little bodies, bulletlike, shoot down into the substrata. This always takes place so quickly that you begin to wonder whether you really saw them. One swoop of the screen left them scurrying around helplessly on the mesh. I sat down on the beach and leisurely picked out fifty of the biggest and the handsomest of the screenful. These I put into plastic bags filled with sand and water.

This operation intrigued the two playful men in the surf. They forgot their game of pattycake and came splashing out.

"What are you doing?" asked one, a bald-headed man with a well-defined paunch.

"Just getting some mole crabs."

"What do you do with them?" asked the other, a long, lanky man, pulling up his slipping bathing trunks over his bony hips.

"Come on, you two, them flies are bitin' me," the wretched woman drawled, walking up to us.

"I use them for bait," I replied shortly, trying to avoid a conversation.

"Well, I declare! I never heard of them being used for bait. I never saw such as that before," said the bald-headed man.

"What kind of fish do you catch with them?" asked the lanky man with keen interest. Both men were ignoring the woman in the bathing suit, who stood coquettishly beside them.

I had to come up quickly with an answer. "Flounder," I replied brightly. "They love it." I dumped the rest of the mole crabs from the screen into a bucket of seawater for my pet flounder.

As I walked away, I heard the woman repeat, "Come on, you all, them flies are biting me." She sounded as if she was about to cry.

"Oh, they sure are," one of the men said, slapping at them.

The other man said, "Let's get back in the water and get away from them."

Turning my head, I saw them splash merrily back into the waves and dive under. I walked quickly, wanting to get out of earshot and away from them. I think I will hear her voice forever, pitiful, almost weeping, saying hopelessly, "Come on, you all."

This was all too familiar a scene in Florida. How I longed for the New England beaches, where I often met interesting people, such as a former professor who became a happy beachcomber, and the bright, alert students from the Northern universities. There were things to talk about, people who had read books and traveled the world, and there were places to go— the theater, foreign films, art exhibits, civilized restaurants. And I could also have all this on the West Coast. I would not meet the same kind of people that I met along the Florida beaches, people who go to a beach and feel that they have to ravage it, strew garbage around, and wear themselves out having fun.

A quarter of a mile down the beach, around a bend and out of view of the playful surfers, I saw the coquina's marks, holes the size of pepper shots. I stopped and watched the surf washing up, foaming, and with the receding wave, a multitude of little coquinas, *Donax variabilis*, thrust out the tips of their valves, then pushed out of the sand, tumbling for a moment in the surf. Their colors and patterns are almost indescribable— brilliant pastels, variegated and combined yellows with green stripes, green with pink bands, soft roses and purples, reds and golds. There is no end to the combinations and designs. Nature went all out to make a fool of any artist when she made these little clamlike creatures.

Each time you return to the beach, the beauty and the wonder of these little bivalves seizes you all over again. You watch one push its white foot back into the sand, hold itself erect, push down, and in an instant it is gone before the return of the surf. They feed on the diatoms and plankton with each return of the pounding sea. They are present in such vast multitudes that I have no hesitation recommending them for a broth—they are delicious, and you can save the shells. With a sweep of the screen I half filled my bucket with them.

The sun goes down quickly in Florida, or at least it seems that way. The hunt for the ghost crabs would begin at dark, although there were plenty scuttling over the white sands while it was still light.

It had taken that time-consuming and costly training called experience to learn how to catch ghost crabs quickly and efficiently. It is almost impossible to collect the ghost crab, *Ocypode*, in the daytime, because its light colors blend with the white sand and it is almost invisible. It runs lightly on its tiptoes, stops suddenly, and seems to disappear. For this reason it is called the ghost crab. You may as well try to catch a bandersnatch as one of these crabs in the daytime. I had done this when I got my first order for live *Ocypode quadratus*. At the time all I knew about *Ocypode* was what they were and where they lived. They preferred the open surf-swept outer beaches and avoided the sheltered harbors. They burrowed way up above the high-tide lines—often I had seen their burrows practically next to a highway. Actually the ghost crabs are the most proficient beachcombers of any seashore inhabitant, even more proficient than birds. A dead gar or a clam when washed up on the beach is immediately cleaned by these crabs. They run up to it swiftly, tear the soft, rotten flesh, and, holding the food with their claws, quickly gobble it down.

When fishermen pull up their seines on shore and cull out the sting rays, skates, catfish, and minnows, the birds, gulls, sandpipers, and herons swoop down and take their fill while the little beach hoppers bounce out of their ropes and strands of cast-up seaweed and gather around the dead and dying sea life. When men and birds have left, out come the shy ghost crabs, who know man is not their friend. On an uninhabited island off Madagascar I have seen naïve ghost crabs who, unacquainted with the terrible creature man, came out, bold and friendly, and accepted the food the members of the expedition threw to them.

I shall never forget when I tried to collect my first order of live ghost crabs, in the daytime. I felt I had earned every penny of that order. I had really more than earned it. It was an insane race. I think I lost all sense of reason. I went leaping after them like a maniac. I tried pouncing on them warily, and when that didn't work, I attempted to tackle them like a football player.

I churned up sand as I sneaked and raced after them with a net, matching the zeal of any butterfly collector. Fortunately, Linda joined in the race and ran them down. What we accomplished that day was to improve the breed by capturing the stupid and clumsy ones.

Ghost crabs are a popular experimental animal, because their high-stalked eyes are a good source for hormones that regulate light adaption. Among the practical points of natural history I have learned about these intelligent crabs is that they are sensitive to glaring light at night.

As soon as night fell, I locked Linda in the car. I no longer needed her help in capturing the ghost crabs, and she would inevitably get into mischief if I didn't have time to keep an eye on her. The blinding white glare of the gasoline lantern held a ghost crab transfixed while I brought the net down over it. Gently, I disengaged its clutching, pinching claws and dropped it into a bucket partially filled with beach sand. If the crab was distracted for one moment from the hypnotic glare of the lantern, the spell would be broken and it would dive into the water and refuse to come to the littoral until I walked a safe distance away. Then it would cautiously emerge, dash over the high beach, and vanish into its burrow. Even while swimming, they were skilled at avoiding the dip net, staying just slightly and maddeningly out of reach.

Despite its size and speed the ghost crab is one of the most delicate of crustaceans. It is high-strung and can die seemingly of shock. As soon as it finds itself in captivity, it becomes frantic and clambers and slips on the sides of the bucket. Failing to escape, it becomes hysterical and dashes about in a frenzy, frequently breaking off limbs and dying. And some just die for no apparent reason. I solved this problem by covering the neurotic *Ocypode* with ample sand, hoping that I could give it the illusion that it was safe in its burrow.

I carried the buckets of crabs back to the station wagon,

where the imprisoned Airedale awaited me with anguished
screams because I had not let her participate. She might have
helped with the crabs, but she would quickly have lost interest
as soon as she heard another animal. This beach was also home
to opossums, raccoons, and skunks. Poor Linda just could not
resist grabbing a skunk by the neck and shaking it. The results
were inevitable—the evening ended up with her in the bathtub
and me scrubbing her down with brown soap and tomato soup,
which is supposed to neutralize the stench. I would curse her
while she cringed, abject and remorseful and making me feel
like a heel.

I was feeling quite pleased with myself. I had finished not
only the day's work but the next day's too, and I would be free
for my date. With all my animals well packed, I drove with
Linda to the airport two hours ahead of flight time, which gave
us ample time to schedule the shipment. At the airport Linda
got into her usual argument.

No dogs were allowed in the air-conditioned freight office,
but Linda could not read and would not obey the rules. As
many times as she was ejected into the stuffy, humid storage
room, she bolted back into the air-conditioned office, curled
up behind the couch, and went to sleep. Finally the freight
agent very sensibly pretended she was not there. This farce
was repeated with monotonous regularity every time we went
to the airport. After the shipments were scheduled and the
freight forms filled out, I notified my customers by phone or
telegram that their specimens were on the way. And then I returned to Arcadia to get a good night's sleep.

The next morning, well rested, I took care of all the details
so nothing would spoil my night out on the town. It was a holiday that was well deserved. I spent the entire day in the laboratory catching up with the routine, taking inventory of preserved specimens.

When the time for my evening engagement drew near, I

took my best suit out of the closet, polished my dress shoes, and ran the water for my bath. Then I remembered that I had not yet fed my aquarium pets. There were the mole crabs for the flounder and frozen rock shrimp for the baby moray eel,

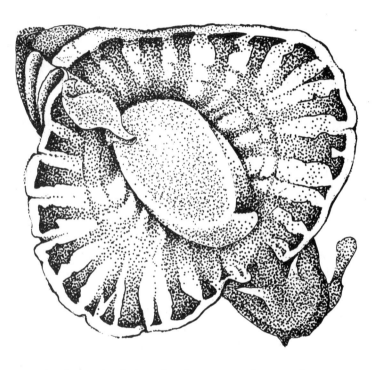

*At the end of the pier I saw my first sea hare
of the season,* Aplysia willcoxi.

but there was absolutely nothing for the sea horse, and he was pecking around anxiously looking for something to eat.

It would only take a few minutes to drive down to Buck's pier for some hydroids. Sea horses do not eat the hydroids, but the clusters are infected with minute crustacea, caprellid amphipods, free-living copepods, and peculiar small green flat-

tened isopods. A veritable feast, enough to keep the sea horse
fed for the next three days.

At the end of the pier I saw my first sea hare of the season,
*Aplysia willcoxi*. Hurriedly I scraped up the hydroids from the
pilings with a special rake and dropped them in a bucket with
seawater. Then I saw six more sea hares with their mottled
bodies come gliding in, lazily and rhythmically, folding and
unfolding their wings, with their necks and heads stretched
out. Sea hares, as they are popularly called, have long pointed
tentacles on their heads which look like rabbit ears, and without
stretching the imagination too far, their facial lobes even resemble a rabbit's whiskers. They were almost fairylike in their
graceful, buoyant movements.

I hurried back to the station wagon, glad that I had not yet
unloaded my usual assortment of collecting gear, my plastic
bags, buckets, and dip nets. I transferred the hydroids into a
plastic bag with seawater. Then I saw ten, then twenty *Aplysia*
winging their way under the pier. Standing at the top of the
pier I scanned the bay and saw shoals coming in with the
rising tide. Oh, how glad I was to see them! I had just about
given up on ever filling the orders; there had been a long-
standing order from the National Institute of Health for a
dozen live *Aplysia*, and several biological supply houses wanted
a total of four hundred. The first eighteen sea hares I caught I
placed in plastic bags of fresh seawater, which they slowly suf-
fused with their rich thick purple ink—as soon as sea hares are
touched they discharge the mucusy ink as a defense mecha-
nism.

Sea hares can suffocate in their own ink, and since I wanted
them alive, I washed and washed them until they stopped ink-
ing and swam restlessly inside the plastic bags.

Then I turned my attention to stocking the sea hares. While
I dipped up one, another floated past gracefully, and without
lifting my net I captured that one too, and then another and

another, until my net was so heavy that I could hardly lift it. And still they kept coming. My three buckets were already filled to the top with squirming sea hares and slimy purple ink. The local name for them was "ink fish."

Every year *Aplysia* came to the beaches, but usually only in small numbers. On a good full day of collecting, covering miles of beaches and tidal flats, I might be able to collect a dozen, and if I were exceedingly lucky I might find two dozen. Once in a great while they swarm to the beaches in vast numbers, but the last time I had seen them in such multitudes had been more than five years before.

As a novice I had thought that they swarmed annually. I was filling an order for two hundred sea hares. The order had stipulated that the animals be fully extended and natural-looking at fifty cents each. A hundred dollars would be an easy fortune to me, I thought, especially when the animals were so plentiful. They were so plentiful that the children, not having snow balls, were having ink-fish fights, which they claimed were far superior because they knew positively when they had scored a direct hit. A big purple slimy splotch appeared on the adversary.

I shudder to think how many *Aplysia* I ruined in the process of learning how to preserve them. I was like an amateur cook with shelves filled with a great assortment of spices and condiments. I tried everything. Perhaps boiling formalin would kill them so quickly that they would not have a chance to contract. Choking and gasping, even with a handkerchief over my nose and mouth, my eyes burning and watering from the noxious fumes of boiling formalin, I tossed a trayful in and watched them turn into round, tough rubber balls. They were hopeless. I tried every ancient anesthetic and fixative recommended by a nineteenth-century publication of the Naples Zoological Station, one of the most renowned works on the preservation of contractile marine invertebrates. The sea hares either contracted or became hopelessly bloated. However, the real missing ingredient was simply patience, which is the chief ingredient in preserving all contractile animals.

By the time I had filled every container I had in my station wagon, twilight had set in. Soon it would be too dark to see. As long as there is light the sea hares stay on the bottom, where they feed and browse among the seaweeds and algae. They slide along like any snail with their mucusy foot expanded and suctioning while they feed like contented cows. They are snails with paper-thin vestigial shells concealed inside their mantles. As the last rays of light linger on the sea bottom, the sea hares become restless; they have a sudden urge to swim. Perhaps it is the powerful mating call. Their wings unfold and they start to undulate, and they curl in their foot and begin rising when the last ray of light has died.

I hurried back to the laboratory to call Ramsy. I told him to get his brother and come quickly, bringing their gasoline lanterns, dip nets, and every container and fish box they could find. The "ink fish" had come in.

When I hung up I saw my dress suit hanging there, and it reminded me of my night out on the town. I shook my head regretfully. A collector, I told myself, is like a doctor—he never knows when he'll be called. And I never knew when the *Aplysia* would come back in such great numbers again. I called my date and tried to explain to her, but she didn't appreciate the urgency. She said she was all dressed up and ready to go out, and she didn't give a damn if there were a billion sea hares. She slammed the receiver down—hard.

By the time we arrived at the pier a big yellow moon hung in the sky. Ramsy worked on the gasoline lanterns, getting them started and glowing. Bubba lugged the pails and buckets down to the dock's boat landing, and I beamed my big searchlight upon the black waters. Gliding on its surface were multitudes of sea hares. It was an uncanny sight as the slow, tranquil, but determined animals rose up from the depth as far as I could beam the light, under the pier, out in the bay, aggregating in thirties and forties. As we gathered them up with our dip nets more and more rose up. With our three nets we dipped and swept the black waters, picking up the ghostly swimming forms as fast as we could, but still missing more than we caught.

Because they swam so slowly we had the illusion we could always get the other groups after we had finished dipping these up on this end of the ramp. Under the glare of our gasoline lantern, I could see ink, which appeared black, staining the water each time we caught a sea hare in the net. Each time we thought we had exhausted the sea hares in our immediate vicinity and were prepared to explore the other end, when a new shoal would rise up from the sea bottom.

Ramsy stationed Bubba at the other end of the ramp and I took the middle. Our arms were exhausted from lifting the heavy dip nets, and there was no cooling breeze. The perspiration ran down our faces into our eyes and our bodies were soaking wet, and we were covered with the sea hares' purple slime and chalky acrid odor, but still we didn't quit until all our containers were filled. It was two in the morning when we walked down the long pier to Ramsy's truck, and still we could see *Aplysia* rising up from seemingly nowhere, forming endless broad rivers.

We stayed up until it was almost dawn, preserving every animal except the eighteen that I wanted kept alive. I paid Ramsy and Bubba for their work and bathed before I got into bed, because I was covered with the slimy purple ink. I tried to think of appropriate apologies to my girl, but I couldn't think of any now—flowers, candy? Perhaps I could make her understand how important my work was. Then I thought about my *Aplysia*.

I had a drum of them packed to the very top. This was a

windfall, real capital. When any firm, school, or university ordered *Aplysia*, all I had to do was open the drum. It was like having money in a vault. It was a wonderful feeling. I wouldn't have to worry if they didn't show up for the next five years. Tomorrow four hundred *Aplysia* and a dozen live ones would be shipped out, and it wouldn't even dent my stock. And the *Aplysia* would pay for dates—my girl. With those happy thoughts I fell asleep.

# 17 The Sea Brings Forth

I had been asleep only two hours when the telephone awakened me. With my eyes still shut, I groped for it. "Gulf Specimen Company," I grunted hoarsely.

"Hello, Jack!" It was Robert Caine from the L. H. Caine Fish Company, and he was yelling into the phone as if he weren't sure the slender telephone wire could possibly transmit an ordinary speaking voice half a mile across town. "Get your behind down to the landing. We just caught a great big old gal sawfish and she's poppin' out babies left and right."

I hung up feeling thoroughly awakened, although I was still aching from last night's sea-hare haul. There was cold coffee on the stove, but there was no time to warm it. I grabbed camera, buckets, and blood-sampling kit, and Linda raced after me into the station wagon.

This was something that was not seen very often, even if you live right on the waterfront. I could say it was the duty of a professional biological collector to be present on such an occasion to record the size, approximate weight, and species of the sawfish for scientific distribution records, but the truth was this was simply something I wanted to see. I would not have missed it for the world, even if I had to stomp all over everything to get to it.

Even from a distance of several blocks I could see the sawfish hanging from the boom of the *Nancy M*. It was a huge brown grotesque creature with a big ugly-looking toothed saw. I was too late; I had missed the delivery. The newborn sawfish were scattered all over the deck. Some still twitched and gasped with

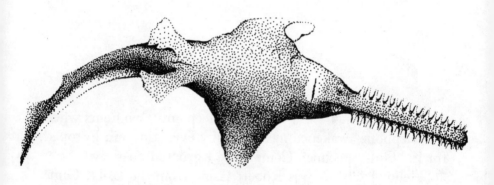

*Even from a distance of several blocks I could see the sawfish hanging from the boom of the* Nancy M.

life. Like other sharks and rays, the sawfish's eggs hatch inside the mother, and when the young are able to fend for themselves they are forced out of her protective womb into the sea.

Fourteen babies had been aborted. Each had its saw encased in a sheath of skin. I had wanted to get pictures of the birth, but it was too late, so I took pictures of the little ones.

I took a blood sample while the mother was still fresh. It was an easy thing to do because blood was trickling out of her gills and only half a cubic centimeter was needed. Then I sampled the blood of the young, drawing the blood out of their hearts so the quantities of nucleic acids could be checked and compared with the mother's. I counted the teeth on her saw and found twenty-eight pairs, which, according to my key to marine fishes, made her *Pristis pectinatus*, the sawfish common in the Gulf of Mexico. Even the old-timers couldn't remember seeing a sawfish this large. Alive she would have been a valuable asset to any of the huge commercial aquaria in Florida, but dead she was only so much crab bait.

By this time the sawfish had attracted an audience of crabbers, fishermen, and early-morning tourists. Everybody was excited and in a good humor. As usual when I got an animal as large as this, I examined it for parasites and growths, then checked the uterus for remaining young, but there were none. I tore open the gills with my pocket knife to look for parasitic copepods, but I was disappointed to find the sawfish clean.

But there was a sizable tumor on the sawfish's tail, and as soon as the tumor was cut free, I noticed a large blood vessel leading into the fist-sized mass of tumorous flesh. Fish frequently develop such growths, but it is not often that one finds a large tumor on a sixteen-foot sawfish for the simple reason that one does not often find a sixteen-foot sawfish. Histologists who were studying the structures of cells and connective tissues would find this item very useful.

One of the Caine kinfolks, asserting his kinfolks' rights, demanded a baby sawfish for a souvenir, as well as the mother's saw. I was compelled to say yes, but I was annoyed at his greed. Robert and Bunko, his brother, cut the huge tooth blade off with a handsaw. It measured almost four feet. Bunko clowned a bit for the crowd; he waved it like a sword, a knight in armor, and challenged menacingly, "I'll take on all comers."

I brought all the other babies back to the lab and turned on the radio while injecting their body cavities with formalin. There was news about a hurricane heading off Cuba north-northwest, which probably meant right into the Gulf.

This could mean a week or even longer before it struck this area—that is, if it didn't veer off into the Atlantic. I made up a fresh solution of formalin, poured it into a vat, and arranged the young sawfish and straightened them so they would harden in a natural extended position rather than twisted or bent. Then I showered to get rid of the sawfish's slime and uremic acid, characteristic of elasmobranch fishes.

I was feeling good about my new collection—there wouldn't be a museum in the country that didn't want one for its fish collection. I heated the coffee and then remembered that I had not fed the animals in the aquarium. The sea horse had been off his feed for a few days, and I was concerned because he had a large, distended brood pouch. He swam around the aquarium, pecking at the coral polyps, sniffing at the sand. The hydroids that I had gathered for him were still in the plastic bag, and they were swarmed with lively crustacea.

When I tossed a cluster of hydroids into the tank, the sea horse greedily began feasting on the copepods and tiny skeleton shrimp, his head bobbing as he snatched them from the protective hydroid clusters. The female sea horse's job is done when she drops her eggs on the abdomen of the male, and his pelvic fins become modified into a brood pouch. My aquarium pet definitely had a pregnant look.

I was pleased to see him eating again and returned to my breakfast. After a few moments I noticed that he was behaving strangely. He was swimming erratically across the tank, bumping into the glass, then dashing back to the other end. I decided to keep an eye on him. In all the weeks I had had the sea horse he had maintained a very placid, easygoing disposition, satisfied to wrap his prehensile tail around a gorgonian and suck in bits of food that floated by him. I was making up a liter of Bouin's solution for the sawfish's tumor, but I put down the graduated cylinder and gave the tank my full attention.

Suddenly the big sea horse spun around and raced back to

his favorite perch, wrapped his tail around it, contracted hard and convulsively, and sprayed out what seemed a multitude of tiny black sea horses. The infants, no longer than a quarter of an inch, floated up to the top of the water. They resembled tiny pipefish more than sea horses. The father, still on his perch, rested after his labor.

Needless to say I was very excited. I had an order for two hundred baby sea horses less than a half inch long to be used for slide preparations by one of the major biological supply houses. But I had no intention of using these infants as specimens, even though it was a good-paying order. I felt somehow responsible for their health and well-being. Had I not helped to raise them, and in a sense brought them into the world?

I was concerned about the flounder on the bottom of the tank, who seemed to show a keen interest in this new development. To prevent any accidents, I put him into the large wooden tank out of temptation's way. At first I did not suspect the father sea horse, but I soon became concerned about his paternal feelings. He sucked the babies through his small mouth. Not liking the taste, he spat them out again in disgust. I removed them to safety in a smaller aquarium. But one by one they began to die, sink to the bottom, and turn white. I realized the hopelessness of saving them. There was nothing to do but preserve them, but rather than throw my charges into harsh Bouin's fixative, I sentimentally prepared a finger bowl of costly MS-222 fish anesthetic and put them to sleep first.

But the parental laboring sea horse was not through yet. Three times he went through the birth agonies, presenting me with two hundred and eleven babies, which was an unexpected bonanza. I had not expected to be able to fill that order—it had been sitting in the unfilled-order file for more than a year. Between the sawfish and the sea horses, I had earned substantial money in one day without going out to sea or combing the beaches in the hot summer sun. The sea was bringing me some of her treasures, and listening to the radio's report of the latest hurricane movement, I thought there might be more treasures to come from the sea. The pounding hurricane waves usually uprooted creatures from the bottom and cast them up on the high beaches. Or would Arcadia get washed away?

After three days of waiting we knew definitely that the hurricane winds were heading north and northwest. They were coming our way. The skies were heavy with dirty ragged clouds. The hurricane had passed Miami and was headed toward Tampa. I thought the tides would be bad, and the tide chart prophesied neap tides, which are not favorable for collecting. Small-craft warnings were up all over the northeastern Gulf, and tides four to six feet above normal were predicted. But contrary to the forecasts and the tide tables, the water in the bay was exceedingly low. Sand and eelgrass flats and oyster bars which I couldn't remember having ever seen exposed, even on the lowest winter tides, were completely uncovered.

No collector worth his salt would ignore a tide that low. After loading the station wagon with buckets, screens, dip nets, shovel, and plastic bags, Linda and I drove down to Pepper's Point.

The flats were completely exposed, and the sea was pushed back so far away that it was barely visible against the horizon. Powerful shrieking winds pushed against me so that great effort was needed in walking. All during the night and all morning the sea had been drawn off. It felt strange walking over a vast stretch that had once been the sea but now was nothing but wet sand, puddles and pools of water, and grass flats. With the sea rushing off faster than the fish could swim, the fish were left flopping helplessly on the wet sands. The luckier fish were in the large pools, depressions in the sand which were filled with water. Batfish were aimlessly paddling around with their flippers, sting rays beat their wings and lashed their tails impotently, gasping for life-giving water. Dead menhaden were everywhere, but there were no gulls to feast on them. All the birds had gone inland for shelter.

The farther I walked, the more exciting were the subtidal communities. There were animals I had never seen by mere beachcombing but only by skin diving or dredging. Hydroids that once had bloomed up from worm tubes hung limply on the damp sand. But their polyps were still alive, so I gathered all I could. There were little clumps of rose coral in places that I never expected to find it. There seemed to be thousands of huge hermit crabs dragging heavy conch shells over the wet sands.

I looked around to take my bearings and saw that I had walked so far away from what had once been a shore that my station wagon was a barely discernible pinpoint. It would be a long and hard way back, carrying heavy buckets filled with specimens, with winds tearing at me. The hurricane was still two hundred miles away and moving slowly, but somehow, I felt uneasy. It was not a rational feeling, because I knew that there was absolutely no danger. But the water which was always so calm and glasslike in the bay was now a frothing, whipped-up caldron of leaden gray at the very edge of the horizon, and the bay itself was now nothing but a vast sand flat with patches of rock.

Linda braced herself against the howling winds and dug into the sands. She seemed to enjoy the battle of the elements and every once in a while managed to bring me over a specimen or two—a thick-shelled black Venus clam, *Mercenaria campechiensis*, or a large, kicking horseshoe crab, held delicately in her mouth by its telson.

Hidden in the normally submerged eelgrass beds were clusters of green grass sponges with networks of worm shells, *Vermicularia knorri*, twisting through them like so many corkscrews. I often found these dead when washed ashore, but it was the first time I had ever found them alive. I was walking over a raised sand bar when I saw a few fat coils of mud being spewed out. I knew it was the much-prized lugworm. I dug up all of the two-foot black lugworm with its tufts of red branching gills.

I was feeling quite pleased with myself with not having broken the lugworm when I saw a silvery pink something explode out of the sand. Before I realized what it was, it dived back just as swiftly with an oscillating movement. An amphioxus! And I had been hunting their habitat for years.

These animals are one of the most important creatures for classrooms and research. They are the only animals that truly represent the link between the invertebrates and the vertebrates. They clearly possess a forerunner of a backbone, a spinal cord, but oddly have no brain and no recognizable sense organs. They have powerful muscles and move swiftly through the sand.

I had occasionally found a few amphioxi, but never enough to fill major orders, so I had to buy them from a collector in Tampa, just as I bought specimens from fishermen. If only this were a good bed! I slapped the sand hard with the back of my shovel, and was thrilled when two dozen amphioxi popped up and dived back in again.

I dumped a shovelful of sand on the screen and washed it in a pool of water, and there were thirty-one pink slivers of amphioxi trying vainly to wiggle through. I was filling my bucket with them when a piercing, agonized scream was brought to me by the wind. I stopped and listened, not sure whether what I had heard was Linda or the shrieking winds. I looked all around the flats and I didn't see her. Between the shrieks of the wind, I heard the high-pitched scream again. It was Linda. I grabbed buckets and shovel and hurried in the direction where I thought I had heard her. The wind was to my back and blew me along rapidly.

A hundred yards away I saw my poor Airedale lying on her

side in a sandy tide pool. I instantly realized why she was screaming in agony. All around her were the hateful spiny saltwater catfish, stranded by the receding sea, and Linda, with her collector's zeal, had slapped one with her paw and got finned for her trouble.

There was a flapping bluish-gray catfish right next to her, with its dorsal spine still erect. I brained it savagely with my shovel and hoisted my suffering, whimpering dog over my shoulder and carried her a half mile over the soggy wet flats to my distant station wagon, with the winds tearing at me. She started out weighing forty-five pounds, but by the time I reached the wagon she felt more like two hundred pounds of wet weight. On the back seat of the car I examined her paws. There was a definite puncture on her left front paw. Panting and sweating, I hurried back for my buckets and shovel and raced the old station wagon home.

The only remedy that is effective for fish stings is hot water, the hotter the better, with a weak solution of bleach to neutralize the toxins. At first Linda was frightened by the hot water, but as the pain eased, she was grateful and made no attempt to remove her paw from the comforting warmth. Of course, I babied her and gave her hamburger while her paw was being soaked. For the rest of the day she hobbled on three legs, then limped slightly but walked on all four, so I knew the treatment was successful.

The hurricane did not strike until two days later, but for twenty-four hours the highway patrol drove up and down the streets of Arcadia and up the sand roads, urging all the inhabitants to evacuate. The village was in a low-lying area, and we were all in danger. Nobody budged! Every time a hurricane was imminent the people were urged and warned to clear out, but only a few timid Yankees obeyed the state trooper.

I suspect that there will come a day when the state trooper

will sadly look over the rubble of what was once the village of Arcadia, look at the few remaining standing walls of the clapboard houses, a shack or two, solitary refrigerators, turned-over cars, and smashed television sets and shake his head mournfully. He will reminisce—here was where C. D. Pearson's house stood, and that was where old Andy lived. And he'll wonder what became of old Andy, his missus and the young'uns. There was all that remained of the both crab plants, just the huge rusty cooking vats. A big drum of formaldehyde and scattered preserved sharks were all that was left of the scientist fellow.

I will even forgive him if he chuckles and says smugly, "I told them so." But in all likelihood he might feel a sense of relief. With the blowing away of that small community, there would probably be a substantial reduction in the number of lawbreakers, thieves, poachers, moonshiners, murderers, and speeders. With the thinning out of the lawbreakers, he might be able to get two days off a week, or at least one day.

The hurricane passed over. And as usual, all Arcadia suffered was two hours without electricity because the power lines were down. A few boats got swamped, and loose branches were blown off trees that needed trimming anyway. But the paved roads on the outer beaches were smashed by the pounding surf, sand dunes were swept away, piers were crumpled, and beaches in Anderson County were radically altered and almost unrecognizable.

The day after the hurricane sparkled and glinted with bright sunlight. The earth had drunk her fill, and the pine trees, water oaks, and palmettos had a fresh washed look. We drove around to gape and gawk at the damaged piers, the crumbled concrete roads, and the stone picnic tables and benches that lay scattered and broken in the sand and on the highways. The state road department's yellow trucks were already standing by as the workers cleared up the rubble. We watched lazily—we could watch at our leisure with the weather pleasant and cool and all the hateful, biting flies blown away by the hurricane, hopefully to hell.

Oh, what a treasure of benthonic life lay on the highest beaches amid knee-deep piles of seaweed! Most of the animals were still alive. If I had waited even a few hours, much good material would have been lost, because the sun would have scorched and dehydrated them. The flooding seas and the pounding surf had swept these animals far beyond the flood-tide level. And every animal there was doomed to die, for the sea would not return to claim them.

With the hurricane-swept seas, the burrowing animals contracted down deeply into the mud and sand. Anemones, worms, sea cucumbers, starfish, clams, and conchs dug fast and deep. Some tunneled far down into the substrate and were safe. Others, who were shallow diggers, were caught in the movement of the onrushing waters. Their holdings, which had once been secure in six inches of firm, hard mud, were swept out from under them. The furious sea carried them along. It uprooted giant sponges, ripped up the massive colonial sea pork, tore up the bryozoans, gorgonians, and profusely branching hydroids. The helpless animals were bounced and jostled in the frothing waters. The sea bottom was gone, and a cloud of mud and sand made the waters brown and turgid. The animals were swept upward, into the pounding surf, and carried on mountainous waves which battered at concrete highways, leveling the sand dunes with the beaches. Finally the hurricane moved ahead, leaving behind all its refuse and debris. The hapless, flaccid sea cucumbers, *Thyone briarius*, lay like empty little round sacks. Gorgonians, looking like varicolored plastic-coated wires, lay tangled up with bunches of hydroids. I recognized the pink flowery branches of *Bougainvillia* among the greenish-brown seaweed. Exhausted heart cockles lay each with its foot lolling out like a large tongue between the ribbed valves. The sunray clams were searching futilely for life-giving moisture, pushing out into the dry white sand. Spider crabs and calico crabs, which are slow animals, feebly flexed their jointed legs. I did not see many fast-swimming portunid crabs—apparently the fast animals were better at surviving.

Thinking about crabs, I wondered how the ghost crabs had fared. I knew they tunneled four feet deep or more. But the sand dunes were leveled. Were they washed out and dashed to pieces, or were they buried under the mountains of sand from the dunes? The intelligence of the ghost crabs never fails to amaze me. Across the road, far up in the woods of palmetto scrubs, were the new burrows of the clever animals. The evidence lay in the freshly spewed-out little pellets of mud and earth. They waited, peeking out of their burrows, until the sight-seers and the road workers had left; in the safety of the darkness, they would feast on the dying and the dead and make new burrows in the altered beaches.

I did not pass up a single parchment worm. They were still alive, encased in their U-shaped white tubes and lying like the other uprooted animals in the massive piles of seaweed. I had to rake through the seaweed to find the sea cucumbers—there were thousands of these, with the multitudes of bivalves and the tubed worms.

Ordinarily I considered digging a parchment worm, *Chaetopterus variopedatus*, little short of a crime. They were not plentiful in my area. These valuable animals are used live by researchers in embryology because they have large clear eggs and the cell division is easily observed under a microscope. The parchment worm is also used live for research in luminology. They glow beautifully when placed in the dark, delighting students who are seeing them for the first time. An uncanny shimmering phosphorescent blue emanates from this fragile worm which protects its delicate form by a tough parchment tube.

The uprooted parchment worms, however, like all the

benthonic animals, were doomed. If I had had the power, I would have bulldozed up the piles of animals with the seaweed, loaded them on barges, and carried them back to the sea.

If I could have returned all the bivalves, sea cucumbers, worms, and starfish to the sea, most of them would have survived, or at least they would have furnished food for the other animals. Many animals, however, were broken from their holdfast and would die anyway, like the massive boulder sponge and the urn-shaped basket sponge—as a matter of fact, all the sponges except the brilliantly colored small lumpy sponge *Xestospongia*, which does not depend on a holdfast to exist. This varicolored sponge has a peculiar relationship with a type of hermit crab, *Paguristes hummi*, which lives in a snail shell that becomes so overgrown with the sponge that only a hole in the sponge mass indicates the crab's entrance.

All day long I gathered specimens, loading my buckets and returning to the beach after unloading the animals in the seawater tanks and preserving drums. There was hard work ahead for me.

# 18  An Offering to the Sea

With the coming and going of the hurricane the summer doldrums were lifted. The fishermen were beginning to talk happily and cheerfully about the coming oyster season. Shrimp boats were chugging back eastward. There were no more pink shrimp in Mississippi and Texas, and the shrimpers were waiting for the white shrimp, for daytime shrimping to open in Shiawassee. The crab market picked up to four cents a pound, and there were even rumors that it would go up to five. Soon the spawning mullet would be making their fall runs, and the seiners would be ready—they were mending their nets and dipping them, repairing their skiffs and outboard motors.

In the eelgrass beds the brachiopod slits were beginning to show, and the muggy hot waters were clearing and cooler. I would soon be able to go skin diving. Tiny colonies of young bryozoans were appearing on the wharfs, and in a few weeks they would be big enough to harvest.

It was time to answer my friend's letter. I had seriously considered his proposal. The job offered security and academic prestige and also being a part of a collective group again. I had failed other times—perhaps it was not my nature to function as part of a group; I had found contentment only as an independent collector. But that I knew could not last. Mail and phone orders had been pouring in during the past week.

The professors coming back from their vacations found my catalogues on their desks. Schools were sending me generous bid lists, and many long-range substantial orders were coming through. I could see that one man could not possibly fill all these orders, run the business and still be free. I would have to begin hiring employees, and they would be dependent on me, so whether I liked it or not, I was no longer a free man.

By realizing that, I considered it a part of my development. I could not stand still, I had to move on and assume responsibilities. And I felt now that I was mature enough to begin. I thought about my friends, the shrimpers, but conditions were no longer the same. Not too long ago these men were the whole of my life after I had excluded the university. Their problems had once been mine: that man was the criminal who had stolen Danny's water pump, and I had disliked Miss Gerty, who cheated all the fishermen of their catch when she weighed in the shrimp, and there was the time when I had untangled Chass's net from the propeller wheel of the *Portia* and thereupon become a hero in the eyes of all the shrimpers. I dived under the boat, twisting and turning until I was blue in the face, then the final twist and the net came up without a rip and everybody cheered.

But now I had moved on. The expedition, the catalogues and the commitments I had taken upon myself, had made these men only a part of my life. I regretted leaving them behind because I saw plainly that their importance to me would diminish even more in time.

As I looked at the harvest of my season's work, my summer

doldrums had also vanished and I could realistically assay the value of my business and its potential. There were drums upon drums filled with sea hares, sea cucumbers, sharks, rays, and other valuable laboratory specimens, packed in my storage shed. And the shelves in my laboratory were lined with bottles and jars of hydroids, sea grapes, polychaete worms, mole crabs, and chitons, and brachiopods.

There was no turning back now. The die was cast. I thanked my friend for his offer, but I could not accept. There would be times when I would regret giving up the opportunity of receiving a formal academic education and collecting on the beautiful rocky tidepools of the Pacific. I knew there would be times when the summer doldrums would return, and there would be annoyances in business and irritations with employees, shipping losses, and bad investments. I also knew these were passing annoyances and would be counterbalanced by the satisfaction I had in building this company, the enjoyment of being an independent seashore naturalist, working enthusiastically with research programs, knowing a little of what research is being conducted throughout the country and even throughout the world, instead of being shut up in a little cubbyhole of one splinter of specialization.

This little company, with its shelves, tables, sinks, drums, bins of fiddler crabs, storage shed, seawater tanks, was all mine. I knew how my shrimper friend George Williams felt. No matter how shabby his Greek rig the *Xenophon* was, at least it was his. He was not working for a fish company. And my laboratory belonged to me. The future looked good. It was what I would make of it.

I realized that the cap, gown, and sheepskin were only symbols, and to many individuals the symbols were meaningless. The kind of education I had been amassing was not honored with a diploma but it had a solid and practical foundation, one that no university could offer. Each of my customers had something to teach me, and I, through my intimate observation of seashore life, had something to offer them. I realized that knowledge need not stop with zoology or biochemistry; man is as much a part of his ecology as a starfish. And no matter where he is—digging ditches, on a shrimp boat, in an office or in a university, he has something to teach me about himself and his world.

Now the time had come to go north to the Marine Biological Laboratory at Woods Hole, Massachusetts, and look at it in a different light. On my other trips I had gone as a student of marine biology to learn collecting techniques and the classification of marine animals, but now my visit would have a broader purpose.

What sort of equipment, pumps, seawater systems did the Marine Biological Laboratory use? How did their supply department handle the huge influx of orders that was growing larger every year? And what were the problems of administration? I had to know all this and more and be prepared for a busy fall season, and I had to know how much money I would need. Since my childhood biology and the study of natural history had been my first love, and I was still in biology the only way I could be in it—under my own terms.

The time to leave drew near, and I emptied my aquarium. It was dark at the boat landing when I returned the flounder, sea horse, anemones, moray eel, and hermit crabs to the sea. A large live sea horse is a valuable specimen—even when preserved it is worth three dollars. I had a jarful of preserved sea horses and I never seemed to have enough to fill the supply house orders. But this sea horse was now my friend.

For weeks he had afforded me hours of amusement, and by presenting me with more than two hundred babies he had given me substantial financial assistance for the trip. It was only right that he return to the sea alive and well. A beaming flashlight on the black water revealed my sea horse swimming as if stunned by not having glass walls to stop him. Slowly he swam down into the depths, beating his dorsal fin, and I said, "May we never meet again. And stay away from people!" The flounder swam rapidly to the bottom. Life was just too easy for him—all he ever did was stuff himself on mole crabs, and he didn't fret a bit about the glass walls as long as he got his dinner.

Before I went anywhere I made it a custom to return some creature to the sea alive. It was my secret superstition that this brought me luck. Perhaps this is a part of our atavistic memories. Primitive tribes in Madagascar who eat dugongs—a large sea mammal—ritualistically return its bones to the sea. An anthropologist once told me that certain Eskimo tribes upon harpooning a seal cut the animal's head off, pour fresh drinking water down its throat, and return the head to the sea, saying "Go tell the other seals that we have been kind to you and we are good people." This ritual is to ensure successful fishing. Perhaps it also placates the gods of the sea.

I have seen the shrimpers pick up one or two struggling, resentful fish—a worthless batfish or cowfish—and automatically, without thinking, return it to the sea with the opening of each net. One time my curiosity got the better of my manners and I asked Chass why he did it. He shrugged his shoulders, looked perplexed, and said, "I don't know why I do it. I just do it!"

Many of us have a pet superstition. Perhaps we are too civilized and too scientific to admit to it. But why tempt fate? I was going a long way in the morning, all the way up to Woods Hole. A collector needs luck, and I believe one way to get it is to give something back to the sea when the sea has been good enough to bring forth her treasures.

I beamed the big flashlight over the black sea. The sea horse had sunk out of sight into the depths, and the bay seemed empty. Only one slow undulating sea hare floated lazily by on top of the water, and finally it too drifted out of sight. Linda pressed up against my thigh and looked up at me and sighed. Then I turned away and she followed at my heels.